Please Remember Me

...a good story...I thought the last twist in the scene between Jade and her father was a wonderful one that I did not see coming.
~ *Literary Nymphs Reviews*

Total-E-Bound Publishing books by Wendi Zwaduk:

Learning How to Bend
Must Be Doing Something Right
My Immortal
You'll Think of Me
Tangled Up
Careless Whisper
What Might Have Been
Ever Fallen In Love
Please Remember Me

PLEASE REMEMBER ME

*To Kelley —
Enjoy the heat!
Enjoy Happy reading"
Wendi ~ 2012*

WENDI ZWADUK

Please Remember Me
ISBN # 978-0-85715-441-5
©Copyright Wendi Zwaduk 2011
Cover Art by Lyn Taylor ©Copyright 2011
Interior text design by Janet Marshall
Total-E-Bound Publishing

This is a work of fiction. All characters, places and events are from the author's imagination and should not be confused with fact. Any resemblance to persons, living or dead, events or places is purely coincidental.

All rights reserved. No part of this publication may be reproduced in any material form, whether by printing, photocopying, scanning or otherwise without the written permission of the publisher, Total-E-Bound Publishing.

Applications should be addressed in the first instance, in writing, to Total-E-Bound Publishing. Unauthorised or restricted acts in relation to this publication may result in civil proceedings and/or criminal prosecution. The author and illustrator have asserted their respective rights under the Copyright Designs and Patents Acts 1988 (as amended) to be identified as the author of this book and illustrator of the artwork.

Published in 2011 by Total-E-Bound Publishing, Think Tank, Ruston Way, Lincoln, LN6 7FL, United Kingdom.

No part of this book may be reproduced, scanned, or distributed in any printed or electronic form without permission. Please do not participate in or encourage piracy of copyrighted materials in violation of the authors' rights. Purchase only authorised copies.

Total-E-Bound Publishing is an imprint of Total-E-Ntwined Limited.

If you purchased this book without a cover you should be aware that this book is stolen property. It was reported as "unsold and destroyed" to the publisher and neither the author nor the publisher has received any payment for this "stripped book".

Manufactured in the USA.

PLEASE REMEMBER ME

Dedication

For my CP, N, who had the faith and drive to stick it out with me.
For KC and MO who read this when it was really rough.
To my editor for sticking by me even though it got a tick rocky.
JPZ — Please Remember Me when I'm gone — I'll be thinking of you always.

Chapter One

I told him I'm coming back to Crawford because I want to see him.

Jade smoothed her hands over her satin jacket and squared her shoulders. Men never got to Jade Weir, movie star. It wasn't an option. She held control...except when it came to the copper-haired deputy with eyes the colour of tropical ocean water. Just the thought of Deputy Marlon Cross made her thighs heat. They'd shared one quick kiss when she'd said goodbye at the sheriff's department but, good grief, how the kiss had stayed with her. The memory of the rasp of his beard abraded her cheeks and kicked her desire up a few notches. She fanned her face. No matter how many sexy text messages and *double entendre* emails they'd shared, a handsome man like him wouldn't be on the market for long.

The lights flickered in his living room. That was a pretty good indication he was home, right? Shit, was he alone? She folded her hands in front of her mouth and peered around the lot. Three cars sat outside his apartment. His? A girlfriend's? Pain seared her chest in the vicinity of her heart, making her gasp. God! Here she sat in a car pining for a man who probably had a woman in there with him.

Glancing in the rear view mirror, she ran her tongue over her teeth to remove the stray lipstick and rubbed the sleep smudges from under her eyes. "I look like I've been on a bender," she muttered, "rather than clean for six months."

Driving sixteen hours straight wasn't her best idea, but it had got her the rest of the way to Crawford, Ohio. Would Marlon recognise her without the heavy mask of makeup? Finger-combing her hair, she considered pulling the strands back into a clip. The last time she'd seen him, the colourist had insisted she looked best with platinum highlights.

With a final look at her makeup—modest by Hollywood standards—she opened the car door. No one recognised the slightly dented Benz or the Topher Azad jeans and hoodie she wore under the jacket. Not exactly glamorous, but not awful. Her phone buzzed as she slid out of the seat. She glanced at the screen before flicking open the phone.

"Hey, Bobby. Yeah, I'm in town, so keep an eye out in case they came, too. We'll meet up tomorrow."

"Yup," came the reply just before the line went dead.

Jade closed the car door with a snick and forced herself towards Marlon's front door. She shoved her phone in her jacket pocket. Each noise, each little movement, put her on edge. A gale of laughter and shouting came from the neighbouring apartment. She nibbled her top lip as her high heels clicked on the pavement. *Please don't let any of Daddy's goons or the press be on my tail.*

From his open living room window came the gentle sounds of his television, accompanied by soft groans. What the heck was he watching? More importantly, was he alone?

She closed her eyes and took a long breath, letting it pass slowly between her lips on the exhale. *I'm visiting a friend.* Opening her eyes, she inched forwards. *No one knows where I am and I can blend in.* Her heart hammered against her ribs. *Don't turn back.* She stopped at the bottom of the short set of stairs and held on to the wrought iron railing. *I can do this.* Thumps came from the other side of his door. Fear and revulsion coursed through her veins as she crept towards the porch. The soft thumping grew louder.

He did have someone there with him. Had to. Hot guys of his calibre weren't alone for very long.

Aw, shit.

"Jade!"

Her hand hovered over the doorbell. Had he just called her name? Shaking her head, she blew off the word she'd heard. A man like Marlon didn't yearn for a woman like her. He probably fantasised about the old Jade, the Jade who took her clothes off to get attention. The Jade who ate drugs for dinner and passed out at parties. The old Jade no longer existed.

The new Jade, with thirty extra pounds, rounder cheeks, filled-out hips and honey-blonde hair, had taken her place. The Jade she'd become was the Jade she'd always been on the inside—Jaden Marie Haydenweir. Sure, she still wore designer and insisted her hair be in a perfect tousle. No need to go totally off the deep end.

Her father's parting words rang in her ears. "You can't make it on your own. Men want the ideal. Without the gloss, you look like the girl next door and not the ones on television. Men want fantasy, not your boring reality. You'll see I'm right."

Taking one more deep breath, she fisted her hand.

"Jade!"

Had he seen her? Without thinking, she spoke. "I'm out here!" Her eyes widened and she slapped both hands over her mouth. Oh God, had she just answered him? What would his girlfriend say?

Turning around, she stepped off the small concrete porch and retreated to the parking lot. The click of her heels echoed in the silence of the evening. No, he wouldn't see her beg or embarrass herself again. When they'd kissed in the parking lot of the airport, her blood had heated. Her mind had spun. Words she'd only spoken in jest before had flowed from her lips, I love you. She shivered. Love at first kiss wasn't possible. Well, not in the real world — only in movies.

When she reached her car, she gripped the door handle and rested her forehead on the cool frame. Tears of mortification pricked her eyes. She had never seen another woman, but he couldn't be alone. Maybe he'd found someone else named Jade.

"Who's out here? Jade?"

Jade froze. His voice sounded strained. Surprised? Worried? Had Marlon come out looking for her? She wasn't sure. Shifting into the shadow of her open car door, she slid behind the wheel.

Marlon, clad in nothing more than low-slung, plaid pyjama bottoms, stood on the porch with his hands on his hips, his gaze darting around the lot. With long, confident strides, he stepped into the splash of fluorescent light. Spiked nipples and a sprinkling of crisp hair decorated his toned chest.

Please Remember Me

Licking her lips, Jade curled her fingers around the steering wheel. Oh, to caress those muscles and nuzzle his pecs. To feel safe in his arms and hear his heart beat as she rested her head on his chest after they'd made love. Oh God. Now she had to explain why the heck she'd ended up sitting out in front of his apartment. Crap. She looked no better than the throngs of photographers who dogged her every step.

He rubbed his hand over his abs as he continued to look back and forth. When his gaze met hers, Marlon strode towards her car, the beginning of a grin on his lips. Did he recognise her?

A light clicked on in one of the units across the narrow parking lot. Tearing her gaze from Marlon's body, Jade peeked over her shoulder. A woman with gleaming blonde hair stepped out onto her porch. "Marlon? What's going on? Is there a prowler? I'm scared."

With a groan only she could hear, Marlon waved. "Hi, Sabrina. It's safe. Go back inside your apartment."

Jade gasped. She'd know that svelte blonde anywhere. Sabrina Jeffries. They'd been up for the same part in Kicks. The speculated closeness they'd shared on set had gone deeper than anyone knew. Jaden shuddered, not wanting to return to the mistakes of her youth. The gossip papers claimed Sabrina had retired. Apparently so.

Sabrina sashayed out into the light. Her diaphanous nightgown shimmered around her body and left nothing to the imagination, revealing perfect swells and curves. "Why don't you come over for a little while and keep me safe?" She wriggled her brows. "I miss our long talks over cappuccino."

Jade's eyes widened. Long talks? With her? She gagged. Maybe she'd better go back to the hotel by the freeway.

There she wouldn't have to look at the Barbie doll wannabe. No wonder women disliked her—she'd been just as plastic as her former co-star.

A shadow darkened her window. When she turned, Marlon stared at her. He tapped the glass with a long finger. "What are you doing out here?"

Jade squared her shoulders and rolled the window down. "I'm sitting. Isn't it obvious?" Wincing, she cursed her cowardice. *Don't slip back into Jade. Let Jaden shine.* Swallowing her pride, she spoke the truth. "I wanted to see you."

Squatting, Marlon folded his hands on her doorframe. "In a beat up Benz? Are you in disguise?"

She stared at his hands. A light sprinkling of hairs covered the backs—enough to be seen without seeming obtrusive.

"This is me." Her stomach dropped to her toes. The nerve of him, to even think she'd come in disguise. Did he think she looked silly? "I thought maybe I'd stop in for a visit—so sayeth my text."

"Got the message three days ago." He cocked his head. "I didn't expect to see you, but it's the highlight of my night."

Clad in a flimsy nightie, Sabrina strolled up behind Marlon. Her face twisted into a frown. "Who's the dump driving the used sports car?"

Clenching his jaw, Marlon closed his eyes. "Sabrina, go home."

Long fingers tipped with crimson nails kneaded his shoulders. "Are you sure, honey? I don't want anything to harm you and she looks sleazy and strung out, whoever she is."

Jade sank down in her seat, not wanting Sabrina to figure out her identity. The strung-out jab weighed heavily on her mind. "I can leave you alone. I just thought we could talk in person." Grief, she sounded cheesy... No, no backing down. "Your lady friend needs you, so I'll see you later."

The beginning of a smile crinkled his lips as he murmured, "You stay. I'll get rid of her." He tapped the rubber lining the window frame. "And she's not my lady friend. Not by a long shot."

With that, he stood and manoeuvred Sabrina to the rear of the car. His words, although muffled, weren't quiet enough. "I appreciate your concern, but it isn't necessary. Why don't you go home? Really, I'm fine and there's no threat. Okay?"

Shrugging, Sabrina walked away. Whatever she said in return remained out of earshot.

Jogging back to her car, Marlon opened the door. "Why don't we talk? I'm sure you didn't show up at my door just to run away." He held out his hand as she slid from the seat. When she stood, a long whistle escaped his lips. "Jade! What did you do to yourself?"

Swallowing past the lump in her throat, she hugged her body. The last bit of bravado she held on to evaporated. "Why don't I just go? You're busy and Sab—she doesn't seem to want me here."

"Not a chance." Marlon brushed a rogue lock of hair off her face with the pad of his callused index finger. The touch tingled her skin and sent electricity to her core. God, the man made her quiver. How unfair! His gaze lingered over her body, but unlike the throngs of paparazzi and fans, his appraisal felt honest. Could she hide the extra pounds under name brands and creatively draped fabric? Not under this scrutiny.

"Marlon."

He cocked his head. "Let's go inside."

Although she wanted to run, she allowed him to show her into his apartment. Even through the layers of her jacket and hoodie, the warmth of his hand on her lower back sent heat and chills through her body. Once inside, she froze. What had she come here for? To talk. Right. Talk. Not sex. Definitely not sex.

"Have a seat. Are you hungry? Thirsty?" Marlon gestured to the couch. "Let me grab a T-shirt and I'll be right back. I wasn't planning on company."

Shaking her head, she sat on the very edge of the sofa. Browns and navy dominated the small space. A knobby navy armchair sat opposite the plasma television. A framed painting of a duck hanging from the mouth of a yellow Labrador hung over the couch. She cringed. Who kept pictures of dead animals on their walls? Gross. She gave an inner shrug. Her father had stuffed fish on the walls of his office. Still, if she had her way, the gruesome image would be out.

She bit down hard on the inside of her cheek. If she had her way? Talk about wishful thinking! Besides, she hadn't come across the country to fall in love.

Marlon shuffled from the bedroom and into the kitchen, clinking glasses and mumbling to himself. Or was there someone in there with him? Squirming in her seat, she folded and unfolded her hands. Leaving. Yes, she should leave before things got out of hand. If Sabrina knew why Jade had come back to Ohio, she'd make it her dying desire to ruin Jaden's life.

Please Remember Me

With a kick, Marlon opened the door and strolled into the room. "I brought you a Coke." He placed the glass on the scarred wooden coffee table and plopped onto the opposite end of the couch. Slurping, he downed part of his can of soda. "What's wrong? You look like you could run out of here in a second. Don't tell me Sabrina's got you flustered. She's harmless—pushy, but harmless. You probably know her. She tried to make it big in Hollywood about seven years back."

"I've heard of her." Hoping he didn't see her tremble, she wrapped her hands around the cool metal. "I had to get away. If I'm intruding, please tell me."

"Nope. This is my night off. I'm the only one here and I was getting lonely. I'm glad you're here." He sipped from his can and smacked his lips. "What did you need to get away from? The hustle and bustle of Tinsel town? Logan says he misses the clubs from time to time, but I think Cass keeps him pretty busy. Actually, I just saw you on television. How is Jeremy?"

Choking on her soda, she covered her mouth and coughed. "Jeremy? Jeremy who?"

He nodded to the blank television. "Jeremy Mears, your current man."

Her heart thundered in her chest. Oh, that Jeremy. "We only dated for a brief time but he's moved on." Grief. They'd had one date and he'd insisted on taking her home by one in the morning—without sex. Jeremy had spoken more about his new clothing line and the record he had in the works than he had about the movie.

"Oh, so there isn't anything going on in your life? No new movie or new CD? You said you needed to get away. What's the matter? You know you can come to me if you're in danger. Door's always open."

15

Clutching the can to prevent herself from reaching for him, she spoke. "I'm in trouble, but not the normal kind." He opened his mouth to speak and she quieted him with her index finger. His lips twitched. The whiskers on his upper lip tickled the pad of her finger. Ooh, what would it feel like to have him kiss her with those scratchy lips— down there? A shudder ripped through her. It'd be heaven. She blinked twice to clear her mind.

"Have you ever been tired of your life? I mean, you have a great life, but is it what you know it could be?" She crinkled her nose. "I mean… Oh, I don't know what I mean."

This time, she withdrew her hand and let him reply. "And you came to Ohio? Yeah, all the celebrities come here for the atmosphere. What's the rest of the story, Jade?"

"Remember how I said I needed to get things right in my head? It took some doing, but things are so much clearer." Her reserve had hit the limit. He wanted to know…so why not tell him? Placing her can on the table, she scooted into the corner of the couch, far away from him. "I hated stepping out into public and knowing everyone laughed. I got tired of being a joke. Turn on any channel and watch the late shows. You'll see someone making fun of me. I am a Hallowe'en costume, for God's sake! I hate it."

Marlon put his hand in the air. "Back it up. Not everyone laughed."

"I'm sorry, but everyone laughed. I saw the footage more times than I can count. Even my father. My father! The man who brought me into this world thought I was a joke. He said so on national television. Logan and Cass were nice about it, but even they had their doubts."

Hugging her knees, she continued. "Anyway, I reached my limit. My life—jet-setting around the world and spending money like it was water—just didn't cut it. I didn't like the woman inside. So...I changed. I cleaned up my act and quit the drugs, alcohol, and random hook-ups. I'm going by my real name and making it on the skills I have, not Daddy's money."

With an appraising gaze, Marlon smiled. "I see."

Okay, his reply didn't exactly reassure her. She shifted in her seat. The door seemed awfully inviting again. "But anyway, I thought I'd stop by to say hi and then go to the hotel."

Bemused, Marlon leant back in his seat. "You don't have to go so soon." He cocked his head and grinned. "I'm sure glad you're back."

As much as she wanted to read into his statement, she bit her lip. A girl could only take so much, and he'd be a handful. He'd want details, and telling him about every nook and cranny of her life would get him closer to her. The closer he got, the harder it would be for her to keep a hold on her independence.

She smiled. "I'll be around."

Chapter Two

Marlon toyed with the condensation on the can. Jade had changed, and how! Her cheeks, no longer sunken, infused with colour when she smiled. Her eyes, once framed by dark rings, now had a healthy sparkle in their green depths.

Her tongue darted out to wet her lips once more. Dear God, he wanted to sample those lips. One kiss had sealed his fate. On every other date since their one lip-lock, no other woman had moved him like Jade. She sat on his couch, in his home. What would it be like to have her in his bed, naked in his arms?

The stiffy pressed against his pyjama pants. Shock rocketed through his veins as he glanced down at the tent. Randy teens didn't get hard so fast after a solo session. He crossed his legs to hide his reaction. If she knew about his predicament, she'd probably run. What was it about her that brought up his primal urge to be with her?

The shriek of his cell phone split the air. He jerked and grabbed his phone. "Sorry. I'm off duty. Let me get that, and we can... Yeah...uh...one sec."

Curling into herself, Jade nodded. "You're important, so I bet you're always on call in one way or another."

With a quick glance at the screen, he groaned and flipped open his cell phone. "It's Mackenzie, my boss. I'll be right back." Striding into the kitchen, he spoke into the phone. "This is Cross."

"It's your off day, but we have news about one of your old cases. Do you remember the Nikita Cline case?"

"Yeah, I remember. What's new?" Marlon peeked though a crack in the swinging door. Jade still remained, but with every passing minute, she looked more as though she might bolt. With her hand fisted around the couch arm, she scooted to the edge of the cushion. Her eyes widened as she gazed in the direction of the windows. Did she think someone had followed her?

"Are you listening?"

Scratching his forehead, Marlon turned away from the door. "I'm here."

"One of the main players is back in town. Do you also remember one Jade Weir? We got a call from the Santa Barbara PD that she's coming your way. I guess her father filed a missing persons report. Crawford was one of her last known whereabouts. She seemed to have a fondness for you so we're on the lookout for her. I remember her having an unusual attachment to you. She's got a drug record, you know. Might not be the best for you two to be seen together. What if she slips up?"

Pinching the bridge of his nose, he gritted his teeth. Damn. He thought he'd regained everyone's trust. "I'll keep my nose clean."

"Don't try to pull the wool over my eyes. You want to help her. I can hear it in your voice. You don't need the trouble the second time around." Mackenzie groaned. "First time I understood. This time I won't be able to save your ass."

Mac had a point. Marlon toyed with the hairs on his chin. Try explaining the need to keep a distance from Jade to his libido. "Even so, what if she ends up here? Has she done something illegal? Last time I checked, there were no warrants out on her. She's supposed to have gotten clean."

"Clean or not, you don't need to chance it. The official story, though, is her father wants her home and he's worried. Keep me posted."

"We cater to celebrities now? We're officers of the law, not babysitters."

"Enough of your tone, Cross. We work for the public, and Rexx Weir is part of the public."

With a sigh, Marlon closed the phone. Mac would probably have his hide for hanging up on him, but some things were worth the trouble.

When he shuffled back through the door, Jade was toying with the strings on her hoodie. He chuckled. The idea of such a glamorous woman in loungewear, albeit sequined loungewear, rocked him. If he'd read her words right, she didn't want to be the glamour girl anymore—well, not all the way. He agreed. Sure, he'd liked her as the Hollywood beauty, but the more wholesome and real look did things to him deep down in his soul. She stirred feelings he'd assumed had been long buried with Addison. Then again, some of the feelings weren't so happy. What if she hadn't kicked her drug habit like she claimed? People lied all the time, and he really couldn't afford to lose his job.

He kicked his apprehension aside for the time being. "So you ran away?"

She froze. Her wide-eyed gaze met his. "I didn't run away."

He sat on the arm of the couch. "Uh-huh. Why don't you tell me the rest of the story?"

"So you can turn me in?"

"Is there something I should turn you in for?"

"I swear I wasn't speeding over in Jarvis. It was a miscommunication."

Wrinkling his brow, he slid onto the couch cushion. "I don't know anything about a ticket, but I'll look into it." God, he needed to be near her. First he needed to control his hormones. "What's the name on the ticket? Jade Weir? Claire Rasmussen? Or Claudia O'Neill?"

"You would remember my stupid alias names." She shook her head. "I gave them my name. Jaden Marie Haydenweir."

Her real name. Ah. Jaden Marie seemed to fit her better than the exotic Jade.

"And I didn't disappear or run away. The officer said I owed him seventy-five bucks for the ticket, which I put in the slot at the courthouse in Jarvis. I can show you the citation—it's in the glove box if you want to see it." She twisted a diamond-encrusted gold band around her middle finger. "I have enough money to get through a week at the hotel and my credit cards for the rest. It's not the norm I'm used to, but I'll make do. If you can point me in the direction of the—what?—job place? I think that's what they're called. Do that, and I'm golden."

Crinkling his brows, he folded his arms. "You mean Jobs and Family Services."

She nodded. "Where is that?"

"What are your skills?"

"Are you one of the service officers?"

"Nah, I'm trying to help."

"Until Parker Pie died, I took care of my dog—sort of. I like kids as long as they don't get messy. I can text, message, and post comments online like no one's business." Her eyes lit up. "I can learn a filing system. Do you know where I can get a job where I can put papers in order?"

"Not at the moment." The department didn't need extra help, but maybe she'd work out at the library shelving books or she could volunteer to read to the little kids. "I'll show you around town tomorrow before my shift starts. Sound like a plan?"

"Yes." She glanced at the time on her phone. "I should go."

As she stood, he shifted his pyjama pants. God, would she see his excitement? "Jaden?" One more moment and he'd be able to get her out of his system.

Who was he fooling? One kiss and he'd be sunk.

In the doorway, she turned. "Call me Jaden Marie. My mom always called me that. I like it better. It seems more like me."

"Well, it is you." Good gravy, he sounded smooth. "I mean..."

"See? My awkward social grace is catching." A giggle swept past her lips. "I'll see you tomorrow?"

"Yeah, come by around ten and we'll paint the town." Oy, that sounded even goofier.

He clamped his mouth shut but still reached for her. As much as his conscience dictated he let her go, he yearned for her. She paused. Should he go for it? Why not?

Jaden beat him to the punch. With lightning speed, she touched her lips to his. Her eyes fluttered shut as she leaned in to him. With his tongue, he traced her mouth, her lips soft as petals on his skin.

Wrapping an arm around her waist, he tugged her close. The stiffy grew. When they parted for air, he gasped, "I'm glad you didn't disappear, Jaden Marie."

Her voice came out in a whisper. "I am, too."

Jaden stepped out onto the porch, into the cool air. Grief, she needed the temperature change. Marlon charged her thoughts and her body. If she stayed much longer, she'd slip into her old self and take advantage of him. Then where would she be? Out on her butt while one of the few men she actually liked walked out of her life. But goodness it felt good to let someone else in on her secret truth and be herself. And the sound of her name on his lips turned her insides to mush.

Behind her, Marlon spoke in a deep tone. "Why don't you let me walk you out? The neighbourhood is pretty good, but I'd hate for something to happen."

The outer layer of her defences melted. What girl could turn down a gentleman? Not her. "If you're worried, you'd better come along."

His hand rested on the small of her back and the sheer power in his body burned her to her core. "How long will you be in town?"

Stopping at the door of her Mercedes, she drummed her fingers on the cracked side mirror. "I thought I'd stay for a while. Cass said this is the best place to be, and when I stayed in her cabin last summer, I never wanted to leave." She fidgeted with her keys. Back in The Hills, she'd simply shut the door and insist the driver speed off in order to end the date. With Marlon, despite the fact that they weren't on a date or even a couple for that matter, she didn't want the night to end.

"I have some time coming this weekend where I can help you move."

The muscles in Marlon's arms bulged as he rested his hand on her door frame. He shifted his feet, resting his weight on his left foot. Even his bare feet turned her on. Criminy, did she need to get laid to get the lusty thoughts out of her head?

"What am I thinking? Living in a hotel for three days would suck." A sheepish grin twisted on his lips. "Just tell me to shut up."

A better means to stop his gibberish came to mind, but two searing kisses in one evening? The old Jade would jump on him and insist on a quickie in the back seat. No, Jaden Marie wanted to wait. She'd rushed the first time around. Still, the feel of his beard against her hand was too much to pass up. Smoothing her fingers over the prickly hairs, she sighed. Even his cologne, deodorant, or whatever he wore drove her senses wild. "I don't have much. It's not like I could throw the mansion in the backseat of the Benz, so I want to try to find a furnished apartment. I'm staying at the hotel by the freeway for now, but maybe we can look for an apartment in the morning."

"Sounds perfect." Taking her hand in his, he kissed her knuckles. Electricity shot from her hand to her heart.

She stepped away from him again and plopped into the bucket seat of her car.

As she pulled out of his parking lot, Marlon stood on the sidewalk waving. Did he want her to leave? Was she a nuisance? She didn't care. Few people who said what they meant came into her life. If he offered even a tiny shred of honesty, then she'd take it. Besides, it wasn't every day she met a man who rocked her to the core and made her think about something other than herself.

After the ten-minute drive to the motel, Jaden settled into bed. Clad in an oversized T-shirt emblazoned with rhinestone J, she tugged the curtains shut and grabbed her cell phone. Phone in hand, she slid between the sheets and thought about Marlon.

Just forget about him. Forget his smile, the goofy way his beard curled up to his sideburns, the gleam in his emerald green eyes, and that body. She licked her dry lips. Even with the T-shirt covering the important parts, a woman could slide over those abs time and time again without getting bored.

The unwanted memory of wild nights spent in the throes of passion and illegal substances crawled into her mind. He knew about her past, but could he accept it? Would he believe that she'd changed? Too many men saw her past as a liability. In Marlon's line of work, a former drug user would definitely not be the right match.

Throwing her forearm over her eyes, she tried to blot out the painful images of her public disgraces—the times she'd flashed the cameras, grabbed Logan just to get attention, run off to Africa claiming to want to help, but instead found new and exotic ways to party. Then there was her disastrous movie career. Did anyone really watch her movies? No. They downloaded that ridiculous Halloween party video where she'd serviced two guys at the same time.

Shit.

Then there was her father. Rexx Weir expected his daughter to parade for the cameras and show skin. Nudity sold magazines. Before her mother had died, her good deeds and philanthropy splashed across the pages of

Delish magazine. Would her mother buy the naughty celebutante act? Probably not.

Instead of allowing her pity party to get the best of her, she sat up and set the alarm on her phone. A shadow hovered by the window. She swung her legs over the edge of her bed. Paparazzi? They didn't know where she was. She peeked through the curtains. The security light bathed the empty walkway in yellow light. Shrugging, she checked the locks on the door and headed back to bed.

Tomorrow she'd meet Cass, shop at the thrift store, and try to find a job. As much as she wanted to hunt Marlon down and spend the day in his arms, he deserved better. From the way Sabrina talked, there was already an affair in progress.

A rush of jealousy surged through Jaden's veins. Tears wetted her eyes. If she didn't know better, for the first time in her life, she just might be in love.

Well, hell.

Chapter Three

The next morning, Jaden showered, dressed, and drove in the exact opposite direction of Marlon's apartment. By the time she reached Cass Malone's driveway, she'd considered and disregarded three impulses to turn around and head back to California. As she pulled up onto the pad in front of the garage, she spotted Logan, or rather Logan's legs, peeking out from under an enormous black truck.

A tremor ran through her veins. Sure, she'd made amends with the object of her puppy-love obsession, but seeing him still brought a tiny twinge of remorse and longing. From his sandy-coloured hair, to his drop-dead hazel eyes and his boyish smile, the ex-movie star could stop traffic and melt the iciest of hearts. At one time, he'd used his assets to woo just about every woman in Hollywood. Jaden grinned. His tomcat ways had stopped the moment he'd met Cass. She matched him in every way without pretension.

Standing, Logan barely reached five-feet-eight inches. But get him angry and look out. If anyone tried to harm Cass, hell hath no fury like a Malone scorned…or really pissed off. Jaden sighed. Maybe one day she'd find that one man who'd fall head over heels with her without a care.

Maybe.

Closing the car door, she strode to his position on the floor. Before she uttered a word, he rolled out from under the truck. "Hello, honey. How are you?"

A laugh bubbled in her throat. Despite her nasty tactics to gain his affections and her affiliation with Cass's ex-husband, Dex, Logan still treated her with respect. Cass had become one of her closest friends. "I'm good. I asked Cass to go with me to shop for furniture. She said the thrift stores around here are the best."

"Yup." Logan wiped his dirty hands on a rag. "She got a sweet deal on the dresser in Julian's room."

"Why are you lying under the truck?" She peeked around him and pointed to the tailgate of the truck. "Don't you have someone to fix it if it's broken?"

Throwing his head back, Logan laughed. "We do have someone." He pointed to his chest. "Me. Working with Ray on the dirt team really helped me out. I knew enough about trucks to change my wipers and the oil, but those guys are hardcore and insisted I learn how to change brakes and anything else that had to do with a vehicle. With Team Jensen, you have to know it all and be fast. Good thing I just wanted to check the rear brakes. I haven't gotten to the lesson on rebuilding an engine block. When that goes, I'm sunk. By the way, Cass should be out in a moment."

As if they had an unspoken link, Cass walked out of the garage door with Julian in her arms. "See, I told you. Daddy's right out here." The crying child brightened upon seeing his father. "He didn't leave you."

Logan wiped his hands on his jeans and held open his arms. "Come here, big guy."

"He's spoilt rotten by his father." Cass shook her head. She pointed towards the road. "Hey, do you know who was in the dark green car at the end of the driveway?"

"No clue." Logan bounced Julian on his hip. "Might've been the mail lady. She drives a new car every day, it seems. Whoever it was is gone now."

"Still bothers me. I'm not keen on strangers showing up out of the blue." Cass turned away from the drive. "So how are you? I already got a phone call, Miss Jaden."

Jaden cringed. First an unknown car and now a phone call. From whom? If her father had felt the need to involve himself yet again, she'd scream and hit the road for Siberia.

Taking Julian's hand, Logan waved. "On that note, we'll leave you girls alone." He kissed Cass's cheek. "Have fun and spend all my money, love."

Cass kissed him on the lips and then kissed Julian on the forehead. "Don't miss me too much, boys." After Logan closed the garage door, Cass spoke again. "Well, now that they're taken care of, I can deal with you. Were you supposed to meet someone other than me this morning?" She crooked a brow. "I'm telling you, he acted like I was your big sister, checking in like that. What you do is none of my business."

Without looking at Cass, Jaden confirmed, "I saw Marlon last night." *Saw him, kissed him, touched him...found my heart.*

"Should you just meet up with him instead? He sounded tired and a little worried."

Wrapping her arms around her body, Jaden walked towards the car. "No. He's just keeping an eye on me. It's nothing." Nothing that she needed to deal with. Marlon wasn't her problem—just a sexy roadblock who could probably love her. Not that she'd give him the chance. Right now, she needed to figure out what she wanted to do with her life.

Behind her, Cass sighed. "It didn't sound like nothing. I got the impression he was pretty shaken up—like a man who's found a reason to smile and can't because she's being obstinate. You haven't done anything you'll regret, have you?"

"He thinks I ran away and he probably doesn't want to get into trouble because he didn't bother to tell the sheriff I was in town. According to my father and the authorities back home, I'm a fugitive. It's all over the national news." Jaden sat on the bumper and stared at Cass. Maybe she'd understand.

"What brought you here to Ohio?"

"A month ago, I decided I wanted to do something with my life. Every other time I got the idea to be a better person, Daddy shipped me off to some third-world country to promote peace or some other worthy cause. And I always managed to screw it up. I ran away from rehab and went on a bender in Beverly Hills. The final straw was when I lied my way out of a movie role because it was nothing more than a porn flick." She waved her hand. "When I was in rehab, I saw these women who had lives and kids and things to look forward to. When the day's done, I have nothing to show for my time on Earth. So I kicked my bad habits."

"You wanted a clean legacy?"

"Sort of. I'm scared my life will have been worthless. I'll never be a great political mind, or cure hunger, but if I can make something of myself, then that's enough. I want to be remembered for the good things I did."

"It's a noble thought." Cass sat down on the black truck's bumper. "I'm sure you could help someone and I have a couple ideas as to who, but what did you have in mind? Since you seem to want to avoid Marlon like the plague."

The plague, the flu, and any other thing that could potentially break her heart and soul. Time to reveal the grand, if rather loose, scheme. "Remember when we went to the bead store in town? They had a little message board with all the want ads. Well, while you and Les looked at beads, I read the board. I saw some ads offering jobs I can do. I'm not perfect with kids, but I can babysit. Do you want a babysitter? I'm sure you and Logan need a night out or at least another pair of hands to help out." She clasped her hands together. She'd plead if she needed to plead. "I'm not totally disgusted by hard work. And if nothing else, I could walk dogs—anyone's dogs."

Raising her brows, Cass pointed to the carpet of drab, olive grass on the other side of the driveway. "You do remember we have snow in Ohio, right?"

"Yeah, a couple inches here and there."

"Sometimes. Other times we get walloped and Logan has to use the tractor to plough us out. Are you sure you want to put up with that? A lot of people choose Florida because they hate our snow."

Snow? She could deal. Lots of snow? Well, she'd learn to cope. Show weakness? Never. "I'm positive I can hack it. I played the part of Claudine in Time Trek. Anything is easier than being a one armed robot—even learning to drive in snow."

"Well good for you." Standing, Cass applauded. "Why don't we go back to the bead store and also try the board at the diner? I know both are full and maybe you can find something by the end of the week."

The heaviness in her heart lightened. Jaden grinned. "Then let's go find the next chapter in my new life."

* * * *

Marlon snapped his phone shut. No answer from Cass except to wait and see.

Dammit.

Okay, so Jaden didn't want to meet. Go figure. Why did she want to avoid him? Wasn't he man enough for her? Was her big change a joke? No, that explanation didn't sit well. She may have lied, but Jade had changed. Jaden Marie had taken her place.

He groaned and stared at the ceiling a moment before he placed both hands on the bench press and resumed his workout. His muscles ached and his mind wandered from the rep numbers. He dropped the heavy weight back into the cradle and sat up. "I'll tear something if I don't get my head back in the game."

Maybe she had plans this morning and his spur-of-the-moment suggestion hadn't fitted in with them. According to Cass, she and Jaden were heading into town. Would he look like a stalker if he bumped into her at the diner? His stomach growled. Getting food held promise—after a shower.

Forty-five minutes after his workout, Marlon headed out to his Jeep. When he opened the door, a familiar voice came from behind him. "Are you headed out this morning? I see your little friend from last night didn't hang around."

Clenching his fist behind the doorframe to hide his frustration, he glared at Sabrina. "You told me to choke on my male anatomy when we split."

Flipping a lock of hair over her shoulder, she shrugged. "You're a sweet guy that I thought I hated, but I made a mistake."

He stared at her for a long moment. Something looked odd about her. Her thin face remained strained, like she had a secret to tell. What was it? His eyes widened. Her hair. "I see you tried a new hair colour." It looked like the exact shade of Jaden's. What the fuck?

Sabrina cocked her head and twisted a honey curl around her finger. "You like it? I thought of you when I bought the box this morning. 'Unleash the real you'."

"Uh-huh." *Thinking of me, or trying to be someone you aren't...* He'd bet the latter. "If you like it, then good for you." He checked his watch. "I have to go."

A slow smile blossomed on Sabrina's coral lips. "Why don't you drop by around lunch? We can share a glass of wine and catch up." Waving, she strolled back up the sidewalk. "I'll leave the door unlocked."

Marlon settled in the bucket seat and yanked his keys from his pocket. Whatever had got into Sabrina's head to make her think he wanted something from her was beyond him. So they'd dated for a year? Lots of people dated with no expectation of a deep relationship. So they'd had sex. It hadn't been earth-shattering. Thinking about her didn't keep him up at night. Sex with her certainly hadn't rocked his world. He watched her saunter to her front door and shivered in disgust. There was no rush, no bone-deep desire to know every inch of her body.

So why obsess about Jaden? There were more than a hundred text messages back and forth between them and only two—no, three real kisses, but the memory of those kisses seared him. His heart had begun to beat again. His blood boiled when he held her in his arms. Did she feel the same? He snorted. Jaden had probably seen him with Sabrina, come to the wrong conclusion, and gone on her merry way. Not that he blamed her... Sabrina didn't walk away quietly from anyone for very long.

What was it about Jaden? Before her transformation, she could stop traffic with her looks. The rail-thin body, the blonde hair shimmering around her face, the wild behaviour... But he wasn't drawn to the glossy image. Yes, he'd liked her—what man wouldn't? But the desire to have sex with the celebrity hottie hadn't surged through his veins.

What had changed?

The Jade Weir persona was gorgeous...but unreachable. Two years ago at the station, when she'd let her guard down and become Jaden Marie, her inner beauty had outshone her physical appearance. When she'd showed up at his door with her curvier body and the natural look, he couldn't help but stare. He longed to run his fingers through the honey-coloured tresses as he kissed her. And those kisses! She had tasted like cola and sin. Intoxicating. What would it feel like to have her astride him, screaming his name as he pumped into her?

Shifting in his seat, he rubbed his groin. The memory of the previous night sucked. Every time he closed his eyes, she smiled at him in a dozen different fantasy scenes. Until he told her how he felt, he'd never sleep. What if the rumours were true? That she'd come to Ohio to escape something other than her lifestyle—like a bad drug buy, or an angry dealer? Shit. Drugs made everything more complicated.

Engaging the engine, he drove into town. Cass had said something about antiquing. Would they be at the thrift store or maybe at the flea market barn by the highway? He'd bet the thrift store, but why would she need to thrift shop if she had money? Unless Jaden really had planned on making it on her own. His admiration for her grew.

The phone call from Mac came to mind. What if she was on the run? From a dealer? She wouldn't have much ready cash. But what if she had taken money from her father? Nah, she made enough on the bad movies and that ridiculous website to fund three middle class households. Plus she admitted to a small supply of funds.

Would it be unrealistic to run her name for a record? She admitted she'd been in trouble a few times as a teen for curfew with related drug charges, as well as a drunk driving charge three years previously. It never hurt to be safe rather than sorry, even if people did change.

He shook his head as he pulled into a parking spot at the thrift store. Jaden wasn't a suspect and she wasn't guilty. Yet. Maybe he'd have Carol Ann run Jaden's name anyway.

He tugged the sunglasses from his eyes and nibbled on the earpiece. If he wanted a chance with her, he needed to think like a man interested in a date, not a cop trying to catch a suspect.

Then what the hell was he doing outside the blasted thrift store? He didn't need furniture and wasn't in the market for gently-used clothes. Sliding down in his seat, he scanned the lot. A jet black Mercedes Benz sat six spots from the door. Hers? He wasn't sure.

Part of him wanted to barge into the store and hunt her down. The greater part of him wasn't so sure. What if she was staying away from him on purpose? She could be up to something she didn't want him to know about. Marlon rolled his window down to let in fresh air. Maybe the stiff breeze would clear his head.

He doubted it.

"I can't help you if you won't tell me what's going on," he murmured.

Chapter Four

Ten minutes of watching the ebb and flow in front of the thrift store bored Marlon to the point of tears. Nothing thrilling happened aside from a green car parking next to the Mercedes. No one exited the vehicle, and since it was a public lot, he had no grounds to question anyone. He gave up his post and headed to the sheriff's department. He strolled inside and made his way to the reception desk. He nodded to Carol Ann Leidecker, the receptionist. "Hi, darlin'. Is Mac in?"

The raven-haired woman grinned. A fresh piercing decorated her right nostril. Thick black kohl rimmed her eyes. "He's in his office and fired up about the rash of auto break-ins. He's got Ronan out checking one of the complaints. How are you?"

"I'm alive and breathing." Marlon grabbed the schedule clipboard off her desk and riffled through the pages. "Good enough for me."

"Right." Carol Ann snorted. "Why are you here, then? You don't usually come in on your days off, especially if Sabrina's off, too. Looking to pick up extra hours?"

"We broke up more than six months ago. What Sabrina does is her business." He reorganised the sheaf of papers and placed them back under the clip. "Last I heard, she moved on to some guy named Tim."

"I heard the same thing and good, too, except his name was Terry. Doesn't matter. I didn't want to have to get rid of her again." Clicking the keys on the keyboard, Carol Ann resumed her typing. "I'm glad you two split. I don't care if she was an actress, she wasn't quite on the level."

"You and me both." He shrugged and headed to his desk. "I've got a name I want you to run down for me. By the way, what's that thing in your nose? It looks goofy."

With a black-tipped nail, she toyed with the crimson jewellery. "Yeah, Daddy didn't like it either, but Craig said it looked hot. I like it." She drummed her fingers on the metal desktop. "I'll bet you want to know about that celebrity suspected to be in town. Possibly a record and her recent activities?"

Stopped in his tracks, Marlon cracked his knuckles. "Who is the celebrity you're referring to?" Like he didn't have a clue.

"Jade Weir."

So everyone knew? Wonderful. "What's she got to do with Crawford? It's not like the rich and famous run off to Ohio when they get bored." He rummaged through some paperwork, not really looking at the words on the pages. The image of Jaden, sitting on his couch grinning and natural, ran rampant through his mind. His sixth sense screamed that she belonged in his life. "Besides, I'm pretty sure she's not here."

Please Remember Me

Footsteps pattered behind him. "So then who is the blonde strolling into the diner with Cass Malone?"

Whipping around, Marlon knocked into Carol Ann. With an, "Oof!" he headed to the window. A blonde? His heart thundered in his chest. Sure enough, Cass stood on the sidewalk next to Logan. The blonde in question cuddled Julian Malone in her arms. As she turned, Marlon knew. Jaden. He'd know her body whether swathed in curve-hugging denim or in sackcloth.

"She's cute."

To hide his shaky hands, he folded his arms. "She's original."

"Do you know her? Taft and I have a bet going that she's Jade and she's slumming." Leaning on Marlon, Carol Ann sighed. "Why she'd slum here is beyond me. There's a whole lot of cow poop, soybeans, and flat land here in Ohio. Think she's making another play for Logan?"

A twinge of jealousy raced through his system. "I hope not. He's not looking. He's happy with Cass." Although Logan was a stand-up guy, he didn't want to think of Jaden and Logan together. The idea of her making love to another man churned his stomach.

"So you do like her!" Carol Ann shrieked and clapped. "Taft said you had a thing for her when you did the questioning. Mac will have your head, you know. He hates when we fraternise with the suspects."

"Taft McGregor wouldn't know his ass from his elbows." Groaning, he widened his stance." As for Mac, he won't care if I don't tell him." Because I won't be with her anyway. She's trouble. "But last time I checked, she wasn't a suspect in anything. Care to enlighten me?" And give him a reason to stay away from her.

"She seems clean. No drugs, no booze. Nothing. I wanted to give you fits, that's all." Carol Ann giggled. "I might need you to do something for me while I'm here. I'm bogged down and could use a favour."

He turned. So she wanted to play dirty, eh? Bring it on. "Oh really? I'd love to make Craig jealous. Meet me at five?"

Crimson infused her cheeks. Her words came out in a rush. "Craig and I…well… I didn't mean you and me… Why don't you go get Mac's lunch at the diner? You can go see her and maybe you can have that tryst you've deserved since Addison passed."

Swallowing a snappy comeback, Marlon held out his hand. No one mentioned his first wife without causing him grief, but since he liked Carol Ann, he'd let it slide this time. Plus, he did want to see Jaden. "Give it here. I won't talk to her in case she's truly in trouble, but I'm sure she's not doing anything illegal." *I hope she's not.* He took the slip of paper and headed out of the door.

Carol Ann cackled. "Go get 'em, tiger. Tag that chick."

Checking the traffic, Marlon crossed the street with long strides. *Tag that chick. Shit.* Blatant words might have fitted Jade, but not Jaden Marie. An afternoon tryst. Hell, getting laid for the sake of getting off wasn't worth it. He wanted a woman to love.

As he entered the glass foyer, he noticed the honey blonde by the community board. He cleared his throat in case it wasn't Jaden.

Startled, Jaden clutched her chest and turned. "I'm sorry. I'll get out of your w—Marlon?"

Despite his common sense screaming not to touch her, he tucked some loose strands of hair behind her ear. Sizzles went straight to his groin. *Dear God, what if they* really did become lovers? He'd never survive—and yet he liked the odds. Dying in her arms sounded rather pleasant. Satisfying.

When she licked her bottom lip, he came close to coming unglued. Her eyes widened. "What are you doing here?"

"Getting my boss's order. I should be angry since you avoided me, but I'll deal." When her gaze raked over his body, he fisted his hand to keep from wrapping her in an embrace. "I see you're checking out the want-ads. Which flyer caught your attention?"

She held her palm open. Three slips of paper lay crumpled in her hand. "One's for a babysitter, one's for a dog walker and the third is for a companion."

Companion? His throat constricted. "Which one?"

"Which one what?"

"Who wants a companion?"

She pointed to a pink flyer. *Elder in the community seeks companion. Must be able to lift a hundred pounds and willing to work nights and weekends. 555-0089 Ask for Dan.* Dan Denoon, local businessman and suspected pimp. Hell, no. She didn't know his story, but he wasn't going to let her fall into his trap. Having a former celebrity would boost his popularity and get Jaden into a world she could probably handle...but didn't deserve.

"You don't want to be his companion. He's not looking for someone to care for his Gramma." Despite his trust in her decisions, he sighed. "He wants an escort-slash-plaything. It's bad news."

Shrinking away from him, she handed him the paper. "Oh. Sorry."

Her sweet nature would be the death of his sanity, but shit if she wasn't cute when she was out of her element. Wriggling in his polo shirt, he shifted. When had the air got so damned hot in the little foyer? It was late October for crying out loud. "You didn't know. Which one is for the dog walker?"

"Maybe I shouldn't tell you. You shot my other option down." The hint of a frown marred her coral lips. "Oh, what the hell? You're a cop. I should trust you." She pointed to a simple, handwritten flyer. "This one. For a lady named Judi Pennywood. Know her? Does she run some sort of prostitution ring, too?" She put her hands up. "I can see it now. Granny's Girlie Show. Come one, come all...or don't come at all. No refunds."

Gritting his teeth, he groaned. "Jaden, honey, I didn't mean that. I just—"

Before he could finish his answer, she clamped a hand over his mouth. "I'm giving you grief. I know how to do that without any training." She scrunched her nose and winked. "So what's the skinny on this Pennywood character?"

Wrapping his fingers around hers, he removed her hand from his mouth. Being with her felt so natural, so right. He wanted to see her more—every day. If she'd let him. "I work with her great niece, Carol Ann. She's a nice lady. Around eighty-six-ish. I believe she still owns a Basset hound."

Jaden cringed. "Do they drool? I hear they make a mess."

Rubbing his thumb over her knuckles, he considered her questions. As far as he knew, Saint Bernards drooled. Did Bassets? "I guess you'll have to call her and find out. Carol Ann loves to tell me stories. I'd say you, Judi and Carol Ann would get along great."

Slowly, her gaze met his. Eyes the colour of sea glass with tinges of azure mixed in for good measure, framed by dark lashes. A man could lose himself in those eyes. "You really think this is a good deal? I don't want to be taken for a ride, but I can do this, Marlon."

"Never said you couldn't." He nodded to the diner. "Although I'd love to stay here and talk, I need to take the order back to the department. Want to come along?"

Before she could answer, the bell on the diner door dinged. Cass, with an armload of squirming Julian, strolled through the passage. Logan trailed only a step behind. "Hey, Marlon. I see you found Jaden. Why don't you two hang out this afternoon? Maybe he knows the guy in the green car."

Jaden's mouth opened a fraction of an inch as she bumped into Marlon, not that he minded. Her warm breath tickled against his skin, sending shimmers through his body. How was it that this woman affected him in such small ways?

His bodily reaction aside, who was this person with the green car? "A new boyfriend in a hunter green sports car maybe?"

Cass elbowed Logan. "You are pushy today, even if you're right." When he shrugged, she turned to Jaden. "The green car seems to be wherever we are, but it's not around now." She glanced at the strips of paper in Jaden's hand. "Did you find something?"

Jaden nodded. "I did. But this foyer is getting cramped. Are we ready to go? I wanted to hunt for an apartment and you said you knew some good buildings."

Opening the door to the outside, Marlon waved Cass and Julian through. "Where were you thinking, Cass? You know the apartments around here from when you helped Les move."

As Jaden edged between him and the glass, her breath caught. He liked that and planned to find a way to bring the reaction back over and over again. Logan gave him a soft punch to the arm. "Go for her," he muttered under his breath. "Keep her off the streets."

Marlon's ears burned. Forget the job, forget his late wife, and forget his hard luck with women. Hell yeah, he wanted to go for Jaden, but at her pace. Better to move with caution than from spur of the moment to regret.

Cass pulled the blanket more tightly around her wriggly one-year-old child. "I thought we'd look at the Brooks Building and the Oceana, but Julian doesn't want to cooperate." She handed her son to Logan. "You might have a better idea, Marlon. I might have helped her look through the phonebook, but you grew up here. You know the town better than I do. What about where you live, in the Abbe Patterson Estates?"

Putting her hands up, Jaden protested. "Absolutely not. The name sounds distinguished, but no. I met some of his neighbours and I don't think I'd be welcome."

The comment rankled Marlon and he filed it away in his memory.

With a snort, Logan wrapped his free arm around Cass. "You ran into Sabrina, I assume."

Cass dug her elbow into Logan's side again. "Why don't we go change Julian and give them some space?"

Logan frowned. "But he's not poopy."

Taking a deep breath, Cass tugged Logan's jacket sleeve. "We'll be over here if you need us," she said and disappeared behind her navy truck.

Jaden dug her hands into her hoodie pockets. "So."

"So..." Marlon fiddled with the paper in his hand. "I'm free until eight tonight."

"You have a date? I'll bet she's pretty."

Jerking his attention from his shoes to her face, he shook his head. "No date. I'm on duty." God, would he have to admit how long it had been since he'd been on a decent date? "I know the Brooks and the Oceana. You'll get a better deal for your money at the Oceana, but the Brooks has better security."

"I've got plenty of security, but what I don't have is stuff to fill the apartment."

"Didn't you find some furniture?"

"Actually I did." Jaden edged a foot away from him. "Cass gave me one of her spare beds if I want it and I found a nice little Queen Anne's chair at the market. I've got my clothes, all my makeup, a duffle bag full of clothes and about twenty pairs of shoes in the trunk—but that's it. I guess for a former celebrity, I didn't plan well, did I? But, hey, I have shoes!"

Most people would have brought things for survival. She'd brought shoes, lots of shoes. "What if I offer to help you move the bed and the chair and the mountain of footwear? I think I can also scrounge up a used fridge and stove if there's room." The more she inched away from him, the more he wanted to pull her into his arms. "And I think I like the woman you are right now better than any old celebrity."

"Like?" A foot from him, she paused. Crimson blossomed on her cheeks. "Thanks, but don't you have to sleep before you go on duty?"

Sleep? Unless he drowned himself in her kisses or watched television with his eyes closed, he didn't sleep well. Not at night or during the day for that matter. "I got enough last night. I'll be good. Why don't you call Mrs

Pennywood and we'll go meet her. I think you just might like the job."

A smile returned to her face, brightening it in an instant. "Yeah?"

Holding out his hand, he reached for her. "I do."

She laced her fingers with his, like they'd been a couple for years. "But what about the food?"

Switching his attention to the piece of paper, he read the scrawl. *Got you. Mac ate an hour ago. Have a fun afternoon.* As much as he'd rather string her up, he applauded Carol Ann's attempt to get him out of himself. Any reason to spend time with Jaden was good enough for him. "Well, damn. I guess the order went out already."

Jade took the crumpled paper from his hand and scanned it. "I think you were set up." She turned when the engine of Cass's Chevy roared to life. "Looks like I was, too."

Snaking an arm around her shoulder, he took a breath of her unique scent. Something flowery and light enveloped him, making it hard to think straight. "Logan's a piece of work. Want me to go?"

She dropped her head to his shoulder, cuddling into him. "He's been a pistol ever since I met him, but he's one I want on my side—just like you. You're not mad I didn't call you, are you?"

"Nope."

"Me, neither."

Her quick response warmed his heart and other parts of his body. He wasn't mad in the least. If he didn't think he'd scare her off, he'd plant a kiss on those lips and savour her sweetness until he had to go on duty. "Good, 'cause I feel great." Better than great. Dancing-in-the-streets, fucking wonderful, perfect-with-a-cherry-on-top great.

"Let's go see these apartments and meet Mrs Pennywood."

Chapter Five

Staring at the keys in her hand, Jaden considered asking Marlon to ride with her, but then what? He stirred desires she'd long overlooked. He made her forget the men in her past. His touch kicked her body temperature up at least four or five degrees, not that she minded. Being in his warm embrace—heaven. With his crooked, furry smile, he reminded her of Ewan McGregor and made her think things she shouldn't consider about a man of the law—not when she had such a chequered past.

The thought occurred to her—would he even fit in the seat?

From the corner of her eye, she spotted Bobby's black truck. At least he stayed true to his word. Just let the paparazzi find her.

Squeezing her shoulder, Marlon nabbed her attention and led her to the Benz. "My Jeep is safe in the muni lot. Why don't we take your car and then I can show you around? You'll get a better feel for the layout if you drive it yourself."

She smacked her lips to break the trance he seemed to put her in. God, how was she going to drive with him so freaking close? "Um, what if it breaks down? I'm not real good with engines and she's been driven pretty hard since I left the Cali state line."

His eyes widened. "You drove here from California? By yourself?"

Squirming under his glare, she edged from his grasp. The security in his size comforted her, but the vote of confidence had unnerved her. "Well, who else was gonna drive? I left my chauffeur at home." She bit the inside of her cheek. Iron-rich blood filled her mouth. "I mean, I wanted to get away, just like that old commercial, so I did. I stashed my credit card, closed my checking account, cashed out the check, and set off. Why? Is that a crime?" Okay, so yeah, she'd done some foolish and illegal things in her life, but not since she'd decided to live life on her own terms. Did he count that speeding ticket? Sheesh.

"Wait." He put his broad hands on her shoulders, engulfing her in his strength and masculinity once again. Even his scent, something woodsy, was wonderful. The green in his eyes softened, reminding her of the ocean off the coast of Florida where the mix of blue and green melded into something beyond description. "I meant that it's dangerous to drive that far if you aren't sure the vehicle is reliable, but you made it and I'm proud."

Her mouth fell open. Wait, had she heard him right? Proud? As in, he thought she'd done well? Hell, yeah. "You really trust me to drive? I did get busted for driving the wrong way down a one-way street in Pasadena two years ago."

He brushed his knuckles over her cheek. "But you can read the traffic signs?"

Slapping his hand away, she chuckled. "Yes, I can. Last time I checked, s-t-o-p spelled accelerate."

"Then we're set. If you get into too much trouble, just listen to me and I'll get you straightened out." Marlon grabbed the door handle. "And g-o means you'd better hit the brake, smart aleck."

A shiver ran up her spine. Electricity crackled in her veins. Maybe he could straighten her out in other delicious, sweaty ways... Fisting her hands, she forced her thoughts towards something more mundane, like kittens, or pancakes...or the sizzle of his lips against hers. Oh, hell.

"You know you sound all official. Do you do it out of routine or to impress women?"

"I'm a cop all the way down to my DNA. Sue me."

"No, I don't want to sue you. I know what cops make." And how they put their lives on the line. Forcing her mind back to driving, Jaden slid into the seat and gripped the steering wheel with numb fingers. Did he know the effect he had on her? Did he care? Did he want to toy with her and break her will to show he could? Enough! No more thinking about what couldn't be.

"Where are we going, again? I forgot."

Marlon handed her his cell phone. "Call Mrs Pennywood and see if she's home. Then we can decide where to go. Deal?"

With trembling hands, she took the phone. Her heart lodged in her throat. She could do this. She could talk to the woman and sound coherent. Landing a job was no harder than taking her clothes off for a modelling shoot, and one heck of a lot warmer.

Please Remember Me

After three rings, someone answered. "This is the Pennywood residence. May I help you?"

She gasped. The words she'd practised each mile of her journey to Ohio suddenly vanished. Marlon must have sensed her fear, and squeezed her hand in one of his larger hands. "You can do this," he mouthed.

"Hello?"

Not about to lose the job before she'd earned it, she forced her mouth to work. "M—my name is Jaden Haydenweir and I'm calling about the dog walker position." Man, she didn't sound anything like the poised woman who endorsed luxury cars on television.

The elderly voice on the other end laughed. "Do you have any pets?"

Pets? Um, did the paparazzi count? They followed her like dogs and chased her like wolves. "No, but I did as a child."

"Good. Do you live here in town?"

She mouthed the question to Marlon and put her hand over the speaker. "What do I say? I live in a motel room!"

He waved away her concern with his right hand. "Give her my address. I doubt she'll check it on such short notice. Sixteen twenty-seven Harvard Street."

With a nod, Jaden relayed the information. Another rush of warmth surged through her. Why did the idea of staying with him seem so nice? Comfortable? Because it was easy and wrong. If they had a relationship, she wanted to have it the old-fashioned way. She wanted to earn it, not be a mercy roommate or a notch on the bedpost.

"Just a moment." The female voice giggled again. "Well, I talked to Sparky and he'd like to meet a Miss Haydenweir. Can you come by around three?"

Jaden glanced at the dashboard clock. Twelve forty-six. She could make three, but what if she found an apartment before the appointment? She'd make time. "We'll see you then."

Her heart thundered in her chest. Three. Until then, she had Marlon to herself and housing to look for. She glanced in the side mirror. The green car sat parked three spaces away but facing in the other direction. Her lunch reversed its course. Someone wanted her whereabouts known.

Marlon rubbed the top of her hand with his callused thumb. "Hey. You okay?"

Okay? No, she wasn't okay, fine or swell. Maybe running away with little more than her sense of pride hadn't been such a great idea. When her father had run her life, she'd just asked and received. What if Mrs Pennywood and Sparky, whoever that was, didn't like her? Her stomach roiled. What if she wasn't cut out to take care of anything other than her credit cards? What about the car that seemed to be wherever she was? What did this person want?

Marlon cupped her chin with his thick fingers, bringing her gaze to his. The heat from his touch warmed her blood. "Hey. You'll be fine. She's a nice lady who probably wants someone to take care of her dog since she can't get out much and her niece works full time. You'll be great, Jaden Marie. I'm sure." His thumb brushed over her lips. "I'm right here and I won't let you give up."

Hearing her name on his lips sent a bolt of confidence ricocheting through her system. She ignored the ill-feeling skittering up her spine and asked, "Then how do we get to the Oceana?"

Although his common sense dictated he should let go and keep his distance from her, Marlon held her hand tightly. God, nothing had ever felt so right in all his life. Was he crazy? Or maybe in love? No, no. Time to switch thoughts before he got himself in trouble and did something he'd regret. He shifted. Damn. An erection pressed against his zipper.

Blowing out a long breath, he switched his attention from the tent in his jeans. He directed her down the side streets to Linden Avenue. "Did she say three twenty-two? That should be right up here."

She afforded him a sideways glance and parked in front of the crumbling brick building. Only after she'd engaged the brake and switched off the engine did she speak. "I guess you probably do know the entire town if you're the sheriff."

"I grew up over in Jarvis, and hung out here in Crawford during high school. I know my way around both towns." She rolled her eyes, making him want to kiss the sass right from her mouth. Running his fingers though his hair, he sighed. "Do you want me to go with you? They might want references."

Her brows furrowed. "References? For an apartment? Why? I can't steal it."

"In case you can't pay your bills. They will want to make sure you're a good risk." Distress clouded her eyes. Hooking his finger under her chin, he placed a light kiss on her nose. "Don't let it scare you. Everyone starts out with no references—even former celebrities. I'll go along and vouch for you."

"Okay." Her lips parted. "Thanks."

He shivered. That one kiss wouldn't be enough. He longed to taste her all over. Aw, crap. He couldn't look at an apartment with a frickin' stiffy. Better back out and get his hormones under control. "Jaden?"

Without warning, she threw her arms around his neck and squeezed. "I know we haven't done anything yet, but thank you."

Rubbing his hands up and down her back, he marvelled at how perfectly she fitted against him. The erection grew beneath his jeans. Shit. Well, no, not bad, but not good for going out in public.

Leaning back a few inches, she stared into his eyes and licked her bottom lip. "Marlon, I think you have a problem. Should we leave? I don't want to get a man of the law into trouble with public indecency."

A belly laugh ripped from his throat. All he could think about was getting into her pants and she took the edge off by making another joke. "I'll try to control myself. Why don't we see these apartments?"

Chapter Six

Plopping down in the bucket seat of the Benz, Jaden blew out a long breath. Grief. The Oceana was nice, but way too expensive for her budget—and without furnishings. The Brooks looked okay and was a better fit for her price range, but no one-bedroom units were available. She could max out her credit card, but with no job, she couldn't pay it off. Drat. Living within her means grew tougher by the minute. She chided herself. *I'm not running back to Daddy. I can do this.*

She checked the dashboard clock. Crap. Two forty-eight. "I wish we had your siren. We need to get to Clarendon Avenue in twelve minutes and I'm not sure where it is."

"The siren's for emergencies, not impatient drivers." He pointed straight ahead. "If you take a left at the stop sign and go two blocks, we should be in her neighbourhood."

Before long, they sat in front of the powder blue Cape Cod. Her hands went clammy and her throat dry. "Is this it?"

"Three twenty-two. Yep, that's it." Marlon crossed his ankles. His wide smile heated the interior of the vehicle, even if he looked uncomfortable with his knees practically up to his chest. "You'll get this job, Jaden Marie, I can feel it."

Shoring up her courage, Jaden stepped from the car. She glanced down at her clothes—jeans and a hoodie with a long-sleeved tunic underneath. Wrestling the hoodie over her head, she finger-combed her hair back into place. Was that dressy enough? At home she'd had a closet full of baubles to accessorise. Here, she was out of luck except for what she'd tossed into her suitcase. She smoothed her hands over the crinkles in her blouse.

"You look beautiful," Marlon whispered.

"Thanks." She slid her gaze over his profile and grinned. So tall and strong, he probably feared nothing. With sure steps, she headed up the walkway. A woman with an unnatural shade of copper hair sat on the porch and a white Basset hound with caramel and coffee-coloured freckles lay spread out on the concrete, warming his belly in the late day sun.

"Are you Mrs Pennywood?"

When the woman nodded, short locks of hair bobbed. "People call me Judi, so if you're working for me, then you can, too."

Fluttering her hands for lack of something better to do, Jaden inched up the stairs. "You don't know me and yet you trust me enough to hire me?"

"I have a great measuring system." Judi pointed to the dog. "You see, Sparky doesn't like strangers, but you're on the porch and he's not making a sound." She nodded to the car. "Why don't you get your gentleman friend from the car? We can talk and get to know each other. I assume he'll be over quite a bit."

Confused, Jaden flailed her hands once more. "Wait. Over? He's not my... He's taken. I'm... We're friends." Grief. She snapped her mouth shut to stop her babbling. Yeah, she wanted him to be more, and that kiss, those cuddles, seemed like more. But really. Coming to Ohio was supposed to get her out from under Daddy's thumb and simplify her life — not make it more complicated. And certainly not for a love match.

Judi smiled. "A nice boy like that isn't a friend for long."

Stunned, Jaden sneaked a glance towards the car. As if he'd known they were speaking about him, probably because he'd overheard the conversation, Marlon was now ambling up the walkway. "Hello, Mrs Pennywood. I'm Marlon Cross. I work with Carol Ann."

Judi snickered, just like on the phone. "I thought you looked familiar. You went with my friend Stella's granddaughter Michelle for a bit, didn't you?"

While Marlon fumbled for an answer, Jaden edged forwards to pet Sparky. She held her hand out and allowed the sleepy dog to sniff before she rubbed the top of his head. Brown eyes the colour of a chocolate bar stared at her. A pink tongue sneaked out of the side of his mouth and licked his jowls. She wrinkled her nose. So his breath wasn't the best and his eyes were a little watery, but weren't Basset hounds known for their droopy eyes? The more she scratched him, the more attached she became. Maybe being a professional dog walker wasn't so bad.

"Do you have a place to stay?"

Her gaze snapped from the dog to Judi. "I'm sorry. I wasn't paying attention."

Another smile crinkled the crow's feet around Judi's eyes, giving her a kind Gramma look. "I asked if you needed an apartment. You look a little lost."

Easing down onto the concrete step, Jaden glanced at Marlon. Better go with the truth. If Judi understood why she'd fibbed and didn't order her off the lawn, then maybe she was meant for the job. "I am looking for an apartment. I just moved into town and haven't found anything I can afford. I'm sorry I lied and gave you his address."

"You? Lie? I'd never guess." Despite her snappish words, Judi's eyes sparkled behind her glasses. "I need someone to take over the second floor and stay with me in case I fall or need to go to the grocery store. I'm seventy-two years old and with my angina, I can't take chances."

"Angina?"

"I had my heart attack at sixty, but the doctor suggested I be careful and reduce my stress." She waved her hand. "Stress…tell that to Steven. He's my son, but I can't count on him to be around if he's in one of his moods."

"I'm sorry." Jaden sighed. She knew all about moody people. "I'd love to help if you're offering me the place to crash."

"Then the bedroom is yours." Judi turned to Marlon. "Although you won't be able to visit all hours of the night, I expect to see you. You see, I do have rules. No men after ten." She giggled again. "Ooh, and that rhymed. I am a pistol."

Jaden exchanged a confused glance with Marlon only to have him smile and look away. What did he mean by the grin?

"Why don't we see the upstairs? It's cosy and already furnished, so you don't have to lug anything up the stairs. They twist, you know, and that's hard for manoeuvring.

I'd hate for you to get hurt before you hit thirty. But I love my quirky house." Judi snapped her fingers. "Come on, Sparks. Let's show our Jaden the room."

With his hand on the small of her back, Marlon followed Jaden into the house and up to the suite of rooms at the top of the stairs. When Judi opened the bedroom door, he whistled. "This is spacious. From the outside, it looked a bit dinky. Nice."

"I'm full of surprises." Judi sighed. "I don't come up here as much as I'd like. The old hips can't take the stairs like they used to." She patted Marlon's arm. "I'll leave you two alone, but no horsing around. I like to keep my walls free from divots."

With a wide-eyed stare, Jaden met Marlon's equally shocked gaze. Moments after Judi left the room, he whispered, "Did she just say something about denting the walls?"

Jaden nodded. She'd dented a few walls in her time and annoyed people in neighbouring hotel suites. But to hear her landlady mention sex... Well, whatever. She'd go with the flow.

"Does she think we'd screw like rabbits while she's home?"

Rolling her eyes, Jaden turned her gaze to the colourful quilt decorating the bed. "She used to be young once, too. I'm sure she and her husband did it when she was married. I'm sure you do it, and I'm not exactly virginal, so what's the big deal?" Not that she wouldn't mind doing it with him, but he'd never offered. Hell, she wasn't sure if his long glances and soft caresses meant more than a casual thing. Most men she knew wanted a quick fuck to mark their bedposts and nothing more. One guy even made his encounter into a T-shirt: I laid Jade. Then there were the lies about the extent of her relationship with Sabrina…

Still, Marlon's fumbling responses jarred her. Maybe he didn't see them spending time exploring each other's bodies.

Interrupting her musings, Marlon spoke in his usual sure baritone. "Why don't we go get that chair so you can get settled?"

With a sigh, Jaden shook her head. "Sure. It's not like I had a hot date tonight."

His eyes widened. "Hot date? You just got into town."

A streak of anger swelled within her. Another man who didn't trust her to take care of herself. He might be six inches taller than her, but he didn't scare her. "Don't get your boxers in a bunch. You have to work, I have to unpack, and it's not like we're a couple. Besides, I'm giving up dating for a while to clean up my act." She clamped her mouth shut. He didn't deserve her fit of temper, but why'd he have to act so pissy when she mentioned another man — even in theory?

His eyes narrowed. "You're right." Jamming his hands into his jeans pockets, he started towards the door. "You're a piece of work. Look, I'm only three blocks from the department, I think I'll walk. Maybe you can con your ex-flame, Logan, or that hot date you claim not to have into moving your God damned furniture."

A howling came from the other side of the door. He tore the wooden barrier open, to find Sparky sitting on the hall carpet, growling and barking.

With a snarl, Marlon turned. "See? You even turned the fucking dog against me and I just met him. No wonder I didn't want to get involved with you."

Stunned, Jaden pointed to the door. "If I'm so repulsive, get the hell out of my room and don't come back. I hate you and never wanted to go out with you."

"I never asked."

Slamming the door, Marlon stormed down the steps. Through the thin walls, Jaden heard him speak to Judi and excuse himself. Good riddance. As she sank down onto the bed, a tear slipped down her cheek and splashed onto her hand. Why did the cute ones always have attitude issues? And to think, she'd rather liked him.

* * * *

As he stomped down the walkway, a gentle voice called from behind. Although he wanted to keep going, he turned. Judi stood on the porch with her arms crossed. "I know you just left, but I have something else I want to say to you."

Forcing his feet to move, Marlon strode back to the steps. "I'm sorry I raised my voice and disturbed you and the dog. I was out of line and I won't do it again. In fact, I'm pretty sure I won't be back."

Judi pulled the terrycloth housecoat a bit more tightly around her shoulders. From behind her, Sparky barked and howled. "I know you won't holler again. I remember your folks—Renee and Michael didn't raise a brat. Too smart, but not a brat."

"Uh, thanks?"

"You're a decent man, and I'm pretty sure you'll be back, but that's not what I need to say." She sighed and gestured to the deck chairs. "Sit. There are a few things you need to know."

Marlon held the chair as she sat, and plopped down on the seat next to her. "I'm all ears."

"You'd better be." Her voice, though soft, never wavered. "You're a police officer, right?"

"Sheriff's deputy. And damned proud of it."

"So you know when a person isn't telling the truth, I assume."

"Most of the time." Where the hell was she going with this?

"Then you know she's not running from the law like they say on all those lousy tabloid shows? Rotten so-called newscasters getting the story all backwards to increase viewership."

"Huh?"

"That sweet woman in my upstairs bedroom isn't running from the law and she isn't running away to be belligerent. She's scared, confused, and trying to figure out who she is without all the fancy, frilly garbage. Don't you remember being young once?"

Young? He might have been eighteen once, but never young. "Judi, my past has nothing to do with Jaden." *And neither does my future.*

She took his hand in hers. Her fingers barely wrapped around his wrist. "Look at the life she's led. My goodness, I wonder if her father cares about her at all. I watch Delish TV. I think she knows her father is a louse, so she's trying to find something...and someone to care about her. She's been embarrassed, harassed and overexposed. Here, she can be a normal, average woman."

He shifted his feet. Was Jaden looking to him for love? As much as part of him wanted to run upstairs and offer her the world, no. Not possible. Men like him made lousy husbands, if Addy's words were right. He worked shitty

Please Remember Me

hours, put himself in the line of fire, and cared about almost everyone in the county. He lived and breathed his job. No, she needed a stable guy who worked a stable job and could give her the attention she craved, the attention she deserved. And there was the pesky issue of her past. Crazy former lovers he could handle—the possibility she'd return to her California lifestyle scared him senseless.

"You're over-thinking this, Marlon." Judi released his hand and laced her fingers. "Give it time. You may not be soulmates or forever loves, but you won't know if you don't give it a chance."

Leaning back in his seat, he studied the porch rafters. Glints of light shone in what should've been a solid surface. Chinks in the armour, so to speak. Could Jaden understand? Would she want a passionate relationship, even if it fizzled? Having her interest, even in theory, warmed his heart almost to the point of melting the ice around it. To keep his mind out of forbidden territory, he changed the subject. "Your porch roof has holes in it."

"So then I expect to see you on your next day off to fix it."

His gaze jerked to meet hers. "What? That's not until next weekend and I had plans to...go fishing." Or something that kept him far from Jaden.

"It's been leaky for this long. One more week won't hurt anything. And don't try to fib to me."

Crooking his brow, he considered her. "Are you sure I can do it? What if I'm lousy with my hands?"

"You aren't."

Her vote of confidence floored him. "How are you sure?"

"Carol Ann told me how you fixed her car when it broke down last winter and how you managed to figure out the wiring on that heater in the sheriff's office. Fixing a roof can't be any harder."

She had a point. He sighed, scrubbing the back of his neck. It'd mean more time around Jade and after his little outburst, she wasn't his biggest fan. Then again, with the right clothes and a touch of finesse, maybe he'd win her over. "When do you want me to come back?"

"Next Friday when you get off work will be fine. I'll have my son, Steven, bring the tools and the supplies."

Though he knew to keep his mouth shut, he forged on. "Why can't he do it?"

Judi smacked his knee. "Where do I start? He's fifty-four and married. He's got his Daddy's cranky streak and he's not fond of my dog. But you, you're…what, thirty-three? You're handsome and I know you aren't married, so what's the problem?"

Problem? No problem, unless a five-foot-eight blonde swathed in designer denim continued to live on the second floor. He dug his nails into his palms. "I don't need dating advice. I've been through hell and I'm not about to go through it again." Not when he could screw his life up on his own.

"Suit yourself." She stood. "But a pretty girl like that won't stay single for long when the wolves are nearing the yard." As she opened the door, she spoke over her shoulder. "I'll see you on the twelfth at ten sharp."

Wolves in the yard? In Ohio? What? Clenching his fists, he strode down the stairs. Well, fuck. Had other men already noticed Jaden? If she walked through the diner, then yeah, half the single male population of Crawford would see her and if any of them got wind that she was the former socialite...

Dammit. Wolves, leeches, and every other lowlife scum wanting to use her to make a quick buck would be right at the door.

Which did he want? To stay in the solitary security of the job, or to succumb to Jaden's charms? The department had never let him down—except during his time with Addy. He'd brought that problem on himself. Jaden had more than her share of problems as well. Distance—he needed distance.

But going to the house to check on her and helping out did mean reasons for seeing her without the threat of trying to make it a date. Plus, then he could see the woman she really was, the woman he'd spoken to at the department on the night of the shooting.

The woman of his fantasies.

Maybe handyman work for Judi wasn't such a bad idea after all.

Chapter Seven

One hectic week of learning how to run a vacuum cleaner, hand-washing dishes, and scooping dog poop from the back lawn later, Jaden collapsed onto her bed. If someone had asked her two years previously how she'd feel about leading the Poop Brigade, she would've laughed and stuck her nose in the air. But knowing that her work kept Sparky not only healthy, but happy, made her day. Hell, it made her year. Someone depended on her, she wasn't letting them down as she usually did, and her father didn't run her life.

She closed her eyes, and her mind drifted to Marlon. His words still stung a week later. Yes, two years ago she'd had the world's biggest crush on Logan Malone. Who hadn't? He made movies, had a hot ass, and had chased her in return. Yes, when he'd fallen head-over-heels for Cass Jensen, it had hurt, but not for long. He was happy, and who was Jade Weir—socialite and loose cannon—to argue? He looked sexier in love anyway. But to have an affair with him? No. Her friendship with Cass was too great to chance it.

Besides, there was Marlon.

How could one man, a cop at that, drive her insane and keep her wanting more at the same time? Because he was different from the men she'd usually chased. He didn't define her by what she could do for him or what her father's money could buy him. He saw the scared little girl who wanted to go home, and until now had shown her a bit of human kindness. So why did he want to tear her down?

Maybe the 'I hate you' remark? She balled her fists. How else was she going to show his lack of confidence hurt like hell? Tell him? Like that ever worked. She'd given her father the truth and he'd acted as though she wanted him to rip his own heart out.

Tears threatened at the corners of her eyes. No. She wasn't about to cry over one man who didn't care and another who wasn't interested. Forget it. The way her luck ran, Marlon probably knew the skeletons buried in her past, or worse, he'd talked to her father.

"Jaden! Can you come down here?"

When Judi called, Jaden sat up. Even her new friend knew she didn't need to cry over stupid men. Pulling her hair back into a rhinestone clip, she rose from the bed and started down the stairs. "You needed me?"

Cell phone in hand, Judi grinned. "Sparks wants to go for walkies and Cass called. You left your phone down here so I answered. She wanted to know if you wanted to go to the dirt races with her. Sounds like fun."

Fun? It sounded wonderful. Jaden took the device from Judi. "Heck yeah, I want to go. She told me all about how they drive in circles and get mud all over everything. She even said there were tons of hot guys in the pits—whatever those are. Now I'm not in the market for a man, but why not look at the goods? I've got nothing to lose and eye candy is fat free."

"You gawk all you want, but realise some of those boys aren't as naïve as they look. We grow them rowdy in Ohio, too." Giggling, Judi grabbed Sparky's leash from the kitchen. "No one has ever got nothing to lose. We all have something near and dear, even if we don't realise it yet."

Okay, what did Judi know? Nibbling her top lip, Jaden clicked the leash onto Sparky's collar. He barked and slapped his tail on the carpet. "Do you know who I was, Judi? 'Cause if you did, you wouldn't warn me, you'd warn them."

Thumps like the tap of a hammer on the roof peppered the conversation. Frowning, Judi shuffled papers on her roll top desk. "If you mean reincarnation, well, I don't believe in that, but if you mean your life in Hollywood, then yes. Saying you were a pill is putting it mildly. You lived enough for three or four lifetimes, but I know that wasn't you."

"No, that was me. I ran with a rough crowd. Would you believe I have more than two million dollars waiting on me, but because I couldn't get my head out of my ass, I can't have it? If that's what you mean by something to lose, I never really had it to begin with."

When Judi frowned, Jaden nodded. "Yep. My mother left me a trust fund, but I can't access it unless I do something charitable with it. Until this past year, I couldn't get past my selfishness long enough to even consider doing something for someone else. I've got money from the last D-list movie I made, but it won't last forever. I'm at rock bottom."

Another round of thumps echoed in the room. "What's going on out there? Are you tearing the roof off or did you give Steven the hammer for stress relief?"

"Steven went to Baltimore for business. His stress is of his own making, but the next time he calls and gripes at you, let me know. He can't holler at me without getting an earful."

Jaden grinned. Having Judi as a mother-figure felt nice, like a treasured gift she didn't deserve.

A smile built at the corners of Judi's mouth. "I didn't want the porch to leak this winter so I have a boy here doing repairs."

Before Jaden could question Judi's statement, Sparky jumped and growled at her feet. Jaden shook her head. "Okay, okay. I guess you're ready to go and I don't want to clean up more piddle. We'll be back."

"I'll see you after a bit." Judi patted Jaden's arm. "Call Cass. I think you'll have a great time at the races. I know I did the last time I went. Plus, Sparks needs a few hours to rest. He's not used to all the exercise."

"You got it." As Jaden strolled out onto the porch, a silver ladder blocked the stairs. At least it wasn't grouchy Steven. Sliding on her sunglasses, she called back into the house. "Um, how am I supposed to get off the porch? The boy has the steps blocked." She added, "The moron," when she turned back towards the street.

A pair of work-boot-encased feet descended the ladder. Dusty jeans clung to the legs. Some men could get away with the grubby workman look. Wonder if the rest of him is hot? she mused. Once the legs came into view, Jaden realised who was responsible for the hammering. "Marlon?"

Peering between the rungs of the ladder, he grinned. "I'm Marlon, not moron, but thanks for shouting it all over the neighbourhood. People wondered and now they know."

Her ears burnt. Great, she'd told him she hated him and compounded it with an insult. Wonderful. "I'm sorry. I didn't know you were up there. She said it was a boy."

Even under the bill of his racing cap, his green eyes sparkled. The dimple in his left cheek deepened as his grin grew. "Would it have made a difference?"

Sparky yelped. Realising the dog wanted to go for his walk, she snapped her attention away from the thick muscles rippling underneath Marlon's tight, dirt-smeared T-shirt. Heat swirled low in her belly. God, what would it feel like to smooth her hands all over his body? To clean him up after a long afternoon of hard work?

"Jaden Marie?"

Shifting her gaze from his chest to his eyes, she blushed again. Damn, he'd caught her looking. Her stomach clenched as the quivers made their way down her spine. She liked his appraisal, even if he said nothing at all.

Marlon nodded at the dog. "You'd better get moving. Sparky just peed on your tennis shoe. Are Azad originals waterproof?"

As she wriggled her toes in her high-heeled sneaker, the dampness seeped into her sock. Swell. She sighed—so much for name brand. Nope, the dog and the man weren't going to break her mood. If Sparky wanted to walk, then they'd walk. If Marlon wanted to laugh at her, then let him laugh. Spying the side exit off the porch, she made a beeline for the second set of steps and shoved her sunglasses higher on the bridge of her nose. "I won't melt. Come, Sparks. Let's go for your walkies."

With a happy yelp, Sparky surged off the porch and into the yard. Although it took a block to calm him down, she let him go at his own pace. At least she'd got away from Marlon and his mouth-watering body. If she'd lingered any longer, she might have told him flat-out she wanted him.

Sparky seemed to like walking three blocks north and sniffing the trash around the bakery before heading two blocks east to the municipal building then back the way they'd come. Along the way, Jaden admired the turn-of-the-century brick buildings lining the main drag of Crawford. Each storefront bore the owner or the builder's name. Grand windows faced the street, some filled with goods, like in the hardware store, while others had plastic taped to the other side, hiding the emptiness.

Unless the stores had clothes, she'd rarely paid attention to the buildings in Beverly Hills. Heck, most of what she'd seen of California had been the inside of nightclubs and the interior of limousines.

As she strolled, her phone rang. Without looking at the ID screen, she flipped it open. "Hello?"

Her father spoke on the other end of the line. "Are you ready to come to your senses and come home? Ohio isn't ready for Jade Weir, remember? We learned that when you chased Logan a year or so ago."

Gritting her teeth, Jaden clenched the phone. "You don't want me home because you care about me. You miss the ridiculous things I did that sold copies of your magazine."

"You're my daughter. I worry about you."

"No normal father gives his little girl the green light to pose nude on her eighteenth birthday!"

"So that wasn't a bright decision. It still doesn't mean I don't love you. But you're a beautiful woman that men want to see. Call the pictorial my gift to the masses."

"Gift? You charged ten bucks for the issue. You love that magazine, not me." She kicked a rock in the middle of the sidewalk. "Now stop calling me. I don't need a shadow."

"I doubt it. Shadows work well in the right circumstances. Then there's always airbrushing. Think about what I said."

Before she could answer, he cut the connection. Jaden slid the phone into her back pocket with more force than necessary. Damn him! Damn Delish magazine. The tabloid rag ruined lives and tore relationships apart. And what did he mean about a shadow? Clicking her tongue, she got Sparky's attention. "Let's go."

When Sparky stopped to nose a pile of leaves and snort, Jaden noticed the slap of footsteps on the sidewalk behind her. When she turned, a blond man with a jagged scar bisecting his right eyebrow like a C stared at her. She shivered. He reminded her of the endless throngs of paparazzi and grunt news people waiting for her to falter. "Can I help you?"

"Are you?"

Narrowing her brows, she wrapped her hand around Sparky's leash. "Am I who?" The dog forgot the leaves and growled low in his throat. Maybe he read her fear. Or he didn't care for strangers.

The man's sky blue eyes widened and his mouth fell open. "You're Jade Weir! Miles wasn't kidding. He said you moved to town because you went off the rails. Fuck, yeah. Can I take you out sometime? I have my own car."

Stepping backwards, she attempted to put distance between the blond fan and her position. "I'm Jaden Marie, not Jade Weir. I have the unlucky coincidence of looking like that blonde airhead." On the inside she winced. Jade was a bimbo. Aw hell.

"No." He shook his head. "I'd know that body anywhere. You chunked on a few pounds and need a diet bad, but you're still doable. How about me and Miles at the same time? I heard you liked kink. He likes to use the video camera. Will that do?"

Sparky growled and barked. Spittle spewed from his jowls. The blond man jerked back a step or two. Her heart thundered in her chest. What a great time to have a dog! Maybe she'd get Sparky a brother or two—or ten.

"She's not doable, into kink or any of that other bullshit you mentioned. You need to leave or I'll make you leave."

Jaden knew that voice. She whipped around and smacked into Marlon. Although the fur on Sparky's back no longer stood on end, he continued to growl. She squared her shoulders and her fear ebbed a bit. Yes, maybe she needed the backup, and Marlon definitely made great backup, but what the hell? Was he following her, too?

"Who the fuck are you?" the blond man spat. "Her lapdog?"

With a sneer, Marlon's lips curled. If it was possible, she'd swear he became larger and more imposing. "That's Deputy to you, asshole."

Ducking behind him, Jaden rolled her eyes. What movie did he get that line from? Sparky, apparently not interested in the fray any longer, tugged her back down the sidewalk.

Marlon's voice, strong and sure, echoed on the lonely sidewalk. "Leave her alone. Jade Weir wouldn't be caught dead in Crawford, Ohio."

Tears pricked her eyes as she allowed Sparky to pull her away. Maybe his words were meant to send the jerk away, but they still pricked her ego. He saw her as worthless. Marlon knew about her party-hearty past and believed she still lived it. She stared straight ahead. The hunter green car rolled down the street before her. Well, swell. Another reoccurring annoyance. She caught sight of black hair and a pointy nose. Mirrored glasses hid the rest of the driver's face. Where the hell was Bobby at a time like this? Instinct dictated she get far away from the cretin in the car — protection or not.

Thankfully, Sparky found his second wind. Shocked that the Basset could walk at such a quick clip, she headed home.

Marlon clenched his fists as the man walked away. He committed the jerk's image to memory. If he wanted to pick at Jaden, then he'd have to go through hell first. The virtue of protecting and serving ran in his blood. "You're safe." Willing his heart rate to slow, Marlon turned. "Jaden Marie?"

No matter where he looked, she wasn't there. How had she got down the sidewalk so fast with the low-rider dog leading the way? He didn't recall hearing a car, so she hadn't been picked up. Damn.

Breaking into a sprint, he headed towards the square. His heart pounded in his chest, and not from the brisk run. He worried that another zany, one with more moxie, would find her. What if another crazed fan decided to get violent? No, he couldn't keep an eye on her twenty-four seven, but he would work like a dog to keep her safe anyway.

One block from the Pennywood house, he saw her. Sparky's quick pace must've petered out and Marlon thanked God. If he could talk to her for a few minutes before she ran inside, maybe he could do some damage control. Throwing caution and his pride to the wind, he called to her. "Jaden!"

Although she didn't turn around, she stopped. Sparky sat at her feet, panting. Her shoulders trembled. Was she crying? His heart squeezed within his chest. No one had the right to make her cry—not even him.

"Jaden? Honey? Are you okay? You shouldn't be alone."

Her voice came out shaky and just above a whisper. "I can't hide and I can't outrun him."

Placing his hands on her shoulders, he rested his forehead against the back of her head. "What can't you outrun? Who can't you hide from?" He had an inkling, but if she'd just tell him, he'd help her. "Tell me, Jaden."

Shrugging out of his grasp, she turned and wiped the tears from her eyes with her sleeve. "I'll be okay. You don't need to clean up after me."

No, he wasn't going to let her dismiss him. It didn't matter that he'd more or less shoved her away the weekend before. Right now, she needed a friend and he insisted on being a rock for her. "The bastard got under your skin. You don't deserve to hurt and I won't let him treat you like shit. I'm not about to let any jerk who wants to exploit some socialite run my town, especially when that socialite doesn't live here."

She shook her head. "No. I am not leaving because you don't want me around. I'm happy here. I like—"

Before she could finish her answer, Marlon sealed her lips with his. Although she fought him for a moment, once his tongue danced against her lips, she opened and softened. Dear God, her taste reminded him of the best wine and sunshine. Was it possible to taste sunshine? Hell, he wasn't sure and didn't care. The whimper bubbling in her throat spurred him on, drawing her closer. He groaned. Who cared that they stood on the sidewalk with a howling dog tangling around their legs?

When the kiss ended, Jaden gazed at him with glazed eyes. "You didn't have to do that—but I liked it."

He smoothed his thumb over her cheek, savouring her silky skin. "Does that mean I can kiss you again?"

She nodded, sending a flood of warmth through his body. "I don't hate you."

"Good, because I'm rather fond of you, Jaden Marie."

"What about that other chick?" Her voice wavered. "Sabrina. Isn't she your woman?"

Sabrina? She hadn't been faithful when they had been together. Why the hell would Jaden think…? The incident in the apartment parking lot came back in a rush. "She's nothing more than a friend with the wrong ideas."

"You don't have to be my personal bulldog. Although no one believes it, I can handle myself."

Marlon brushed a rogue hank of hair from her eyes and cupped her skull. She felt so small in his hands, but so strong. She could handle whatever life dished out and yet he wanted to be there. "You're tougher than nails." He glanced at Sparky who thumped his tail against the ground with a steady beat. "I don't want to start any rumours, but I'm pretty sure Sparks would like to go home, so why don't we drop him off? I want to make things up to you."

As they began to walk towards the house, Jaden stopped and gasped. "Man."

He froze and scanned the area for anything or anyone out of place. "What? Who do you see?"

"There he is again."

"Who?"

She nodded down the street. "That green car. It's been everywhere I am."

"The one on the corner?"

"Ford…Mercury, maybe. I couldn't tell the make, but it has a dented rear fender and a bent rear bumper—like a frown."

Noting the car she pointed to, Marlon committed the make and model to memory. "He's leaving, but I'll look into it."

She slapped her thigh. "Dammit. I was supposed to call Cass. She wanted to know if I wanted to go to the races. Why don't we take a rain check?"

Not wanting the good feeling to end, Marlon scooped her into another embrace. "My detail tonight is the races, so why don't you call her and I'll meet you there? I owe you a good time after my behaviour last weekend."

A smile crept across her lips. "I'd like that."

Strolling with their fingers entwined, they stopped in front of Judi's house. Marlon released her hand and cupped the back of her head. "I'll see you later? No running away from me, even if you don't like me much?"

"You do realise there is a real chance we won't work out? My track record sucks." Jaden punctuated her words by poking her index finger into his stomach. "I'm rather shitty with commitment."

"Are you throwing down a challenge?"

"Just don't expect to win."

"Why?"

"Because you won't."

Chapter Eight

Cass smoothed the blanket on the hill and placed the baby seat in the middle. Clumps of grass popped up around the edges of the crocheted cotton like little tufts of hair. Jaden crossed her legs and sighed. Mason, one of the engine builders for Cass's dirt racing team, sat next to her and talked non-stop about gear ratios. Her head span. Maths had never been her favourite subject with her tutors. Then again, the only science she understood was biology, and that came from putting the knowledge into practice. So much for practising.

Propping her head in her hands, she scanned the crowd again. People dressed in various team colours littered the stands. Everyone seemed to have a favourite. She leant over the baby seat and nudged Cass. "Are you going to expose him to all the noise? Seems really loud for an infant."

Cass held up a thick set of earphones. "He wears these and tends to sleep through the races. I think the earphones diffuse the sounds into a low buzz and it lulls him to dreamland. Plus, I cover the carrier with a blanket to keep the dirt off him. He'll be fine. Speaking of a buzz, have you seen Logan?" She checked her watch. "I thought he'd be here by now."

Jaden shrugged. "Where did he go?" Since Logan had dropped off the national radar to be with Cass, his life was of his choosing. She coveted his decision to be his own man without the cloak of celebrity. Someday she'd make the dream a reality in her life as well.

"The local news wanted him and Corbin for an interview." Cass stretched and crossed her ankles. "You know how he loves the cameras. He says it doesn't faze him, but the man primped for an hour to make sure he looked good at every angle. He's a dork, but I love him."

Logan, a dork? Not hardly. He made women swoon when he smiled. But, yeah, he probably posed in front of the mirror to make sure he made the right visual impression. Above the superficial act, he loved Cass and Julian and no others.

"He'll be here."

"I know." Cass placed the earphones on Julian and re-crossed her legs. "So, how was the first week with Judi? I don't know her personally, but she seemed like a really nice lady. She called to ask me about you. I gave you my thumbs up."

Waving her hand, Jaden bobbed her head. "Well, she takes a little getting used to, but it's a good adjustment. By the way, thanks for the reference. And before I forget, she's got a stack of your books she'd like autographed, if you don't mind."

"Not a problem at all. I love meeting my fans." She grinned and tucked her dark hair behind her ears. "Did you know you made the tabloid shows?"

"How? I haven't done anything."

"That's it. You haven't done anything. Your father got on Movie Time Tonight a couple of nights ago, I think, and pleaded for you to come home. He thinks you ran off to Tibet and shaved your head. The scandal media ran with it and sent crews to at least three retreats trying to find you. This morning he pleaded for you to refrain from tattooing your body just for the sake of rebellion. You do understand that once he realises where you are, you won't be able to hide here."

Jaden snorted. He knew full well where she was, but trust him to make a couple of anthill stories into mountains. "You know he only wanted me around to boost sales for the magazine. When I behave, then he has to look for stories and pay his reporters to do their jobs. God forbid he spend money to make money." Or love his child just because she was his child. "Hey, does your mail carrier drive a green sedan?"

"Nope, she's in one of those funny little mail trucks. Why?"

"It's nothing." Jaden pieced together the sightings in her mind. Once at Cass', twice at Judi's, and once on the main drag. Could be a coincidence. Could be something more.

"Are you happy in Ohio?" Cass asked.

Before Jaden could answer, Marlon, decked in his putty-coloured sheriff's department finest—complete with tall black hat—strolled along the fence in her prime line of vision. Her heart fluttered and her mouth ran dry. Some men simply wore their clothes. Marlon made the uniform work. With the gun and radio decorating his belt, he oozed strength. Even the badge gleamed in the setting sun. Marlon made her more than happy—he made her feel safe. She tried to bite back the grin curling her lips, even as her stomach flip-flopped. What would it feel like to strip him out of his uniform after a long day protecting the public?

A hand waved across her field of vision. "Earth to Jaden."

She whipped around to see Logan laughing. The tips of her ears burned. Could they tell she had visually groped Marlon? She hoped not. Well, maybe she did care. Thinking of Marlon sent sizzles through her veins and left her fevered in delicious ways. A blonde trotted along the fence line and snagged Marlon in a tight hug. The little green-eyed monster in the back of her mind reared its head. So they weren't a couple—barely friends. Seeing him with someone else gnawed under her skin. The blonde turned. Sabrina. Well, shit. Jaden shielded her eyes from the track.

As Logan plopped down next to Cass, he knocked knees with Jaden. She turned away from Marlon to snicker at Logan as he rained kisses all over Cass's face. "I missed you, Cassie Love." He nodded to Jaden. "Hey Jaden, I see you made it. The way you gaze at Marlon makes me think the cars weren't the draw. I should be jealous, but I'm not."

Jaden rolled her eyes and forced her attention to Logan. He still had an ego the size of a European country. "Sorry, I didn't come here to stoke your self-esteem." She shrugged. "So? Did it go well?"

"It's all right." Logan cracked his neck and pulled a hoodie sweatshirt emblazoned with a race car on over his head, covering the dress shirt. "Team Jensen will be on the eleven o'clock news, but don't expect to see me."

As she laced her fingers with his, Cass frowned. "Why not?"

"The reporter, Aurelia Goshen, the saccharine sweet one, thought that I drove the car and got miffed when I told her I worked behind the scenes. Apparently, she thought she'd get the interview of a lifetime and tried to put the moves on me. Grabbed my ass and everything! When I didn't take the bait, she balked and walked out." He smoothed a hand through his hair, patting it back into place. "Thankfully an intern named Tennille Black jumped in and talked to Corbin for over an hour. Good thing Ray's driving in the first heat race. We just made it."

Shifting her attention from her friends to the fence, she searched for Marlon. Where was he? She cracked her knuckles. So being on-duty meant no contact? Damn.

"Looking for me?"

Her heart clenched. Jaden turned, face to face with Marlon. The tangy scent of his cologne wrapped around her as he knelt next to her. He'd trimmed his beard close to his face, making his dimple stand out more. She licked her lips. "Sort of."

In the standard sheriff's uniform, every muscle and curve of his body stood out. Even with the hat and dark glasses, he took her breath away. It wasn't fair how he affected her.

"Heya, Marlon. Thanks for getting me through the traffic. You didn't have to do it and I appreciate it." Logan stuck out his hand. "I see you and Jaden found each other." He wiggled his brows and clicked his tongue. "Good for you."

Even through her bit of embarrassment, her thoughts moved to more romantic ideas—like being alone with Marlon.

As the men shook hands, Marlon's forearm brushed her knee. The momentary connection crackled between them. She pressed her knees together to quell the building heat between her thighs. Before she could say anything, Marlon laced his fingers with hers. "Want to check out the track?"

Fine—gave them time to talk about the Sabrina situation. Jaden glanced at Cass. "Do you mind if I stretch my legs? I feel the sudden need for a walk."

Cass disengaged from Logan and waved. "Have fun! That's the whole point of coming to the races."

Logan frowned. "I thought it was to watch the cars and then make out afterwards. I always do."

Clamping her mouth shut, Jaden closed her eyes and stood. Leave it to Logan to be blunt and honest. "I'll be back in a few." She wobbled on her feet, reaching out. Marlon's strong hand clasped hers. Without opening her eyes, she'd connected with him. Blinking, she slid her gaze up his body to his face.

"Good?"

"I'm okay."

Leaving Cass and Logan alone with the baby, Jaden followed Marlon through the crowd. Her mind wandered. What would it be like to be his girl? Would other women stop and stare, wishing they could be the woman with him? Nibbling the corner of her mouth, she cracked a smile. She wanted to be his girl. Moments later, he led her to a small shed next to the ticket booth. Opening the door, he held out his hand. "It's not much, but it's a good place to take a break—especially during a rain delay."

Although no one said her being there was against the rules, Jaden hesitated. The Jade from Hollywood would have him pinned against the wall in a kiss or propped in a corner as she opened his fly. She drew a long breath, liking her improved sense of resolve and restraint. Was it possible to get into trouble with a lawman in charge? Probably not, but still... What if his boss or another deputy showed up?

Marlon propped the door open, shoving a thick wedge of plastic under the edge with his booted foot. "If Bobby or Saul stop by, they'll see us talking and sharing a cup of coffee. You're good."

Empty save for the shelf full of rain gear, a couple of radios and two Styrofoam cups, the shed looked a bit lonely. "So you stand here? Seems a bit boring." She toyed with her ring, sliding it around her finger. "Although I think the slower pace is refreshing."

He shook his head. "Trust me, things start to jump when the main races get underway and egos get hurt. Complaints increased when the concession stands started offering beer. People get worked up when they've had a few and their driver loses."

"You're getting all professional-sounding again. I kinda like it." Jaden knotted her fingers together. "So...have you brought other women here? I—Forget I asked that. It's not my business." Averting her gaze, she stared at the particleboard floor. What a foolish question! What he did on his own time wasn't for her to know. The electricity flowing between them didn't have to mean an attraction. Back home, she'd perfected man-catching allure. Who knew? He might just be working his own sexy mojo.

Dipping to meet her downcast gaze, Marlon grinned. "You're my first. Honest."

Her eyes widened and searched his face. He'd shaved. If she had her druthers, she'd take him with scruff.

"Really? I'm honoured." Long ago, she'd had a first. A first kiss, a first sexual experience, but love? Maybe Marlon was supposed to be her one and only.

A female voice from over her shoulder interrupted the conversation and her musings. "Hey Marlon. I hoped I'd see you here and you brought your lovely friend. Having fun?"

Rubbing his hand over his face, Marlon groaned. "Hi Sabrina. How are you?"

With a tug on her ponytail, Sabrina adjusted her hair high on the crown of her head. She smoothed her hand over his breast pocket, spending extra time on his pecs. "You're smart to hide out here. Looks like a great place to make out." She giggled. "Chalk it up to my man in uniform fantasy and overactive imagination. Don't I know you?" Sabrina stepped back and squinted. "I know you, but where from?"

Jaden cleared her throat. "I'm just the third wheel." A peal of jealousy rang through her. She and Marlon weren't an actual couple. She had no claims, but the thought of Sabrina's slimy hands all over Marlon made Jaden want to puke.

"I do know you." Sabrina's eyes widened and a slow sneer curled her lips. "Jade Weir, no shit." She clicked her tongue and wrapped both arms around Marlon's biceps. "As I live and breathe, I never expected to see you ever again." Her gaze flicked over Jaden once more. "Went on a bender, didn't you? A little detox and you'll drop the weight no problem. Want me to make some calls?"

"I'm fine on my own." Jaden scuffed the toe of her high-heeled boot on the floor, biding her time. The moment Sabrina left, she and Marlon had to talk.

"Marlon, a word?" Sabrina disengaged from Marlon's arm and hooked her fingers into his belt loops. "Excuse us." She dug her elbow into Jaden's side, shoving her from the building.

Shit. Jaden chewed the corner of her mouth as a pair of officers strolled up to the shed. She tipped her head in a silent nod to Bobby. They'd have to meet up in public eventually with him still at the station, but the other man…where'd she know him from? Black hair, like coal. The nose on the officer looked right. Kind of.

Behind her, the shed door opened with a creak. "You can't tell me anything new."

Jaden's blood ran cold. Sabrina could tattle lots of secrets and what she didn't know for sure, she'd easily invent. Jaden inched to the side of the shed. Once out of Marlon's line of sight, she made a run for it.

"Hey Hutchins, Carver, want to escort Sabrina to her seat? She's scared of crowds and likes men with thick…muscles."

"Dick." The raven-haired man grunted and wrapped a meaty hand around Sabrina's upper arm. "Let's go, Ms Jeffries. I thought we had this discussion before. The only danger here is a man in uniform."

"Your lines are cornier than Marlon's," Sabrina spat. As he led her away, she pinched the officer's butt. "This could be the start of the best cop fantasy! Ever thought of doing stunt work?"

Jaden trusted Bobby Hutchins, but the other guy? Not a chance. She cringed. Carver. She'd have to keep the name in mind. She stared at him as he walked away and committed his visage to memory.

"Want to tell me why you're out here hiding?" Marlon leant against the corner post of the building and folded his muscle-corded arms. "Sabrina doesn't bite hard."

"I remember."

He cocked his head and opened his mouth. His radio crackled on his hip, interrupting whatever he wanted to say. A frown creased his lips and forehead. Speaking into the tiny mic, he grunted instructions. When he looked back at her, he cracked a half-smile. "Shit. I'm sorry to cut this short, but I have to get back out there."

Jaden smoothed her hand over his collar, adjusting the lapel Sabrina had knocked askew. "I know this is probably disorderly conduct or something, but I can't let you protect the county with one side up and the other down. You look silly."

Closing the gap between them, he grabbed her hand and drew circles along her inner wrist. "Thanks. Now tell me why you came out here. What if the infamous green car guy showed?"

"It got stuffy in the building and Sabrina booted me out." Her heart fluttered in her chest. If she didn't just spit out her issues, she'd burst. "Sabrina, for as nice as she acts, isn't what she seems." Jaden paused and nibbled her inner cheek. "Neither am I."

"If there's one thing I dislike, it's a liar." Marlon's radio crackled. Apparently a drunk by the north bleachers was throwing cans onto the track. "I have to go." He squeezed her hand. "Oh, before I forget, I'll be at Judi's tomorrow. She wants me to fix the sink in the kitchen. Will you meet me for lunch? I want to talk about what you said and what happened tonight."

He hated liars and he wanted all her truths.

"Oh, sure."

* * * *

The next morning, Marlon woke up sore. The drunk race fan from the night before had not only tossed his refuse onto the track, but also insisted on doing his impersonation of a mixed martial arts fighter and used his fists for protection. After a couple of cheap shots, and a bloody lip, Marlon had subdued the man and hauled him to the county lockup. His head still throbbed like a son of a bitch.

A knock at the door jolted him from his semi-slumber. Who wanted him this early? He grabbed the alarm clock and peered through blurry eyes. Ten twenty-seven. Shit. He'd overslept. Was Jaden on the other side of the door trying to rouse him? Just the thought of her sent blood rushing through his body. Heat pooled in his belly. Crazy thoughts rolled around his sleepy brain. She could wake him every morning—with nothing but a smile. He fell back against the sheets and palmed his growing erection. She made him come alive in so many ways. He sighed. He needed to get her alone very soon to discuss her cryptic comments—then learn every inch of her delectable body.

Wrapping his fingers around his cock, Marlon stroked and relished the jolt of electricity through his veins. This won't take long. His actions became more frantic as he roughly caressed the tender skin. His balls tightened and his hips bucked off the bed. His groans filled the air. He clenched his teeth and fought to drag air into his lungs. "Oh, shit." With a moan, his body tensed and cum smeared on the sheet.

He lay there for a moment, basking in the weightlessness of the orgasm. Damn, she had him on edge. At least now he could face the person at the door without a raging hard-on.

The knocking grew louder, breaking his train of thought. "Marlon? Are you in there? I know you're home."

He rolled his eyes. Trust Sabrina to come looking for him. What the fuck? Didn't she get the hint?

Behind the door, she continued to shout. "Marlon? I heard about the fight at the track. I want to make sure you're okay."

Groaning, he sat up. The sheet fell away from his body and cool air slid over his nipples like a lover's caress. He cracked his neck. If Jaden were there, then she could roam his body and make him her own. The thought of her naked curves curled against him renewed the supply of blood to his cock.

"I'm going to break down the door. I'm worried and scared."

Shit. Sabrina could move far, far away, or at least find herself another man to pester, and he'd be thrilled. He stood and yanked on some pyjama pants. Forcing his mind to anything but his time with Jaden, he willed his dick to cooperate. No need to give Sabrina the wrong idea. She'd acted as screwy as Jaden the night prior. He rummaged through his top bureau drawer for a clean T-shirt. "Hold on."

With a long sigh, he made his way to the front door. A quick peek through the peephole revealed Sabrina in a trench coat. A trench coat? What the hell…another Hollywood affectation? He opened the door and braced for the fallout. "I'm fine, so trot back home."

Barrelling past him, she whirled around in his living room. The coat opened and pooled on the floor at her stiletto-clad feet. "When we split, I know I said I wanted to move on. I did, but seeing you last night with her, so happy, made me really examine my feelings. I never should've walked away." She paused, murmured something inaudible, and snapped her gaze back to his face. "There isn't a man alive who'd turn me down."

He clamped his mouth shut and stuffed his hands into his pockets. She was not naked in his home. Not now. "Sabrina, you need to leave."

Cupping her breasts, she blew out a long breath. Her nipples puckered. "How about I up the ante?" Her thumbs flicked over the pink tips. "You like the fantasy, a woman who dazzles and sparkles. I am that girl."

Something about the precise wording she'd used. Why did it sound…

Jade's movie, Clover Perception.

Lord help him, she'd recreated the beginning of the sex scene in the film. He rolled his eyes and turned away from her. "Don't do this."

Slinking across the room, she rubbed against him. "I'm ready for my boy in blue — more than she ever could be."

Marlon groaned. Why did the good things in his life always have to have speed bumps? "Go find your boy toy."

"Other men don't compare to you. It's so much nicer to walk in the summer breeze with you. I miss cuddling under the blanket and counting the stars."

"Summer breeze?" He turned around and stared at her. "Counting stars? What the hell are you talking about?"

"Silly me, I got caught up in the moment. I read for that part, you know." She clapped both hands over her mouth and tittered. She dropped her hands and shrugged. "I just finished watching Kicks and Clover Perception and got caught up in the stories. Don't you want to play with me? It'll be a lot of fun. I know things she's never even tried." Wrapping his fingers over her hands, he edged her back. He kept his voice level. "Sabrina, enough."

A squeak erupted from her throat. "You're not giving me a chance. I know things about her. Things you need to know."

He grabbed the coat from the floor and draped it over her bare shoulders. "We're done here."

She whimpered. "She's good at hiding her habits—like who she's sleeping with and what she's taking."

He wrangled her arms through the sleeves of the trench coat. "Wait. What? Sleeping with?"

"On the set of The Mythical Beast, she snuck off a lot without her boyfriend. We found out later it was to…powder her nose with the lead actor."

Opening her apartment door, he held out his hand. "That doesn't mean she's still using."

Sabrina kicked off her pointy-heeled shoes. "It's just the tip cf the iceberg. I spent time with her in Hollywood. We worked together on the set of Kicks. I know her secrets—all her secrets. Secrets that will ruin your career."

"Enough, Sabrina." He headed for the door. No more roadblocks. "Go home."

Licking her lips, she grinned and let the coat drape open to her concave navel. "You bet, neighbour."

Back inside his apartment, Marlon raced through a shower and shave. Did men normally shave to fix a leaky sink? If a hot honey blonde waited, ready and able to test the faucet when he finished, then yes ma'am—he'd be there and smooth to her touch.

Even the feel of his own hands on his body made him think of Jaden and her light caresses. What if he played out the scene from the movie with the real woman? He shuddered and stroked his length. Dear God, Jaden invaded his life, his dreams…hell, his fantasies. If it took rubbing one off every day to keep from coming across as a sex-driven man in her presence, he would without complaint. She warmed his days and steamed his nights.

Rinsing away the soap and the result of his fascination with Jaden, he turned off the water and dragged the towel down his torso. With as much as he hoped for with Jaden, Sabrina's comments bothered him. She knew Jaden from Hollywood. What if the crap she'd said was actually the truth?

But relationships failed without trust.

"Shit," he muttered. "God help me, I don't want to fail…again."

Chapter Nine

Jaden ran the canister vacuum over the hall carpet the next morning, humming to the last song she'd heard earlier when her alarm clock went off. As she worked, her butt vibrated. Pausing, she looked around. What the hell? When she'd cleaned the living room, she'd dusted the silent radio... She cocked her head. Her phone!

She clicked the power switch and slid her phone from her back pocket. She'd called Bobby earlier in the morning to check in—no sight of the paparazzi or her father's band of henchmen. The number didn't look familiar. Despite the notion of letting it go to voicemail, she flipped open the device. If her father wanted to harass her, then fine. She could ignore him. "Hello?"

"Hey Jaden. Did you enjoy the races last night?"

Her hand trembled as she wiped the loose strands of hair from her forehead. "Fine, but I'm a little fuzzy. You are?"

"It's Corbin—I drove the car. Maybe I should've waited to call you."

"Hey, Corbin." Holy hell, the blond Adonis behind the wheel was calling. An electrical jolt went the length of her spine. "You made hash out of the field." She mentally replayed that. Why hadn't she paid attention to the race lingo? "I mean, did I say that right? The field? I'm not big into racing." She rolled her tongue around her dry mouth. Corbin Moss, the handsome and very single Late Model driver for Team Jensen. He had called her.

On his end of the line, Corbin laughed. "Honey, you got it just right." He cleared his throat. "Um, are you free tonight? Cass said you and Marlon might be involved, and I don't want to stick my nose in where it's not wanted."

Squeezing the vacuum hose, she nibbled her bottom lip. A date? Involved? Hot damn! "I'm not involved with anyone exclusively. Why do you ask?" Marlon said he liked her, but he hadn't asked for more than flirtation. Would it be wrong to give him a run for his money? Would it be fair to Corbin if her true desires lay with Marlon? And what if the fanatic showed up?

"Hillbilly Boots, Ray's band—I'm on the drums now since Levi quit—is playing at the Ricochet. Cass said you liked to dance. She gave me your number, so I thought you might like to come out for the concert."

Her heart thundered in her chest. A semi-date sounded fun. "So is this an official night out? Because I haven't been out of the house save for last night and each afternoon to walk Sparky."

His voice cracked. "Umm…I hadn't planned on a real date but yeah, this can be a date. I'm a little rusty at dating, myself. If you don't want to, I understand. You barely know me and you probably think I want something from you." His voice faltered. "I mean...shit...I'm babbling. We could keep it loose, instead of a real date."

A night on the town sounded like fun. She could be carefree and decide what she wanted. Maybe it'd give Marlon a reason to make a move. "Then why don't I meet you at the Ricochet?"

"That works, since I have to be there at seven." He chuckled and static fizzled on the line. "I'm looking forward to hanging out."

"Yeah." She said goodbye, clicked her phone shut and kicked the switch on the vacuum to bring the machine back to life. A night out meant she could dress up. She could dance and forget her worries.

Two more passes over the hall carpet and she shoved the canister into the dining room. She glanced through the doorway into the kitchen. A pair of jeans-clad legs stuck out of the cabinet under the sink. Marlon? Oh no... Judi had asked him over to fix the sink. Had he heard her conversation? Damn, damn, damn.

Sneaking further into the dining room, she hoped he didn't know she'd seen him. But what was she to do? It wasn't like he'd actually asked her to go out...had he? She cringed. No, he'd said something about being his fashion patrol, not a night on the town. For all she knew, he wanted to be friends. She smacked her forehead with the heel of her hand. Wouldn't her Cali friends laugh! Jade Weir indecisive about a date and lovesick over a man!

Angling around the corner, she sneaked a glance at the sink. The doors, once open, now sat shut. The tools weren't scattered on the floor. Even the towels no longer lined the edge of the countertop. What the hell? How had she not heard him cleaning up? And how'd he manage it so fast?

A pair of strong arms wound around her. "Looking for me?"

She screamed. The instantaneous surge of fear passed as she realised who held her. Marlon. She dug her elbow into his stomach, barely making a dent in the taut flesh. "Don't freak me out like that!"

Warm breath tickled her ear. The rasp of whiskers abraded her cheek. "Check. Hands off if I want to keep my lunch down." When she elbowed him again, he backed away. "Hey. What's going on?"

Raking her fingers through her hair, Jaden closed her eyes. "I thought you were under the sink. I didn't know you left the kitchen." *I had a panic attack thinking you were one of Daddy's goons here to kidnap me.* She rubbed her temples and opened her eyes. Telling him the whole truth now wouldn't help her cause. It'd prove her to be a liar and would certainly push him farther away.

He leant on the wall and crossed his boot-clad feet. "I finished and saw you'd moved into the dining room. I'd like to know why you're jumpy but I'll settle for asking about the dog. Where's Sparks?"

She nodded to the back door. Sparky was a topic she could deal with. "He's doing his business."

"I'll check on him in case—" He waggled his fingers in the air. "—the green car bogey man is hanging out in the backyard."

As he edged past her, his touch made every hair on her body tremble. The man reminded her of sin in the flesh. So why commit to a night out with someone else?

Even a former party girl needed options.

Her phone rang again. This time, she checked the screen—her father. Dammit. She pressed the button to ignore the call and shoved the device into her back pocket.

Please Remember Me

When Marlon returned with Sparky, the dog jumped on her. Muddy prints marred her sequined ballet flats and the carpet. Infusing fake irritation in her voice to cover her frustration, she pointed at the dog. "Sparks, I love ya honey, but you messed up my vacuuming."

Marlon's cheeks streaked with crimson. "Don't blame him. I forgot to wipe his paws." Hooking a finger under her chin, he met her gaze. "Are you going to go?"

Her eyes widened and her jaw dropped. "Go?" Her voice broke. "I'm—" No, no lies. He deserved the truth, even if he wasn't acting as fast as she wanted. "I'm going to the Ricochet with Corbin Moss. He asked and I accepted, but it's not a real date. And I'm not afraid of you. I just don't like people sneaking up on me. Never know who it could be."

Rubbing his chin, he nodded. "Well, good."

She huffed. "Well, good?" She wasn't a doormat and she wasn't about to let him get away without an explanation. "What's good? Are you going to go out with someone? We could double up."

He shrugged. "I might. You don't know who I have lined up for a hot date."

"Oh really?" The gall! The nerve! She knelt to pet Sparky. The no-good, sexy jerk could live his life. She wasn't about to interfere. "Then have a good time, since you didn't bother to ask me. May I ask who she is?"

His eyes narrowed. "None of your business. But since we're being nosy, who was that on the phone while I was out back? I heard the second call. Is that the person you're afraid will jump you? Or someone else? Lie to me and I can't protect you."

She snorted. The jerk. "As you put it, none of your business! I don't have to answer to you."

His eyes widened. "It might not be my place because I didn't act first, but you cut me deep. You infuriate me and yet I still worry something might happen to you." He snorted. "Doesn't matter. You've made up your mind."

He started to walk away and paused. "And to think I really came over here to ask you on a candlelit supper and dancing kind of date. I'll have to try later when your social calendar is free."

His words stung. The ice in his eyes bored into her soul. She fought back tears. He could cut her down, but he wasn't going to break her. Sparky nuzzled her face, licking the tip of her nose. At least the dog understood.

Just after the front door slammed, Judi poked her head around the corner. "So, that was interesting. Is my sink fixed?"

Wiping her eyes with the back of her hand, Jaden cleared her throat. No more weeping over a jerk. "I assume it's working. He cleaned up his mess."

Judi pulled out a chair at the table. She folded her hands and licked her lips. "Why don't you sit down with me? I wanted to share a few things with you."

Patting Sparky's head, Jaden stood and brushed away the residual tears. She had nothing to say. Maybe she was the spoilt rich girl Marlon made her out to be.

As she sat down, a grimace fluttered across Judi's face and her right hand clenched.

"Judi? Did you take your meds this morning? You look pale."

"I have my good days and ones I want to forget." She sighed. "But I'm fine. Fact is, I'm more worried about you."

"Me?"

"Despite what that boy says, you're a nice, decent girl. You have a big heart." Judi patted her hand. "Sparky loves you and I love you. He'll come around—even if it takes a while. He knows what kind of woman you are inside."

"Woman inside?" No matter how hard she tried to hold it back, the rush of emotion engulfed her. "I ran away because I didn't want to spend the rest of my life showing off my body to feed my addictions and sell my daddy's magazine! I just wanted to go out and have a life, and when I made that choice, my past came back to kick my ass."

Sparky whimpered and cowered at Jaden's feet. She bent to scratch his floppy ears. "I'm sorry, baby."

"So are you done feeling sorry for yourself?"

Jaden wiped her eyes. "What?" Was this a sob fest? Revulsion and embarrassment warred within her. It was.

"Give up the pity party. We all have things in our past we wish we hadn't done. I sometimes wish I hadn't been so hard on my son. If I'd taken the time to talk to my sister on a regular basis, I might have made amends before she died. Damned heart attacks run in the family. But that's all in the past and I have to live with it. Are you done crying over spilt milk?"

Jaden tucked a lock of hair behind her ear. "I'm done."

Judi giggled. "Good. I don't like being worried, but don't you dare fib to me to save my feelings. I'll find out. Same goes with someone looking in my windows. I don't like nosy-bottoms. Got me?"

"Did someone peek in the windows?"

"A photographer, but he won't be back. I had a hot flash in front of the window." She winked and the fluorescent lighting glittered in her eyes. "I wanted to talk about more exciting things, like my will and what I'll do with Sparks when I go."

"Your will? That's not exciting!" Jaden covered her mouth with her hand as the import hit her. Judi couldn't leave. Not yet. Maybe never. "When you go? You can't go!"

Judi scratched Sparky's back. "The document is very stimulating when it comes to Sparks. I want someone to care for him in the event that I can't. To that end, I chose you. Mr Tibbets came over while you and Marlon had your argument. He changed the will, naming you as Sparky's guardian. I even set up a small trust for his care."

Gasping, Jaden grasped Judi's hand. "You have faith in me?"

"It's not that I have faith in you, necessarily. I do, but this is about Sparky. He believes in you and he's never wrong."

"Then Sparky's guardian it is." Jaden sniffled. "I won't let either of you down."

Wiping away more tears, Jaden grinned. Funny how thinking she had nothing to lose had changed the moment she crossed the Indiana-Ohio line. Besides her own independence, she now had Judi and Sparks to lose. They believed in her. Good start on the road to living with her choices.

Now to deal with the man situation.

* * * *

Marlon stormed into his apartment. For the love of God. To spend the morning working under a stinky, leaky sink and then have the woman of his dreams decide to date another man! Fuck. Okay, so yeah, Corbin Moss was a nice guy, a decent guy. The kind of guy any level-headed woman would love to go on a date with. So why get so worked up?

He wanted her honesty. If she was struggling with something, he'd make sure she got the help she needed. Why? In the grand scheme of things, she was little more than a good friend. Wasn't she?

He plopped down in his easy chair and stared at the couch. She'd sat with him. Told him she'd come to see him. Was it a lie? She still hadn't said why she'd come back. He stood and crossed the room to his free weights. As he dry-lifted the dumbbell, he could almost hear his mother's voice. "Your rational brain wants an explanation. Your subconscious wants the woman. Which do you want?"

"I want to stake the first claim." He replaced the weight and grabbed another. The more his muscles burned, the brighter his fury blazed. Jaden wasn't a mountain to chuck a pole into and claim for the USA. She was a vibrant, sexy woman—soft and curvy and beguiling. He wanted to make her happy. To see the smile light up her face. she was woman any man would jump through hoops for. Like Corbin. Or Bobby.

He continued pumping the weights in both hands as a mental image of his tirade came to mind. She needed to slap him and hard. When had he let irrational emotions take over his life?

About the time she walked back into Crawford. If his mother could've seen him, she'd more than likely groan, after giving him a lecture. When he screwed up his life, he did it on a monumental scale. First with Addy and now with Jaden.

Time to start getting things right. Time to show Jaden what she'd be giving up.

He placed the weights back on the rack and wiped the sweat from his brow. He'd dated since Addy's passing, but no woman had compared to Jaden. None mattered. So why was he standing back and letting her get away? He had no idea what she'd do or who she'd choose. But Corbin couldn't dance with her all the time if he was up on stage...

He shook his head and walked into the bathroom. "I've played it safe way too long. Safe sucks ass."

Chapter Ten

Jaden applied another swipe of mascara and pressed her lips together. So she didn't know Corbin that well. If Cass thought he was a nice guy, then she'd give him a chance. She'd pissed Marlon off. Any chance with him had fizzled the moment she'd opened her mouth.

She narrowed her eyes at the reflection in the mirror. Marlon. The two-faced jerk in muscle-hugging blue jeans. He didn't trust her. Didn't own her and didn't have the right to get so cranky. She sighed. Why did he have to be so blasted sexy? Why did she have to care about him?

Judi knocked at the door. "Honey, you have another visitor. He's a sweet-looking young man." She sat on the edge of the bed. "So is he your date?"

"I was supposed to meet him there, but whatever." With a nod to the mirror, Jaden turned. "Wait, another visitor? Who else was here?"

"Bobby Hutchins came by. He wanted to make sure you got home all right. I didn't think you knew him."

"We met when Logan was shooting Broken Wheels. Bobby did set security and we were close." She cocked her head. "Was he driving a green car when he stopped in?"

"Nope. He came in his cruiser. Is someone bothering you?"

Jaden gnawed the inside of her cheek. Bothering? Bobby did his job and kept an eye on her without being obvious. The stalker could be another goon or a well-disguised paparazzo. If she didn't continue to stand on her own two feet, she'd never stay independent.

"It's nothing really." Jaden smoothed her hair from her eyes and dropped her hands. "Be honest, will this do?"

Judi's brows rose. "You're asking me? I wear pink polyester to bingo. I'd say I'm not a good choice to be the fashion police, as you call it."

Jaden's shoulders sagged. "Maybe not, but the last time I went out, really went out—you know, with a guy I liked—I wore the teeniest dress I could find and the highest heels I could stand up in. I made it to home plate, but I never found out if he liked me for me or if he just wanted to be seen with me."

"So what do you want out of this night?"

"I don't know." She stood and strolled to the bay window. "I want to have fun. I want to meet people. I want to drink and not get drunk. I want to dance and not have to worry about my clothes falling off because I'm incapacitated." Tail lights faded down the street. If Corbin hadn't run yet, she'd be surprised. No wonder men got sick of waiting for women before dates. "I want to stay true to myself."

"Well, then you'd better get moving." Judi stood and brushed off her pants, like she'd sat in dog fur. "Try to be yourself and if competition strikes...then use it."

Jaden crooked a brow. "Are you telling me to flirt with both men?"

"It's like ice cream. I'm suggesting you try more than one and see which you like the best. You might like one and detest the other, but then again, you might find you aren't real thrilled with either."

As she descended the stairs, Jaden squeezed Judi's hand. "You're right. I'll give them something to miss."

Against his better judgement, Marlon dug through his closet for his cowboy boots. If Jaden wanted to see a man in action, then she could watch him. When he climbed into his Jeep, he checked the mirror. The windows in Sabrina's apartment were dark. Maybe she had a date and wouldn't give him grief.

He doubted it. Lately she seemed to come on like the plague. He shifted into gear and zipped out of the parking lot. Every time Sabrina made a move, nice or not, he wanted to puke and run the other way. And what did Jaden think? He wasn't sure.

Could the injustice of his words be erased with one slow dance and a bit of cuddling? Probably not, but it wouldn't hurt to try. Anything had to work better than catering to his constant worry.

At the Ricochet, he nodded to the bouncer and slipped him a five. "Thanks, my man."

"We got a new girl here tonight." The tall man cleared his throat. "She's ripe for the pickin'."

Stopping short, Marlon whipped around. "Oh, yeah? What's she look like?"

The bouncer rubbed his chin. "Five-eight, dirty blonde hair, big boobs, nice ass."

Marlon bit back a growl. "That sounds like a lot of women." Who else checked out her boobs? And why was he so damned jealous?

"True, but this one was hanging on Corbin Moss like a vine. Cute face, but could stand to lose a few pounds."

Hanging on him? Was she really attracted to the lanky man? With a grin to disguise his irritation, Marlon rubbed the taller man's belly. "And you're svelte? I'm sure she's cute no matter how many pounds she has." More cushion for the pushin' if he had his way. "But you said she was a dirty blonde? I'll have to keep my eyes peeled."

"Decide for yourself. She's with the band."

"I will."

Inside the dancehall, the hum of conversation bombarded him. People drank and cheered at the long bar while couples peeled off to dance on the gigantic wooden dance floor. Sparkles from the mirror ball in the roof glittered on the crowd. He glanced at the darkened stage. The DJ danced behind his counter, clutching his earphones and chomping on a wad of gum.

He scanned the dining area and the dancers. No Jaden. Well, fuck. A blonde at the highboy tables caught his eye. Was that… no, not Jaden. Another glance at the blonde made him duck behind a pole. Shit. Sabrina had followed him to the dance hall.

Or maybe she'd got there ahead of him and hadn't seen him. Maybe she had a date with another poor sap. God, he sounded paranoid.

Edging around a throng of drunken farmers, Marlon headed to the pool tables and away from his ex. At least there he could watch the dancers and stage without looking like a stalker. A spotlight flicked over the crowd as the announcer took his place in the middle of the stage.

"Ladies and gentlemen, it's the time you asked for. We couldn't hold them off a moment more. You asked for the best, and we brought the best. Raise the roof for Hillbilly Boots!"

On cue, the room went black as Ray Russell thundered into the beginning strains of the first tune. The spotlight shone right on him when he stepped up to the microphone. Women shrieked and rushed the stage. Preening, Ray sang the first lines of the song, "Back to You".

Chalking his cue stick, Marlon gritted his teeth again. His jaw ached from the combination of worry, regret, and frustration. As he'd expected, Corbin was perched behind the drums. Where the hell was Jaden? Yes, there was a little room off to the right of the stage where the band stowed their gear. Was she sitting back there waiting for Corbin like a groupie? He hoped not.

Something icy pressed against the back of his neck. Tossing the chalk onto the pool table, he turned. Bobby Hutchins sipped from a frosty glass of beer, a devil's grin dancing in his eyes.

"What the fuck, Bobby? I gave you something to do last night and this is how you pay me back? Asshole."

The younger officer shrugged and downed the amber liquid. He smacked his lips and scrubbed the back of his wrist across his mouth. "I'm not a billiards player, but you blew the game before you even picked up your stick. What's eating your ass? Is it that chick from the races? She was cute. I'd tap that. Strike that. I think I will."

A growl ripped from Marlon's throat. "Not a chance in hell."

Bobby put his free hand and the mug in the air and backed up. "Touchy, touchy. If she's yours then I'll lay off for now. But I don't see what the deal is. She's spent the last hour dancing with Moss and me. I thought you were sorta back with Sabrina."

"I set you up with Sabrina so you'd get some action, dumbass." Marlon chewed the inside of his cheek. "You danced with my Jaden?" Shit. He hadn't meant to add the extra word.

"Every man in the joint noticed your Jaden when she strolled in with Corbin Moss. She happened to be standing alone during the first set, so I asked her to dance. Seemed to me like she liked me."

"Who likes me?"

Marlon pinched the bridge of his nose with his thumb and forefinger. "Hello, Sabrina."

"I'll be right back." Bobby ducked his head and disappeared into the crowd.

Snaking her arms around Marlon's body, Sabrina rested her chin on his shoulder. "Your sweet little girl's here, but she's not sweet."

"Oh?" Marlon removed her fingers from his front pocket. "You know something I should know?"

Sabrina turned him around in her embrace. She rubbed her pelvis against his groin. "Have you noticed she's more combative then touchy-feely? If you ask, she'll say it's her temperament, but a little E never hurts."

He snapped his attention from the stage to Sabrina's eyes.

"Those aren't mints in her purse."

"Oh and you know this how?"

"Once a user, always a user."

Bobby returned, fresh beer in hand. "Sabrina."

"I hope it was worth it." She pressed a kiss to Marlon's lips. "She's trouble you don't need." She waved and turned to another man playing pool.

The comment stuck in Marlon's mind. He'd heard the exact same words from Mac. Shit. Things had to get sorted out or ended.

"Bobby, you went to the bar. Have you seen Jaden?"

"Last I saw, she was headed out to the patio with Cass Jensen." Bobby chalked his cue stick. "Go easy on her. Sabrina could be full of shit."

Shoving Bobby aside, Marlon strode to the side door. He tamped down his caveman tendencies. If he hauled her over his shoulder, she'd run and never look back. Play it cool, man. Cool. He stopped in the doorway. Bobby hadn't been around when he'd talked to Sabrina. What the hell?

Just as Bobby said, Cass and Jaden stood on the wooden patio rubbing their arms and chatting. "I'd suggest heading back in if you're cold."

He chuckled. Trust Jaden to wear a thin tank top on an October night. Two thick black bracelets jangled from her wrist. Where was old Corbin to keep her warm? On the stage showing off with Logan. Time to make his move.

Both women turned. Jaden blushed. Cass smiled and said, "Why thank you, kind deputy, sir. It's good to know you're looking out for us."

"Besides being dark out, it's almost Hallowe'en. I don't suggest anyone go out by themselves." He bit back a groan. Why did he seem to slide into preachy cop mode when around beautiful women?

Cass dipped her head. "Then thank you again. We need a burly cop to keep us safe."

Jaden muttered something he couldn't hear, making Cass slap her on the arm. "Behave. He's just doing his job," she snapped. "Don't say what you don't mean and can't take back."

Meeting his gaze, Jaden's green eyes narrowed. "I know what I'm doing and no, I don't want to take any of it back. Two-faced is two-faced no matter who's wearing the mask."

Shoulders slumped, Cass sighed. "Then I'll leave you two to work this out. There's nothing better than being forced together if something needs discussed." She paused at his shoulder. "And find her a jacket or something. She'll freeze to death." Before he could stop her, she strolled back into the bar and shut the door.

Silence enveloped them. Silver clouds of Jaden's breath dissipated in the air around him. What should he say? I want to see you naked and straddled across my lap? Um, no. Chilly weather we're having? Want to borrow my department issue jacket? Wrong. Please tell me the mints in your purse really are mints. Hell.

"Are you having fun?" Smooth. Real smooth.

Her gaze hardened. "I was."

With a wince, he decided to bare his heart. "Jaden Marie, I'm sorry."

"For what?"

Inching closer to her, he smoothed his hand over her arm. "I'm sorry for jumping on you about the date. I'm sorry for not asking you first. And I'm sorry I'm acting like a grade-A ass. There are a lot of things you don't know about and I'm not sure how to tell you."

"That's a lot of 'sorry's in one breath." Averting her gaze, she notched her chin in the air. "You didn't do anything wrong. It was just a date. I'm twenty-three. I like to go out. And your 'things' aren't my business."

She didn't pull away, but she didn't surrender to him either. He wrapped his left arm around her shoulder and tucked her against his body. If nothing else, he'd share his body heat. As though they'd been a couple for years, she rested her head on his shoulder.

"I like you, Jaden Marie. A lot. I'm drawn to you and want to know you better. When I'm around you I say goofy things and act like a smartass because you fluster me." He groaned. No wonder women laughed at him. His lines sounded cheesy. "I mean..."

Raising her head from his shoulder, she pressed her finger to his lips and stopped the flow of foolish words. "I like you, too."

Ego no longer deflated, he threw caution and his common sense to the wind and dabbed his tongue over the pad of her finger. Her eyes widened, but she didn't withdraw. Taking her surprise as a go-ahead, he sucked the digit into his mouth. Dear God, she tasted good. A moan split the air. Was it her? No, another moan rippled from his throat.

Her lips parted a fraction of an inch. Desperate to taste her everywhere, he relinquished her hand and swooped in for a kiss. She whimpered, opening for him and taking the lead. Her tongue danced over his. His head span. She affected him like no other. He twined his fingers in her hair, drawing her closer. Her groin rubbed against his, sending a tremor through his body. They needed to find a bed and fast—like yesterday.

A door clicked behind him. Jaden screeched and jumped. "Go away."

"Hey, hey. I'm not the stalker. I come in peace."

He gritted his teeth. Fuck. She was still out with Corbin. Marlon released her, giving her the option to choose her own partner for the evening.

Jaden ran a shaky hand through her tousled hair. "Corbin. I'm sorry. I got overheated and came out here to regain my breath. Cass was with me, I swear. I didn't mean to ditch you."

Bracing his feet shoulders' width apart and folding his arms, Corbin shook his head. "Overheated? You don't have to lie. I understand—I think."

Knotting his brows, Marlon forced his gaze from Jaden to Corbin. "What do you understand?"

"She's taking risks because she's into you."

Jaden fumbled, waving her hands in the air. "Now wait a minute."

Cocking his head, Corbin puffed out his chest. "Tell me the truth. Who do you think about late at night? I'm willing to bet my drum set it isn't me."

"I want to tell you differently, but I can't." Her shoulders drooped and the bracelets clanked together. "I'm sorry."

"Who'd you seek out for"—he hooked his fingers in the air—"body heat?" The words rolled off his tongue like an accusation.

With the tips of her ears a bright crimson, Jaden toyed with the hem of her blouse. "You were on stage. What was I supposed to do, yank you away from the band to keep me warm? I don't think so."

Marlon hooked his thumbs into his belt loops. Well shit. He hadn't meant to throw such a large monkey wrench into the works. He'd be the bigger man, even if it killed him. "I'll leave you two alone to work this out."

Corbin put both hands in the air. "No man, you stay put. You need to settle the score with her, since you've got it as bad as she does." He glanced at his watch. "I have another set any second, and I'm not big on getting involved with taken women." He nodded to Jaden. "I had a nice time, but if this guy breaks your heart, you come find me. I will jump off that stage in a heartbeat. And if the cretin shows up, scream. You've got lots of backup in this town. Okay?"

Scarlet tinged her cheeks. "I got it. Thanks."

Point made, Corbin strolled back through the door, leaving them alone again.

Jaden wrapped her arms around her body as she trembled. From embarrassment or to stave off the chill, Marlon wasn't sure. "Did you mean what you said?"

"I mean every word." Curling both arms around her, he nuzzled her hair. Too much, too soon? He didn't care, though he should. He'd vowed not to get lost in her. Too many more kisses and his good intentions to stay at arm's length would be shot to hell. He loosened his embrace and stared at her, ready to put the brakes on this thing they'd started.

Jaden's green eyes sparkled in the soft light cast by the multiple strands of white Christmas tree lights. She slipped her hands down the front of his jeans and cupped his growing erection. "Make me feel the way you see me."

So much for good intentions.

Chapter Eleven

Jaden licked her dry lips. Dear God, had she really just volleyed the first serious challenge? If the heat in Marlon's eyes was any indication, she'd met her match. Most men took her advances with a grain of salt—they stole what they wanted and ditched her when her use fizzled. Would Marlon? She hoped not. Emotions akin to love snaked through her brain.

Something prodded her lower belly. She shifted against him. Was that his...? Good gravy. His cock nudged her hip, sending a rush of heat to her core and her heart. Oh grief, it felt good.

Sprinkling kisses over her cheeks and lips, he pulled her more tightly against his large body. "Come home with me."

It wasn't a question, but rather a command. Well sure, the man was an authority figure. He dealt in commands and those aggravating fatherly tones. People swore by his word. Was she up for the test in taming a deputy? Hell, yes.

Despite the rush of boldness, she held back. She shouldn't drop her pride and fall into bed with him. She should head home or at least back into the bar and spend the rest of the evening with Corbin. She owed the drummer that much. But being with Marlon and his gentle caresses and searing kisses seemed to be her undoing. Each nudge, every touch, brought a new and heightened sensation. Every good-girl cell in her body urged her to take her time, whilst her libido, out to sea for the last couple of months, screamed at her to let go.

Shivering, she made her decision. "Lead on and I'll follow."

Even reformed bad girls had a limit.

Marlon twined his fingers with hers and led her to the access gate on the side of the patio. Pressing a few keys on the worn keypad, he unlocked the door.

Baffled, she stopped in the exit to the parking lot. "How'd you do that? I mean, I know you must know the code, but you don't work here—do you? Don't we have to go back through the bar?"

"We can leave right here from the patio." With a grin, he shrugged. "I was a bouncer here for a couple months four summers ago after my buddy Angelo took over management. I had time to kill, and he needed competent security staff. It worked out for the best."

With a combination of wonder and respect, she murmured, "I see."

As he tugged her across the overcrowded parking lot, the image of him as a bouncer—clad in all black, with shiny sunglasses, arms folded, doing his dead-level best to look menacing—developed in her mind. She sucked in a ragged breath. Men in command turned her on, and how! If he'd been the bouncer at one of the clubs she frequented, she might not have left California.

When they stopped a moment later, he pinned her between the door of the Jeep and his body. He blotted out the world around them with his sheer size.

"Oh my!" She jumped away from the chilly metal. "Yikes."

"What, babe? What's wrong? Is someone watching you?"

"Freezing door plus bare skin equals really-freaking-cold Jaden." She rubbed her arms to get the blood moving. "No one's following me. Promise."

"Oh. Just a moment." He pressed a button on his key fob and opened the door. While he rummaged in the back seat, she brought her hand down on his ass. Nice and firm.

"I could leave this sweatshirt in the car and let you ice over." He held his hand up out of her reach. "What would you prefer?"

"You have a nice ass. I had to touch it. I might even spank it if I'm given the chance."

Marlon yanked the zipper down the front of the sweatshirt and held it open. "Arms." The single word held so much weight.

Thankful for his gesture, she complied. She moaned. "I knew I'd be underdressed, but I wanted to look sexy. Thank you for rescuing me from a case of bad fashion."

"I live to serve beautiful women named Jaden." Drawing her back into his embrace, Marlon kissed her cheek. "Babe… Do you realise you can bring a man to his knees with just a smile?"

She smoothed her hands over his chest. "Really? Any idea who he is? I want to meet him." Marlon reminded her of iron encased in flesh. She trembled, wanting to grope him everywhere. Still, she couldn't just give in—yet.

Raining kisses on her lips, cheeks and nose, he cupped the back of her head. "You're a bad girl, Jaden and it's so good." His breath came in short puffs. At least she had him on edge. She hated being horny alone.

"Honey, you caught my eye a long time ago, but it was nothing like the ache I feel right now. I know the woman in your heart and want to feel her moving with me. I can't catch my breath when I'm around you because I want to please you." His kisses became rougher, more consuming, as his hands moved beneath the sweatshirt and encircled her waist. "I want you like I've never wanted a woman. Fuck, I think I need you more than I've ever needed anyone."

"You talk too much." Sliding her hands under the soft cotton of his T-shirt, she learnt the dips and valleys of his body. His firm nipples seared her flesh. The rasp of crisp chest hair against her palms sent pinpricks of excitement racing through her body. "Take me home."

He panted against her neck. "Home. Yes. Now." Fumbling to open the door, he helped her slide onto the seat. "Yes, home."

Marlon raced across town, cursing each stop sign and red light. Was it bad for a cop to break the speed limit when there wasn't an emergency? Hell, being with Jaden felt like standing next to a four-alarm fire. How would he survive making love to her? He'd go down in her blaze of glory.

Screeching into his parking spot, he chastised himself. She wasn't a disaster waiting to happen. She was sultry woman, primed and ready to accept his advances. The badge, the danger, the crazy schedule—nothing else mattered.

When she held him, he felt invincible. He felt something deeper, something he couldn't put his finger on. Love? Maybe, but he wouldn't hold his breath. Love meant pain and suffering and he refused to succumb again.

As soon as he switched off the engine, he jumped from the Jeep and raced to her side. God, did he look antsy? Remind her of the shallow men she dated in the past? He wanted to be different from the rest, but she made it hard to gather his thoughts, much less stifle his Neanderthal urges.

Her voice broke through his sensual fog. "Marlon, we don't have to rush. We have all night to touch, cuddle, and pleasure each other."

On the porch, he stopped and forced his brain to function in a gear other than sex. "I only have a couple hours."

Concern infused in her voice. "Why? Are you on duty?"

He shoved his key in the lock and twisted the handle. "No, sweetheart. I promised Judi I'd have you home at a decent hour."

With her hands on her hips, she cocked a brow. "You did? How chivalrous—I think."

The feeling that he'd sent the mood south gnawed at him, but still—he might as well come clean now. "I…she knows how I feel about you and suggested I throw it all out for you to do what you wanted. I'm laying myself bare."

"You aren't bare yet, but you will be." She walked her fingers up his chest, making him shudder. "She suggested the same to me in different words. So why don't we find out where things will lead?"

Point taken, he shoved the door open and led her inside his dark apartment. Had he tidied up the place? He couldn't remember. Too late. God help me not to fall on my ass.

Taking the lead from him, she snicked the door shut and pressed him against the cool barrier. The chill from the steel barely diminished his fever for her. Her hips ground against him, while she licked a path of heat along his neck. The only light in the room came from the security light above his picture window. The yellow glow splashed over her body, her skin glistening with a fine sheen of perspiration.

He fisted her hair in his hands, clutching her to him. "Baby girl. You're dangerous." If she continued on her present course, he'd finish in his pants.

Nibbling his chin, she giggled. "Good." Both of her small hands edged beneath his shirt and roamed his torso once again. Her touch sent shockwaves straight to his groin.

Releasing her hair, he slid his palms over her ass and cupped the perfect globes. He slapped her ass and thrilled at the cry from her throat.

"Yes, Marlon." She whimpered as he picked her up, guided her legs around his waist then headed to the couch. Although making love to her pressed against his front door sound like one hell of a good idea, he wanted their first time to be special.

He plopped down on the sofa with her still wrapped around him. "Yes, baby girl. Tell me you want this. Tell me I'm doing something right." To make you mine.

Jaden wriggled around to plant her knees on either side of his waist, rubbing her pussy against his cock. Easing back for a moment, she clutched the hem of her sweatshirt and tank top and whipped the soft fabric over her head.

Her hair fluttered over her shoulders as the shirt flew across the room. Her nipples pebbled in the cool air and struggled against the delicate lace of her bra. He licked his lips. She wasn't overly endowed, but just enough to fill his hands. Perfect.

She traced her index finger over his lips, toying with him. "Make love to me. Show me I'm sexy." Her husky bedroom voice was his undoing.

"With pleasure." He sat up and yanked his T-shirt from his body.

Every inch of him yearned for her. Her breath feathered over his skin, knocking his control off-kilter. He didn't care. The straps of her bra slipped from her shoulders, revealing the tops of her breasts. The primal need to claim her returned. To make her his.

With a groan, he tugged the delicate fabric down and bent to take a rosy nipple into his mouth. Each tiny moan heightened his need. She murmured his name, easing him further down the path of destruction.

She leant back and jammed their bodies together. Her sharp little nails dug into his shoulders as she ground against him. "Marlon! Oh, God."

Switching to her other nipple, he feasted. She tasted like honey and sensual woman, a lethal combination made just for him. As he licked and sucked, he worked the button on her jeans. When he freed her from the denim constriction, he smoothed his hands between her lacy panties and her ass.

"Stand up, babe. Let me see all of you."

With strands of hair falling over her eyes, she stood. Her breasts rose and fell with her laboured breaths. He'd seen nude pictures of her, but nothing compared to holding his woman in the flesh. His. He liked the sound of that.

"Sweetness." Sliding to his knees, he grinned and guided the denim and lace down past her hips. What she called extra pounds filled her out and evened out her body. He licked his dry lips and leant forwards to nibble on the slight roundness of her stomach. He tugged at the piercing in her navel.

She shivered and ran her fingers through his hair. "Marlon, it's too much."

"Not yet," he murmured against her belly button. "Let me play a bit longer. I've waited a long time for you." He cupped her ass once again and nuzzled her slick lips. The soft thatch of dark curls tickled his nose. Her aroma rolled over him like a gentle wave. He gasped and laved his tongue along her labia, savouring the softness of her body. His brain misfired and his thoughts honed in on her pleasure.

"Marlon." Her grip on his head tightened as she screamed. "Yes, yes, yes."

Dear God, she was wet for him. His cock pressed painfully against his zipper. He ignored his needs and focussed on her. It had been so long since he'd truly pleased a woman, seeing Jaden come apart in his arms was sending him to the ragged edge. But he'd finish in his jeans like a randy teenager before he ruined the moment by forcing the pace. He added another slap to her ass, enjoying the red marks on her tender flesh.

More emotions he couldn't name welled to the surface. Was it love? The real thing? He wasn't sure, but he wasn't about to trade it either. The idea of spending the rest of his life with her twirled around in his mind.

Each lick, each caress over her clit, brought another tug until she shivered and groaned. "I. Can't. Hold. Back."

Releasing his grasp on her hips, he gave her nether lips one more lick then sat back on his heels. He cleaned her juices from his chin and grinned. Holding back wasn't high on his priority list either, until she whimpered.

"Don't leave me this way." A glazed look clouded her eyes as she wobbled on her feet.

"I'm yours, babe." He eased two fingers into her slick heat, pumping in and out. Wrapping his other arm around her for stability, he pressed the tip of his tongue against the bundle of nerves at the apex of her thighs. He toyed with the pucker of her ass with his free hand, eliciting a shiver.

"Oh my God, yes, do that. More." Jaden thrust her fingers into his hair, pulling at the strands. Her hips rocked in a less-than-rhythmic fashion as she quaked in his grasp. Her breathing hitched. "Marlon." She shivered and collapsed against him. "Wow. Just wow."

"Good?" Tolerable? Something she wanted to experience again?

"I love it." She rested her head on his shoulder and snaked her arms around his waist. "Do it again, stud."

Love it? Stud? The words pulled all the happy strings in his heart. "Easy, sexy girl. You'll make me think we've started an inferno."

Drawing her into his arms, he carried her down the short hallway to his bedroom. Once on the bed, she curled onto her side and smiled drowsily at him. "I think you're trained to deal with this fire. You've satisfied me."

"Satisfied is good, but no sleeping yet."

She mock-saluted him. "Not tired, just waiting on you."

"Never make a lady wait." With fumbling fingers, Marlon unbuttoned his jeans and shoved them to his feet. He retrieved a condom from the nightstand.

Please Remember Me

Giggling, Jaden sat on her haunches and snatched the foil packet. "I'm resilient. Now, let me take care of you." In a matter of seconds, she had slid the latex over his penis, caressing him as she went. "You're so soft, yet hard. I like it." She paused, holding his manhood in her grasp like a treasure. "It's easy, since I like you."

He groaned. No woman had ever sheathed him. The move, compounded with her words, turned him on and turned his senses inside out. Then again, the idea of making love to her without the barrier kicked his desire up a few notches. What would she look like round with his child? Dynamite.

Squeezing his eyes shut, he switched mental gears. Who knew how long she'd be with him? Or if she loved him in return?

"Take me in, love," he murmured.

"Slap my ass again. Feels so good." Jaden braced her shoulders against the sheets and angled her hips off the bed. With slow strokes, he nudged her pussy and gazed at her through lust-filled eyes. She gasped and guided him along his journey with both hands. Her hair fanned around her face, reminiscent of a halo. Jaden was no angel, though, and her devilish needs held him fast. She knew what she wanted in bed, took it without question and held his heart. Forever-thoughts swirled in his head. He needed her. Not just her body, not just her friendship—all of her, for the rest of his life.

Words teetered on the tip of his tongue. I love you.

Groaning, he held back. Too soon.

Slowly, slowly, he eased into her and dug his fingers into the creamy flesh of her ass. With each increasingly rapid thrust, he fell further into the great unknown.

Rational thought left his brain. He added a couple of swats to punctuate each pump into her.

Her eyelids drooped shut and a long sigh escaped her lips. "Yes."

He slammed his hips into hers, fusing with her. Screams ripped from her throat. More and more, he delved even deeper. Her inner muscles grasped him like a fist. He shivered. Making love had never been this powerful, this primal. Sweat beaded on his forehead and moistened his back. Her small hands scraped his shoulders, marking him, claiming him. She arched into him. "I'm coming. Oh, my God!"

He threw his head back and groaned. Light pricked behind his eyelids as he came. She trembled and gripped him tight, milking him of his seed. Thank God for the condom.

Marlon braced himself on his hands and slumped to her side. His heart thundered in his chest. Could he truly be in love? The possibility flashed in his mind. At the same time, a tiny voice in the back of his mind threw doubt on his feelings. He'd fallen too deep and too damned fast for his own comfort. Too many things hadn't been said—her past, her true feelings for him, her plans for the future.

He squeezed his eyes shut. God damn, love sucked as much as playing it safe.

Chapter Twelve

Moments after coming down from the orgasmic high, Jaden collapsed on the bed—Marlon's bed. Her mind reeled. Oh my goodness. They'd had sex, but not just run-of-the-mill sex. Raw, bone-deep sex. The kind of sex that seared itself into one's brain forever.

Whoa.

His breath tickled her shoulder while he drew lazy circles around her belly button, occasionally bumping the piercing. The rasp of his whiskers abraded her skin, yet it didn't hurt, but rather heightened her awareness of him. As she licked her lips, his masculine taste lingered like a fond memory. Her inner thighs were chafed, but in a delicious way she wanted to experience over and over again. Who knew a man's beard could be such a mood-enhancer?

Everything about him suited her—the facial hair, the rippled muscles, the determination in his emerald eyes. In his arms, she felt safe. But for how long? Her tastes always changed once she'd sampled the forbidden goods. Was Marlon now a folly or a favoured mistake? She smoothed her hand up his back. No, he was the kind of mistake she'd remember when the rest of her world collapsed.

Moving against her, he chuckled. "I have to get up, Jaden Marie. I don't want to, but I need to chuck the condom."

Meeting his gaze, she wriggled. The emotion in his words left her speechless. Making love wasn't a one-time, attention-grabbing move for him. Commitment, thy name is Marlon Cross. His eyes, still wide and dark, roved over her body. She didn't want the night to end either. Refused to let him linger as a mere blip on her radar. How could she make the moment last forever? Confess the words in her heart?

Yeah right, and watch him bolt.

"Go." She brushed her semi-erect nipples against his arm, the move turning her on almost as much as she intended to tease him. "I'll still be here."

"If this is a dream, I don't ever want to wake up." Marlon shuffled and rolled out of bed, tossing the sheets over her naked body. Not that she wanted to stare, but the sight of his bare ass transfixed her. Her mouth watered. Her hands clenched. If she sneaked up behind him, she could grab a handful and feel her fill—again.

The sound of water running and rustling met her ears. Biting the inside of her cheek, she went with her urges and crossed the thick-carpeted floor on silent footsteps. As she got to the door, the shrill ring of her phone startled her. She shrieked. Marlon bounded from the bathroom and smacked into her with an, "Oof!"

Catching her as they plopped to the floor, he chuckled and wrapped both arms around her. "You know, you can get my attention without waking up my neighbours. I wanted a round two, three...or maybe even six."

Biting back a laugh, she elbowed him and kissed the hollow of his neck. "It's my phone. Only a few people know the number." She rummaged through her jeans pockets for the device and marvelled at how relaxed she and Marlon were together. He didn't even rush to cover himself when he got out of bed. He felt comfortable in his own skin and, boy, did the image rivet her.

Sitting on her shins, she glanced at him. He'd already stretched out beside her on the floor, propped up on one elbow. "I'm the one people try to call all hours of the night. What's the emergency?"

She frowned and pressed the keys to retrieve the voicemail. No one who knew her number had anything to say that she couldn't share with him—even her father. Switching the phone to the speaker setting, she grabbed the rumpled sheet from the bed.

"Cold?" Grabbing her hand, Marlon pulled her into the crook of his arm and kissed the underside of her breast. "I can warm you better than the blankets."

Although his actions challenged her grip on control, the voice on the other end of the line made her pause.

"Jaden, honey, this is Judi. I'm not good at leaving messages on these things. Honey, if you'd call me. I—do you remember me talking about Pearl McKinley? She has that sweet little terrier, Riley. Oh, my time is probably up. Drat. Bobby called. Come home, okay?"

With trembling hands, Jaden switched off the speaker setting and dialled Judi's home number. Something felt off. True, Judi wasn't the best with technology. She hated the timer on her crock pot, but still. Calling at one-thirty in the morning wasn't her style. Jaden's heart clenched in her chest. If Judi's angina was acting up... What a time to have let her emotions get the best of her.

"It'll be okay. We'll get through this." Marlon sat up and wrapped his body around hers. "Why is someone named Bobby calling you?"

"He's being cautious." Jaden rested her head on his shoulder. After two rings, Judi answered. "Hello? This is too late to call someone. Go to bed."

Jaden sighed. "Judi, it's me. You wanted me? What's wrong?"

Although flat, her voice still held a hint of her usual humour. "I'm fine. My arthritis is acting up, but the ticker's fine. Sparky's wandering around looking for you like he does, but that's not why I called. Is Marlon with you?"

The tips of her ears burned. "Yes. You said you wanted me to come home. What's wrong?"

"Bring Marlon. I'll have the coffee on. We need to talk—the three of us."

Before Jaden could answer, Judi clicked off the line. She snapped her phone shut and pressed her face against Marlon's neck. "She wants to talk. I don't know why."

Whatever Judi needed to tell her couldn't be good. She swallowed past the lump in her throat and repressed nervous laughter. Marlon stroked her arm, offering more silent comfort. A rumble vibrated low in his chest. "So I heard."

Jaden nodded. Duh, she'd had the phone on speaker. People in the next apartment probably heard. "She wants to talk to you, too. I know we aren't super close, but please come with me."

He cupped her jaw, rubbing his thumb over her cheek and bringing her gaze to his. His eyes darkened once more. "Jaden Marie, we are very close. Yes, I'll go with you. You drive me crazy and don't tell me all the details, but I can deal—unless you're sharing your affections."

"Bobby's...never mind." Her resolve broke. Someone cared about her—really cared. Tears streamed down her face. Although he hadn't said the words she longed to hear, he shared her feelings. He wanted to be with her. "Thank you."

* * * *

Ten minutes later, Marlon raced back across town. Though no longer crying, Jaden held onto his hand with an iron grip. Whatever Judi needed to say at two in the morning had Jaden on edge.

Coming to a stop in her driveway, Marlon threw the Jeep into park and surged to Jaden's side. A single light in the living room cast pale light out onto the front porch. Jaden trembled and dug her sharp little nails into his palm. "I have a bad feeling. I'm scared."

"I'm right here beside you, babe." Marlon wrinkled his nose. Judi didn't seem like the type to throw someone out in the middle of the night. Heck, she reminded him of his grandmother—a gentle smile, a fresh batch of cookies, and a warm hug when life went south. Still, the unnerving feeling remained in the back of his mind. He needed to get down to who the hell Bobby was. Did she mean his fellow officer? He'd been burned by Hutchins before. Never again.

When Marlon opened the door, Judi sat perched on the couch, tissue in hand, stroking Sparky's fur. The snoring dog kicked in his sleep, probably chasing a rabbit or something in his dreams. Removing her glasses to wipe her eyes, Judi looked up. "Hi kids."

Sparky, instantly interested in the commotion, sat up and growled. Wriggling, he slid off the couch and plopped at Jaden's feet. She knelt to pet the dog. "What's wrong? You're crying." With one hand on the dog, Jaden grasped Judi's hand. "I can call Steven."

"Don't bother him He's got enough to worry about what with his cholesterol." Judi blotted the corners of her eyes with the balled up tissue. "Do you remember me talking about my friend Pearl? She had Riley. I have no idea what his specific breed is, but you took him for a walk with Sparks when we played cards. Well, the cancer won this evening and she's finally with Francis. Her family knew it was coming, but not how fast."

Marlon sat down next to his friend and wrapped an arm around her. "I'm sorry for your loss, but she's in a better place and she's not suffering."

Judi sniffled and nodded again. "I agree, and thank you, but that's not the shitty part."

Taken aback by the coarse language, Jaden looked up.

"Her son doesn't want Riley. That little dog was Pearl's lifeline. He kept her company and comforted her while the cancer ate away at her. With Francis gone for so long, Riley helped make her last few months more enjoyable. And that rat wants to have him put down!" Judi turned to Marlon and slapped the arm of the couch. "He can't do that. I won't allow it. Riley is a sweet dog who deserves a new family."

Jaden stroked Sparky's fur. "He did get along with Sparks real well." She nibbled her bottom lip. "Do you know someone who can take him?"

Marlon shifted in his seat. He wasn't sure what his place was in the conversation, but if both women hurt, he'd try to make things better.

"What if we take him?" Jaden waggled Sparky's head. "Can we have a friend come over for a long time—like an extended sleepover?"

Marlon rolled his eyes. "You talk to the dog like he's a person, too? He's just a dog."

Her brows knotted together. Gentle colour infused her cheeks, as she squared her shoulders. "He's not just a dog, he's part of our mish-mash family and yes, I talk to him. If he wants a brother, then we'll take Riley. I won't let someone put him down."

"Having Sparks has been the best therapy for me. I don't see how another dog would be a bad idea." Judi patted his knee. "Can you make him turn the dog over to us? Or do we have to go through the Sunny Retreat Shelter?"

Marlon shook his head. "I'm not sure. I'll ask Carol Ann to look into it and talk to Summer Tyler over at the dog warden. She's a good friend and always willing to help. Been a godsend to me."

Jaden averted her gaze and snickered, making his heart clench. Okay, so that sounded strange to say in front of a woman he'd just made love to. Then again, he wasn't exactly the king of smooth. Never had been. And Jaden constantly kept him on the verge of making a fool of himself.

"Godsend?" Jaden squeezed his thigh, a gleam twinkling in her eye. "I'm glad we can count on her."

With a grunt, Judi stood. "These late nights are going to be the death of me if the old ticker doesn't give out first. My hips can't take the stress either." She clapped Marlon on the shoulder. "Thank you." At the doorway, she spoke over her shoulder. "I'll make an exception to the rule tonight. Bobby can't come back."

Before Marlon could process her statement, Judi disappeared to her bedroom. Jaden chuckled and plopped down on her butt. "You know, I think she's trying to throw us together. That and the little curfew idea. Stroke of genius, if you ask me."

He rubbed his chin. "Oh, probably. Now about Bobby…"

She stood, her long legs stretched before him. He rolled his tongue around his dry mouth. Dear God, she was sexy. He held out his hands. Jaden pulled him into a standing position. "She's got a lot of friends with animals, you know."

He wrapped his arms around her waist and nuzzled her hair. "I'm sure she does. But I wanted to know—" She sighed and his mind reeled. He was thinking of sex and Jaden, no doubt, had her mind on something totally different.

"Marlon," she murmured, "who takes those animals when the people die?"

Her innocent question and blatant avoidance knocked him off-kilter. Hell. He wasn't sure where the critters went. His mind hadn't diverted from the Bobby situation. Damn, he needed an intelligent answer. "I'd assume the dog warden or Sunny Retreat. I don't handle many cases where the person dies of natural causes. With homicides, if there were pets, they go to the next of kin or the shelter. If someone passes naturally, then it's up to their next of kin. Why?"

"Seems like a shame."

Something more lay under the simple comment. He cupped her jaw, tilting her head to meet his gaze. "Why do you ask?" What was going through her mind at warp speed?

She shrugged and looked away. "I don't know. It's just disgraceful and mean." Wriggling from his grasp, she strolled to the opposite end of the room. "I know how it feels to be left behind and it sucks."

Marlon sat down on the arm of the couch. Whatever she needed to say, he'd listen. "Tell me what's on your mind, Jaden Marie. I'll help you through it."

She smiled and her eyes shimmered with unshed tears. "That reminds me of my mom. Each time you call me Jaden Marie, I think about how she'd say it and smile. And in a strange way, I think that's how Riley and Sparky feel. When Judi or Pearl talks to them, they feel important. With Pearl gone, Riley has no one. And think about all those folks out there who want to keep their pets, their babies, even when they themselves are sick. Animals do have healing powers."

Without a second thought, he stood and crossed the room. He scooped her into his arms. "I agree." Her words, though a jumble of thoughts, made sense. Sparky brought out the maternal, selfless qualities in Jaden. The walks kept them both healthy and sociable.

"When Mom died, I felt like my world collapsed. As it did for Daddy, though he never said it outright. He changed and nothing I did was good enough," she sobbed, wetting his shirt. "Maybe this is what I'm supposed to be good at."

Okay, now she'd lost him. "Explain it to me, baby. You're good at plenty of things."

Leaning back within his embrace, she wiped the tears away with the back of her hand. "When I did all those crazy stunts in California, it was because I thought I could outrun my problems. If I did drugs, I was numbing the pain of not fitting in. When I drank and partied, people noticed me. My actions served the purpose—up to a point. I belonged. Then everything hit the skids and the people didn't care. The fiasco with Logan and Dex showed me just how far I'd run off the rails." She sniffled. "I was a mess until I met Cass. She took me under her wing and let me be me. If I hadn't had the cabin for a detox-slash-retreat, I'd be dead."

He reeled. Yeah, he knew about the deal with Logan. The file on Dex Rose had her name all over it. During the interview, she'd spoken about her drinking problem and her substance abuse. But to think she'd be dead... His heart clenched. "And this translates to the dog...how?"

"I wasn't any good at being a party girl. I suck at modelling and my acting skills aren't even acceptable enough for the gag reels. I put so many things up my nose it's a wonder it's in one piece. But now that I'm here, I'm pretty good at taking care of Sparky." She gestured to the dog. "I'm responsible for someone other than me and I like it. I'll bet Riley would like to be in a home where he's loved. Here, he can be. I figure, if I can channel my energy into making other people's lives better rather than my addictions, then why not?"

Her words turned over in his mind. A place for the unwanted animals? Sure, he'd always wanted a dog, but with his crazy hours, it seemed unfair. If she could handle the chaos, then maybe the idea of taking in the occasional animal wasn't so bad. But to take in the masses to combat addictions? He wasn't so sure. Still, his respect for her rose along with parts of his anatomy.

Squeezing her tightly, Marlon sighed. "You can do whatever you set your mind to. I know you will give him the best home possible." The scent of her shampoo wafted to him. "But right now, I'd like to know who Bobby is."

"A friend who keeps an eye on me, kind-of-sort-of."

Her words didn't ease his apprehension. "Jaden..."

"He's in my past and nothing you have to handle. Really."

"You frustrate me, babe."

A smile lit up her face. "So you will stay? I know Judi gave the green light, but I was afraid to ask."

He chuckled. "Miss Bold was afraid to ask? You didn't seem to mind taking charge back at my apartment." Meek and demure suited her. Then again, he liked her bold, sassy, and willing, too.

More colour rushed into her cheeks. "I didn't want to sound like a wuss. I mean..."

He silenced her with a kiss, enveloping himself in her scent. She clasped his shirt in both hands, pulling him flush against her body. When they parted, her eyes fluttered open and a lazy smile blossomed on her lips.

"I'm needy, aren't I?"

"Sweetheart, I'm standing here, trying to hold off a damned erection and you talk about needy?" He rested his forehead on hers. "You've got me wrapped around your little finger."

Jaden wrapped her fingers around his length, stroking him. "How about you stay tonight and snuggle me?"

"You got it."

Chapter Thirteen

"Just try to tell me pets don't have feelings." Jaden stormed into the shelter. Her voice shook the glass foyer. "Everyone has feelings!" *Including me.*

She'd spent the previous week arguing about Riley with Pearl's son Leonard through a series of phone calls and personal visits. He wasn't about to let her adopt the dog. His words at the diner cemented themselves in her mind. "Drop him in the pond for all I care." Thank God Marlon had heard the nastiness. As soon as she'd found out the dog had been dropped at the shelter, she'd rushed across town. According to Summer, Leonard abandoned Riley on the doorstep with the opinion that animals were nothing more than disposable 'things'.

An eerie feeling wrapped around her heart. She took a quick look over her shoulder. The dark green sedan sat in the parking spot next to her car. A man lounged on the hood, his ankles crossed. At first glance, he appeared casual. She inched backwards towards the inner door. He wore sunglasses again. Who knew what he was looking at.

He can't take my independence and he won't break me.

Once inside the sky blue building, she stopped cold. Puppies, full grown dogs, kittens and cats peered at her from inside wire cages. Some of the cats mewled and batted their paws through the holes. Others sat and stared. Some of the dogs barked, while a handful whimpered. Her heart clenched as she forgot her problems. Many of the dogs were purebreds. She swallowed past the lump in her throat. All of them needed homes other than the chilly confines of the wire and cement block.

"There's so many of them," she murmured and folded her hands in front of her mouth.

"People give them up because they lose the cuteness. The dogs get too big to control and the cats cause allergies. It's sad but true."

Jaden jumped. When she turned, a petite woman with hair the colour of milk chocolate crossed her slender arms.

"Didn't mean to startle you."

"Are you Summer?"

The woman grinned, displaying dazzling white teeth. "One and the same. I assume you're Jaden. Marlon spoke highly of you when I took some forms over to the county office. It's a little strange because he doesn't talk about anyone except for the guys he works with. You've made an impression."

Jaden fumbled for a response. He thought highly of her? She'd made an impression? Wow. He knew the woman she wanted to be—not the celebrity fuck-up. She owed him the biggest kiss and more than one night of devotion.

"You don't believe me?"

Jaden tucked a hank of loose hair behind her ear. "I—it's just crazy to hear it from someone else."

"Get used to it, girl. He's usually a pretty quiet guy, but he's got a great big heart and he's loyal. He's in love with you and I am thrilled." Summer clicked her tongue, calming some of the dogs. "I tried to be the kind of woman he needed, but I couldn't overcome the memory of his wife. I still see him from time to time."

The wind rushed from her lungs. The 'in love' part she could deal with eventually, but wife? The man had a wife? Jaden grasped for anything to keep her upright. The glass door worked fine. She prayed it didn't swing open. Okay, so they really didn't take much time to talk about stuff, but really. A wife? Hell.

Summer touched Jaden's arm. Her voice dropped to a low tone. "He didn't say anything, did he? I'm sorry. It wasn't my place to shout out his past." Putting one fist on her hip, she frowned and tapped her chin with her other hand. "That might have had something to do with why our dates are further and further apart. I tend to talk without thinking sometimes. It's a gift and it gets me into so much trouble."

Jaden squared her shoulders. She tended to speak before thinking, too. "I understand and it's fine." Sort of. On to more important things before she had too much more time to think. "I—I came here to pick up Riley."

Summer's frown brightened to a wide grin. "Ah, Riley. He's a pistol, but he'd be a great family dog. He tore up the squeaky hamburger toy in about ten minutes flat. Lots of energy, he'd like kids to play with." She sighed. "But then all of them would make great pets. I want to save them all, but I can't. Not enough room. If I'm lucky, two-thirds of them are adopted."

Forgetting her personal discomfort, Jaden slipped through the glass doors to the kennels. She'd always wanted a kitten. What about a full-grown cat? The first cage held two grey tabby cats. She stuck her finger through the holes in the cage. One of them purred. The other butted her fingers with the top of its head. "I think I'd like a cat, but how do you know if they tolerate dogs?"

Summer snorted. "What cat does? It's a case of coexisting and a matter of temperament. In here, they're all lovey and adorable. At home, some change. Some cats are distant. It's like they do what they have to in order to get out and when they succeed... Well, you'll have to see for yourself. I know a couple of cats who took to their master's dogs with no issues, but they were adopted."

The duo slithered around each other in a desperate attempt to get her attention. Would Judi mind a pair of cats? What if she was allergic? Two sets of greenish-yellow eyes peered at her. Her heart melted. My life, my choices. "I'll take Riley and these two. They seem to need me."

"I have to get preachy for a moment. Four animals is the limit in town, you know. Marlon won't enforce it because he's with the county, but he will tell the city cops if you change your mind and think you want more. Unfortunately, he has to tattle."

"Oh." Tears misted behind her eyes. Not because of the rules, but for the loss of the opportunity to do the right thing.

"Enough sermons." Summer opened the cage and handed Jaden one of the cats. "I know how you feel. I've seen too many older people have to give up their pets because they can't take care of them anymore. Then there are the ones who outlive their owners, like Riley. It stinks. I want to take them all home." She tapped her chin again.

"Both of these guys have had their shots and the local vet neutered them, so you'll only have to take them in for a check-up. While I'm thinking about it, did you bring a crate?"

Jaden froze. "Crate? For what? Can't I just put them all in the car?"

"You'd be surprised, but no." Summer laughed, the sound ringing around the room. "I know Riley likes the car because Leonard told me. Cats tend to ride better when in a crate. Although I had one lady who drove with her orange cat draped around her shoulders like a shawl, not that you probably care. It's kinda funny to see old Doris Folger tooling around town in her Caddy with Farkus sleeping around her neck."

Jaden nibbled the corner of her mouth. Keeping cats entailed a whole new set of equipment… Still, she couldn't leave them. "Okay, so where do I get a couple of crates?"

* * * *

Whistling the last song he'd heard on the radio, Marlon strolled out of the courthouse and through the parking lot to his patrol car. Each time he'd had got a chance over the past week, he headed to Judi's to see Jaden. She didn't insist upon dissecting his day, but listened until he had nothing else to say. She took away his stress when she smiled. Each time they made love, his desire for her grew. He'd rip out his own heart and bronze it for her if she asked. But letting her go? Damn. Letting go might be more than he could handle.

His phone beeped with an incoming picture message. He grinned when he read the identification screen—Jaden. He pressed the buttons to retrieve the message. Could it be a risqué picture to tide him over? She might have shrugged out of the Hollywood façade, but she knew a thing or two about turning a man on. Sliding behind the wheel of his cruiser, he peeked around the parking lot and brought up the file.

In the image, she smiled with a wide-eyed grey tabby in her arms. The caption read: "My child, Tantrum!"

He shook his head and laughed. Only Jaden could name a cat after a temper fit. Another picture popped up. In this one, she held another cat while Sparky peeked over her shoulder. The caption for this image read: "Here's his sister, Unruly. Sparks and Riley love them. Well, sorta."

Somehow the sight of Jaden with multiple pets seemed right. As right as her with children—his children. Laughing, he drove to the muni lot. The smile on his lips warmed his heart and spread through his chest. She took all the dull greys in his life and gave them pops of vivid colour.

Once he'd traded the cruiser for his Jeep, he engaged the engine and headed to his apartment. After he'd retrieved a change of clothing, he planned to spend the evening with Jaden—and now her furry children. He couldn't wait to hear the adoption story.

Hell, he couldn't wait to hold her and be near her.

He rummaged through the top drawer for a fresh pair of socks. Each time he showed up at Judi's, she found yet another odd job for him to complete. If it wasn't a leaky toilet, it was a broken step, or the smattering of leaves in the back yard that needed tending. He didn't mind, but the work meant he got filthy. A man couldn't cuddle with his girl when he smelt like sweat and rotten leaves. Jaden never crinkled her nose or pushed him away, but as far as he was concerned, the scent of garbage disposal waste was not sexy.

As he stuffed the socks and a black T-shirt into his duffle bag, his doorbell rang and echoed through the silent apartment. His heart leapt. Jaden? She didn't generally come to his apartment because Sparky insisted on riding along. He rushed to the front room and yanked open the door, expecting to see the love of his life. His good mood fell flat.

Sabrina.

She fluffed her hair, running her fingers through the thick, honey-coloured curls. "Hey you, you're never home anymore."

The deep V of her lavender blouse drew his attention to her ample cleavage. Holy shit. She'd mimicked Jaden's couture look, complete with rhinestones on her curve-hugging jeans and heels so high she'd likely topple over. Well, hell. He groaned. She obviously wanted to trap him. But now was not the time for her shenanigans. "I'm not your concern."

Crinkling her brow, she stepped towards him and gripped his shirt. "I didn't come over here to maul you. I've missed our friendship." She released his shirt and smoothed her hands down his sides to his hips. "You're one of the few people I trust."

"Uh-huh."

She cocked her head. "You look pretty lonely and there's no one in this whole huge apartment. I don't like seeing you so down." She peeked over his shoulder. "I do like the extra muscle. You're working out more." She squeezed his arm. "Your strength turns me on. Let me nibble every part of your body until we both collapse."

His cock shrivelled in his jeans. The scent of her perfume churned his stomach. She wasn't the woman he wanted to impress. He spoke through clenched teeth. "Sabrina, go away. I'm not interested." His phone interrupted him, frustrating him no end. "I need to answer this."

Faster than he could fumble the buttons to connect the call, Sabrina grabbed the phone. "No way, baby." Her eyes lit up. "Ooh! It's Jaden. You even have her name highlighted with a picture when she calls. How sweet." Giving him a shove, she flipped down the receiver. "You've reached the very involved Marlon Cross residence. This is his girlfriend Sabrina speaking. Let me direct your call." With that parting shot, she snapped the phone shut. "Oops. It dropped the call."

"What the fuck?"

"Oh, my. You'd better go get it before something happens to it." Turning, she gave the phone a hefty fling, sending it into the middle of the parking lot.

Marlon swiped his hand through the air in a vain attempt to grasp the phone. An oncoming car connected with the phone, shattering the device against the asphalt. Bracing himself, Marlon winced. "Shit." So much for modern technology.

Sabrina cackled. "See? You didn't need to talk to her anyway. She's a waste of your time. She causes things to break."

Marlon had hit his limit. "Sabrina, there is nothing between us. There used to be and it died when you fucked Tex Anderson and God knows who else." Fury coursed through his body. He'd pent up the feelings for almost a year. "I'm tired of your shit. You wanted just sex and then cried because I never took you home to meet my folks. I can't because they're both dead! But you won't believe me." He grabbed her shoulders and directed her out of his apartment. "I don't know what you want, but I'm sure it's not me."

When she turned, he shivered. Her eyes narrowed to angry slits. "Did she tell you about the drugs? The dealers? She won't because she's good at hiding things."

Without thinking, he gave a snappy retort. "I doubt it."

Her voice dropped to a dull roar. "Do you realise who she's seeing when you aren't there? Bobby Hutchins isn't just a sweet old friend of ours. He banged her on the set of Broken Wheels just like he had that affair with Addy. Jade's got a history with the asshole."

A peal of unease rang through his system. He'd finally worked out a life he liked with a woman he cared for, but the lethal combination of mistrust and reality showed up to screw it all to hell.

Well, fuck. Marlon stewed a moment and regained his bearings. "You had no problem strolling off with him the other night."

"It's called making an exit." She rested her hands on her hips. "So what are you going to do? I know Jaden. I was in her shoes for a while."

What? His hearing was off. Had to be. Damn. "Make an exit now." He'd have to hit the sparring bag to calm down.

"I will." She winked. "I'll watch you like a hawk. You've always been one of my favourite, if rather blunt, men." Sabrina sashayed off the stoop and crossed the parking lot.

Behind the wheel of his Jeep, Marlon forked both his hands into his hair. Where was his loudest heavy metal CD when he needed it? Son of a bitch. First the mention of drugs, then the mention of Bobby. With Jaden he'd be playing with fire. Was he up to the potential burn?

Chapter Fourteen

Jaden stared at her phone. What the hell? His girlfriend Sabrina? She snapped the phone closed and shook her head to clear out the ugly thoughts. She needed a moment to gather her wits. *I trust him. I don't know about her, but he's got the benefit of the doubt.*

Tantrum and Unruly sat on the bed staring at her. When Unruly swished her tail and bopped Tantrum, he pounced on her. The ball of grey tabby fur rolled on the comforter until Tantrum gave up and stopped to clean his paws. Sparky, though not totally sure of the cats, lolled on the floor. Riley sat next to his new canine pal, nosing Sparky's ear. Jaden puffed a long breath. Why did life have to throw curve balls? She hadn't planned on falling head-over-heels for Marlon. Maybe a weekend fling or friends with benefits, but not love.

A soft knock at the door created a clamour in the room. Riley and Sparky barked while the cats surged under the bed to hide. Judi peeked around the door. "Goodness.

Now I see why my friend Rosemary never wanted a security system. These guys are loud enough to wake folks down in China." She leant against the doorframe. "You look lovely. Marlon must be stopping by. Well, good. I need him to check the belts on my Buick. It's squeaking and I don't want to get stranded at church with a bum car."

Jaden shrugged and smoothed out the wrinkles in her cotton prairie skirt. "I can't get him—it keeps going to voicemail." Because a certain busybody ex-actress butted in. "I don't know what's going on, so I'll give him an hour. If I don't hear from him, I'll call Logan or Ray. They can fix the car, too." Not Corbin, though. Grief, she wasn't totally sure where she stood with him after that date. And not Bobby. He might be great extra set of eyes, but anything more wasn't going to happen.

"Well, all right." Judi nodded. "I want to have it fixed before the snow comes because I have the feeling this winter will be rough."

"You okay? You look a little pale."

"I haven't put on my foundation today. I didn't feel like getting gussied up. Just one of those days." Her shoulder moving a fraction of an inch, Judi shrugged. "Speaking of fun things, Halloween's the day after tomorrow. Have you given any thought to your costume? I love to dress up in my witch costume and pass out candy during trick or treat."

Despite the amount of money she'd dropped to buy the cats' supplies, Jaden had made a special trip to the mall for a suitable get-up. The silky crimson gown, paired with sheer black stockings and sky-high heels, would be perfect for her plan to portray a she-devil. She grinned. "I have a great idea for the party tomorrow night and a tamer version for trick or treat tomorrow afternoon. I found a sweet little set of devil's horns for Riley and a child's track jacket for Sparks. He'll look like a professional runner!"

Judi clapped her hands and shrieked, the rosy colour returning to her cheeks. "I love it! Sparks, you've never dressed up before. I can't wait!"

"You do realise I've never actually passed out candy? Daddy usually made the help do it..." She giggled and scratched Riley's ears. "But since I'm the help, I guess it fits."

"You're the best help."

The doorbell rang, echoing up the stairway. Judi pointed to her head and then to the door. "My ESP says a handsome deputy stands outside my door. I'll go let him in."

Once Judi had disappeared down the steps, Jaden slid off the bed and knelt on the floor. When she moved the comforter, two sets of green eyes peered at her. "Come on out, kids. It's safe. If it's Marlon, he's a good guy. He's got some issues, but I still like him—a lot. I'm not sure how to tell him because I've never been in this deep." She stroked Tantrum's head.

"I'm scared that when I tell him I'm in love, he'll leave. Everyone else I've loved finds a reason to run away. Sure, Cass and Logan still care, but..." She sighed. "It's not the same. I think they have to love me because they feel sorry for me. Not Marlon. He's the first guy who seems to like me for me and I'm falling head-over-heels for him."

Marlon stood just outside her bedroom, transfixed. There sat the woman who made his heart beat, talking to a room full of animals—quite the motley crew—and telling them the contents of her heart.

She loved him!

He considered throwing the door wide open to proclaim his love. No, the over-the-top approach wouldn't work, especially not when he had so many questions. He wanted a relationship built on mutual devotion and trust. But damn, she looked hot as hell in a skirt and fitted tunic. If he lifted the hem of the skirt… His mouth watered and his cock sprang to life.

Sparky, no longer interested in what Jaden had to say, barked. She jerked around. "Hi." Her gaze darted to her shaky hands. Her face paled as her voice wavered. "Um…how long have you been out there?"

He eased the door open and strode into the room. "Long enough to know a few secrets, but nothing I'll press you for right now."

Jaden turned away from him and ran her fingers through her hair. She snorted. Her voice came out curt. "Don't quit your day job so you can write greeting cards. That was pretty corny."

He nodded. "It did sound mushy, but I also eavesdropped on a private conversation. Not cool." A grin tugged the very corner of her mouth. He placed his hands on her shoulders. "Why don't we go watch that marathon of scary Halloween movies? I want to hear all about your costume since you refuse to model it for me, but first, why don't you introduce me to our kids?"

Jaden turned around and tipped her head. "Our?"

"If I've said it once, I'll say it a million times—you're not in this alone, babe."

One of the cats slipped out from under the bed and sat like a statue next to Jaden. She smothered her smile behind her hand before regaining her poise. "Despite his calm attitude, this is Tantrum. When I got him out of the cage, he wriggled and squirmed. Once we let him loose here in the house, he ran around like a kid on a sugar high. Judi wanted to name him Havoc, but I liked Tantrum better, so we compromised. Havoc is his middle name. He pouts when he thinks he isn't going to be fed." She raised the comforter. The other cat, more black around the eyes, peered at him. "This is Unruly. She's not fond of the crate I used to bring her home. She cried and protested the entire way home. She hasn't gone ballistic, but she's still wound up—on the bed, off the bed, in the window, kneading her claws on the bedspread. She ran laps around this room for a solid five minutes. You already met Riley. Kids, this is Marlon."

Marlon knelt next to Jaden. Every day and in every way she amazed him. "So you went to get Riley and you came home with them, too?" Without thinking, he rubbed his hand over her spine. The scent of her shampoo floated around him, reminding him of making love to her in his shower. His erection pressed against his pants. He tugged her into his lap and kissed her shoulder.

"They looked so sad in the cages." Her bottom lip jutted out in a pout. "But I also found out that their previous owner went into a nursing home. Summer didn't want to split them, so I took them. Judi loves it. She wants a whole house full, but I hear we can only have four animals."

Bobbing his head, he nodded. "Yes and no. Yes only four, but it's really a four-dog limit. She's got a big enough back yard that there should be enough room for them to run, but I wouldn't suggest adopting everyone from the shelter either."

"I won't, but I felt so sorry for them. It was like each animal begged with its eyes, saying "Please remember me—come back and take me home". And let me tell you, I wanted to. It took a lot of guts to walk out of there without crying my eyes out."

His heart melted. "I have no doubt it did." She cared so much for others, yet didn't see it. He liked the way she became the real woman within—the woman he loved. Still, he wanted to beat the shit out of the person who had stripped her pride to nothing.

Her laughter broke his thoughts. "What are you staring at?"

Marlon grasped her tighter. "You." He glanced out of the window for a split second. A flash near the street caught his attention. He stood and edged to the window. "So, you met Summer. What did you think? Or should I be afraid?" Scoping the street, he saw nothing, but filed the information back for later. Was the jerk from the main drag back on her tail? He hoped not, for her sake. He shifted his interest back to her.

"Well...um, yeah." Jaden stood, patted the cats, and whistled for the dogs. "Come on, boys. Let's go downstairs. Marlon and I have to talk."

Why did her words make his skin crawl more than the issue in the street? Because he'd committed his heart into her hands—without words, yes, but she flowed through his veins. If things hit the fan with Jaden, she'd push him far, far away. Living without her would suck.

Letting the dogs through the doorway first, Marlon followed Jaden down the stairs. "You didn't answer my question. What did you want to talk about?" Besides the fiasco with his cell phone...

"You'll see."

When they reached the bottom of the staircase, she stopped. First sneaking a peek into the living room, Jaden yanked him into her arms and planted a wet kiss on his lips. Not content to keep the kiss platonic, he tickled the satiny flesh with his tongue. On a sigh, she opened for him. She tasted of mint toothpaste and sensual woman. His hips seemed to move of their own accord, pressing in to her to relieve the ache in his groin. Judi could walk in at any time, but he didn't care. The thrill of potentially being caught spurred him on.

After what seemed like forever but was only a few moments, Jaden eased away from him. "You're addicting. I wanted to do that all day." Her breath came in short puffs. Crimson streaked across her cheeks. Her green eyes darkened to dark pools with thin hazel rims. At that moment, she looked primed, ready, and gorgeous.

With one arm around her waist, he threaded the fingers of his other hand through her hair. He pressed his forehead to hers. Her scent, a mix of flowers and vanilla, twirled around him. His brain went fuzzy on the Jaden contact high. "Good. I'd hate to suffer alone."

Behind them, the sound of claws on upholstery filled the room as Sparky and Riley jumped onto the couch. Jaden giggled. "As per normal, the most important members of the family have chosen their seats. Do you mind sitting on the floor? I vacuumed this morning."

He glanced at her feet then into her eyes. "In heels and diamond earrings?"

She shrugged. "The great diva, Carley Moreno, taught me well. She said, 'a girl has to look good at all times'. She wasn't kidding. What if you came over and I looked like a frump? You'd turn tail and run to the hills."

"You don't need to follow the mandates of some has-been actress. You're always beautiful to me, babe. In full makeup, in sweats, it doesn't matter. I look at you and turned-on doesn't begin to describe how I feel."

"I think you're hot, too, even when you get all bad-ass cop on me."

"Smart ass."

Stepping from his embrace, Jaden bent to retrieve the remote for the television. Her ass could stop traffic. No wonder she'd posed in that nudie magazine. She could model for him any day. Swimsuits, lingerie, hell, even turtleneck sweaters—he didn't care as long as she gave him attention between wardrobe changes.

When she turned, she flashed him a disarming smile. "Speaking of looking hot, will you go with me to the Hallowe'en mixer tomorrow? Cass said it's a great time and since the band's playing, I thought maybe we could have real date."

"You beat me to the punch." When she looked away, he cupped her chin. Something else brewed on her mind. "What are you thinking about?"

"Something from earlier, not that I can hide much from you." She let out a long sigh. "You wanted to know about Summer. I'll say this. Summer Tyler is quite the talker."

Biting back the groan, he sat down on the edge of the couch. "She is. And?"

"This probably isn't the time, but were you going to tell me you have a wife?"

He winced. "Had." Minor technicality that had the potential to cause major damage. He sucked in a ragged breath. Trust Summer to blab things he wasn't ready to deal with, even four years later. "There's a big difference."

Sitting on the coffee table opposite him, Jaden tangled her fingers together. "Summer said you two dated, but she couldn't wipe out your wife's memory. Sounds like she was one in a million—your wife, not Summer. I'll stop talking now."

"It's fine." Marlon sighed. How to answer without sounding like a shit? He rubbed his chin with the pads of his fingers, as if the nervous gesture would help him find the answers. "Some women make good friends. Others make good lovers. Summer is a friend. You are my lover and my girlfriend."

Her voice remained low. "Oh, well, that's good to know. What about Sabrina? I trust you. If you say there's nothing there, then there's nothing there. But, man, she's persistent."

"I admit it. She's clingy." He tilted her head to catch her gaze. "Jaden Marie, look at me. I need to see those beautiful eyes of yours."

"You stink when you try to rhyme. Go back to cop mode." Slowly, she shifted her focus. "Really, the greeting card industry is not the place for such a smooth-talking man."

"Back to cop mode? Try to rhyme?" He feigned surprise by clutching his chest. "I don't try to do anything. I succeed."

"You do." Those two words turned his guts inside out.

"Baby girl, I have a past just like you. It's not as colourful, but it's mine. I won't make excuses." He rubbed his thumb over her bottom lip. "I'm a man who wanted physical affection and I found a couple of women who fit the bill on a temporary basis. But when it comes to you, it's different."

"Really?"

Pulling her onto his lap, he wrapped her in his arms. His cock pressed against her crotch, causing delicious pressure. "Do you feel that? I think about you and have to work like hell to hide the stiffy. Making love to you blows my mind. Yes, I was married once and one day I'll explain, but not right now. Addy's a wound I don't know how to heal or deal with, but being with you helps. I thought I loved her, so I married her. I was wrong."

"How do you feel about me?"

Her question, simple but powerful, rocked him to his core. He ached to be inside her again, to make love to her again. Why not tell her the truth? He wiped a tear from her cheek with the pad of his index finger. "This is so unlike anything I've ever felt and it took me too long to understand it. There's some things I need to get sorted out, but I don't want to be without you."

"I love you, Marlon." Although she continued to cry, she laughed. "Screwy, huh? Here you're being all covert and confused, and I was afraid to tell you I love you."

Fusing their lips, he sipped from her. The ache in his groin increased, only to find relief in her. Her small hands clutched his shoulders. A whimper ripped from her throat. He pushed the kiss further, caressing her breast. She wriggled and pressed her chest into his hand. Her nipple pebbled. Determined to turn her on as much as she affected him, he pinched the hot flesh. She gasped and held on tighter. "Yes, Marlon."

"God, I want to fuck you right here."

Jaden gyrated her hips and licked his bottom lip. "Why else do you think I wore a skirt?" She fumbled with her skirt and produced a condom.

"Smart woman." Marlon whisked his hands under the skirt and palmed her thighs. The higher he touched, the silkier her skin became. He clawed at her panties and shifted them to the side. Her cream coated his hand. "Hell, yes."

Jaden worked the zipper on his jeans and withdrew his penis. Using measured strokes, she worked the condom onto him.

His breath stuttered. "Fuck, I won't last."

"Then don't." Jaden eased down on his latex-encased dick and her head lolled on her shoulders. She clutched the sleeves of his shirt in white-knuckled hands. Whimpers floated on the air.

His thrusts became frantic and sweat beaded at his temples. Damn, he'd love to be lost forever in the tight heat of her pussy. Grabbing her hips, he slammed into her body and muffled his cries against her neck.

"Come for me, baby," she murmured.

He shuddered and released his seed. Her words rocked straight to his core and resonated in his balls. He gasped to catch his breath. "Yeah."

She whimpered once more and collapsed against his chest. "Yeah's right."

As if they thought she was being hurt, Sparky and Riley began to bark. Soon, two wet noses butted in to the kiss. Jaden jerked back and wiped her mouth with the back of her hand. "Sparks! Riley! Really! I know where those noses have been on more than one occasion."

Marlon laughed, really laughed. Yeah, so the dogs interrupted things. Oh well. She loved him and he loved her. Things were good. "See? When I want to be smooth, I do just fine. I even got the dogs' attention." He slapped her bottom. "Scoot. I want to chuck this before Judi comes into the room."

Jaden wriggled off his lap and handed him a tissue. "It's fine. She's lying down. We scrubbed the kitchen this morning and it wore her out."

After tossing the tissue into the waste bin, Marlon strode back into the living room. His Jeep sat alone in front of the house. Still, the earlier odd flash in the street unnerved him. "Have you noticed anything out of order? Any people following you for too long or people on the sidewalk staring? I need to know. Has that jerk bothered you again?"

Her brows knotted. "No, I haven't seen him since. Why? Things have been pretty boring and peaceful, save for arguing with Leonard and avoiding Steven's grumpy attitude when he checks on Judi." She caressed the top of his hand with her index finger. "No phone calls or anything from the weirdoes this week. I'm not complaining, but you're scaring me."

"Phone calls?"

"Yes, someone prank called the house a few days ago, but it stopped. Why? Did you see something?"

"Nothing important." He shook his head. "No, there is something. Are you seeing anyone else?"

Smoothing the wrinkles in his shirt, she nibbled the corner of her mouth. "No one but you."

Marlon rubbed his thumb over her chin. Bits and pieces of his conversation with Sabrina came to mind. Was Sabrina trying to sabotage the relationship or had she told the truth? His response to Jaden felt too right, too bone deep to be wrong. Changing the subject, he smoothed his hand to the back of her head and cupped her skull. "I need some Jaden love time."

Scooting closer to him, Jaden smiled. "Then kiss me, sexy man!"

How could he say no to a direct order? Marlon nipped her lips as he succumbed to her charms. She sucked his tongue into her mouth and the suction sent sparks and flames to his erection. Holy hell, he'd never last if she kept teasing him so.

"Jaden!"

Judi's scream from the other room made him pause. When she stumbled into the living room, both he and Jaden broke apart and jumped up. They spoke in unison, "What's wrong, Judi?"

"It's my heart." The older woman gasped for air. She leant against the doorframe. "My chest hurts. It's tight. My left arm aches and the room is spinning."

He turned to Jaden, his adrenaline surging through his veins. "Call 911 and tell them Judi's having a heart attack." Focussing his attention on Judi, he checked her fluttering pulse. "Do you have any aspirin?"

Jaden raced into the room with a purse. "In here. She keeps a bottle just in case. The ambulance is on its way." Her voice rose a couple of octaves. Panic infused her words. "Oh God, Marlon. Save her."

Moments later, when the red and white lights flashed through the windows, Marlon allowed himself to breathe steadily. Thank God the fire department and ambulance service were only a couple of blocks away. Adam Stafford and Greg Brewer were some of the best EMTs he knew. They'd take care of Judi until she arrived at the hospital.

He held Judi's hand. "Sweetheart, can you hear me? Two of my friends are going to take you to the hospital. Jaden and I will be right behind. I'll have her call Steven, okay?"

As Adam whisked Judi into the ambulance, she nodded. Her eyes closed and the monitor beeped more loudly.

Marlon reached for Jaden, who stood clutching Bobby Hutching. What the fuck? Both Sparky and Riley howled. His heart dropped to his toes. Sure, he'd seen accident victims, shooting victims, and people with health issues, but never anyone he was so close to—other than his parents. Other than Addy. The thought of losing Judi bothered him almost as much as losing his folks. Losing Jaden.

"Bob—"

"Don't get your pants in a wad. I was at the station with Adam." Bobby stroked Jaden's arm and nudged her towards Marlon. "I'm just here to help."

Jaden's voice broke through Marlon's anger-induced fog. "Put Riley in his crate and we can go. He tends to chew on the dining room table legs if no one's watching, and since I don't want Judi to be alone, he'd better be confined."

"You got it, honey."

Marlon kissed her temple and held her close—a sign to Bobby she belonged to him. The thought of sharing Jaden with anyone didn't sit well with Marlon. She trembled, blotting out his frustration. "I'm scared. She's the closest thing to a mom I've had in a long time. I don't want to lose her. Hold me."

He stroked her hair and kissed her head. "I'm holding you, Jaden Marie."

Her voice cracked and her words rushed together. "I can't feel it."

"I promise, baby. I won't let you down."

Sparky continued to howl from his spot on the rug while Riley jumped all over the couch. Jaden wiped her face with the back of her hand. Her voice dropped to a low octave, the raw sound twisting his insides. "We'd better go before she thinks we forgot about her."

Marlon scooped Riley into his arm and strode to the crate to place the dog inside. Turning circles on the navy and black blanket, Riley barked and whimpered.

"We'll be back, big guy." Marlon checked the lock on the back door. When he entered the living room, Jaden fumbled with her purse. The contents spilled onto the floor. Her hands shook as she tried to put the loose bills and makeup into the leather bag.

"Slow down, baby. We'll get through this." Marlon knelt next to her and held the scratched metal tin. He toyed with the catch, opening the container. White tablets. No lettering, but blue flecks.

"Mints. You know, the cool breeze that knocks out the worst breath?"

He looked up and caught her gaze.

"I liked the tin, but you can check. Just mints."

He handed her a pink tube of lipstick, the tin, and her license. The picture was of the blonde Jade. He chuckled. She'd changed so much in the month since she'd arrived. Compassion and concern enhanced her beauty. Her smile, once plastic, now shimmered when she laughed. Once things calmed down, he'd confront her properly concerning Bobby and her past habits. Then he'd get down to loving her.

Chapter Fifteen

Two hours after Judi had been rushed to the ER, Marlon paced the waiting area in the hospital's critical care unit. Crawford General wasn't the largest hospital in the area. The building had stood in the centre of town for over fifty years, serving the residents of Crawford. The pale blue paint on the walls, though clean, needed an update. The vending machines lining the far wall had seen better days.

But none of that mattered.

Crawford General had the best staff. Few hospitals could boast such an attentive group of doctors and nurses. He wasn't fond of the place, only because a hospital visit meant questioning a banged-up victim or, worse, talking to a woman who had lived through spousal abuse. Like the animals at the shelter, the abuse victims reminded him that some people were blameless while others were plain evil. The women always had the same pleading look in their eyes. Help me.

He glanced at the doors to the main hallway. A nurse pushed a man in a wheelchair past, but there was no sight of a doctor. Marlon turned his attention back to Jaden, who sat in a ball on one of the couches. Her eyes, puffy from crying, had lost their sparkle. Bobby sat across from her with his hand on her knee. There to help... Marlon wanted to believe him, but come on. He was too damn close and the coincidence was too easy.

In three long strides, Marlon reached her couch and sat down. "I'll get you through this. Judi still has things to do. She's not ready to go home to her husband."

Clutching a tissue, Jaden sniffled and curled in to him. "I believe you, but I can't stop thinking. What if she passes? Riley lost his home when Pearl died. I came into Sparky's life by accident. They're the lucky ones. Who will help the other older people who want to keep their pets? I can't adopt them all."

He sighed. "Honey, you're right. You can't take them all in, but you can pray that Judi gets better."

Bobby stood and cleared his throat. "I'm going to check on Judi. Be back in a bit."

Marlon allowed himself to relax a little once the other man had departed. "Things will get better."

"And what about me? I have a little money, a huge credit card bill, and four animals who depend on me. I took care of her, but if something happens, I have nowhere to stay! God, I'm irresponsible!"

Tucking her safe within him arms, he kissed her temple. "Don't say that. There's more to you than a glossy magazine page. Besides keeping the animals happy, you keep Judi from betting too much when she goes out to play bridge and bingo. And I trust you with my life."

"You do?"

"I do." The vision of Jaden in white murmuring those exact words flicked into his mind. His bride. Jaden Cross. Even her name linked with his sounded perfect. Once things with Judi settled, he'd propose to Jaden. Life was too short to waste it with uncertainties and gossip.

"Thanks for the kind words, I needed it." She sat up and wiped more tears from her cheeks. "Bobby might be around, but Daddy doesn't care what happens to me. Momma's been in heaven since I was little. All I have left of her is their wedding band." Her voice caught and exhaled slowly. "Maybe that's why I came back here to Ohio. Between you and Judy and the kids, I feel like I've got a snuggly warm blanket shielding me from the shit I lived through in California. You know what I mean?"

"I know exactly. Mom and Dad weren't too fond of the choices I made, but they never gave up on me. I'll be damned if I let anyone hurt you." Even Bobby.

"I must sound like I'm helpless." She twisted the ring around her middle finger. "Will you tell me about Addy someday? I don't want any secrets between us."

He froze. His past wasn't up for discussion. How to detour the conversation? "You don't want my ancient history. There's so much I don't know about you."

She nodded. "I know some of it from Summer. I'd rather know the truth from you when you're ready. Lies and assumptions just get people into trouble."

She glossed over her own past, but wanted to know about his wife. Well, hell. He fidgeted in his seat, staring at his work-roughened hands. Scars from a recent scuffle marred his knuckles. "It's nothing exciting." He sighed. When Jaden squeezed his fingers, he found the strength to tell his story.

"I'm thirty-three years old and not real suave around women. My idea of a hot date was going to the Wing Hut and sharing a soda over a bucket of hot wings."

She cocked her head. "Nothing wrong with that."

"Not in this town. The bar scene is the place to be, except it's not my thing. But you asked about Addy." He wrinkled his nose and sighed. "When I was fresh out of the academy, I met Addison Davids. Until that point all I wanted to do was be a cop, but she blew my mind. All long legs and blonde hair. I wanted to run away with her." He paused and toyed with the thick band on his watch. "But being with Addy wasn't exactly easy. She liked men—all men—without commitments. I wanted her for myself, and it took convincing. That right there should've told me she wasn't wife material, but I was young and dumb and horny. Even my parents hated her."

Jaden giggled, breaking the heavy mood. "Everyone has to be young and foolish at least once in their lives. Don't kick your ass because things weren't parent-approved. Look at my life. I'm not an after-school special."

He nodded. "You're right. Now I know why I care about you so much." He kissed her temple. Being with her made telling his past so much easier. "Looking back, I thought I loved her. I fell hard for her and told my parents where to get off. But now I realise I loved the idea of being with someone. She laughed, drank, and made no excuses. I proposed after three dates and she said yes. I thought I knew what I was doing."

She smoothed her hand over his cheek. "You didn't?"

"Not a clue." He rubbed his forehead. "I bought her a house, a new car, and offered to help her care for her daughter. At first, it was the best. She helped me deal with Mom and Dad passing within a couple weeks of each other and cheered when I was hired on here at the department. Sydney's father was in the picture and cool about the situation. Syd, Addy, and I were a team. But then nine months into the marriage, Addy changed. She said it was a sickness, but I found out later that she wasn't telling me the whole truth."

He sighed. His heart felt lighter, but the devastation of his relationship with Addy tore at old scars. "She had a boyfriend on the side as well as a pretty serious addiction to sleeping pills and alcohol."

"When you found out, you stopping trusting, didn't you?"

"It wasn't when—it was how." Once again, he nodded. "I wanted things to work with her so bad. I figured that if I loved her enough, then she'd change. I took care of her daughter, Syd. It took me five years, two totalled cars, and my being busted for drug possession to realise I wasn't man enough for her to overcome her addictions."

"You?" Her brow furrowed. "No."

"Normally I took the cruiser to work because it was easier. No big deal. But earlier in the week I'd been in a fender bender as part of a high speed chase, so I had Addy take me to work. In Crawford, she floored it through the square. She was stopped and the officer recognised the both of us. Because she complained she needed to get 'something' from the glove box, he searched the vehicle. He found two dime baggies of cocaine and a needle. I was livid." He clenched his fist. The past still pissed him off.

"I know how that feels. I was busted for drug paraphernalia when I was sixteen. It sucks."

"Sucks? They weren't mine, but dammit, Mac didn't believe me right away."

Jaden inched away from him. Her eyes widened.

"It took me six weeks of work and the complete destruction of my life to clear my name. I got my job back by a thread. I'm not going through that again. Addy thought the whole thing was a joke until I served her with divorce papers."

Although her voice dropped to a whisper, Jaden's question was clear. "What happened?"

"She took the papers and threw them on the lawn before she set the house ablaze. When she drove off, she headed for the Halden Reservoir. Bobby Hutchins found her body three days later. She'd mainlined too many drugs and passed out behind the wheel. She made it far enough into the water that the cabin filled. Even if she'd regained consciousness, she would have had little chance of surviving."

Jaden pressed her head against his shoulder. "I'm sorry. I shouldn't have made you tell the story. I shouldn't have been so flippant."

He cleared his throat. Damn, the past sounded bad. "What did Summer tell you? The stories went around town like the plague. In one, I made her leave. In another version, I chased her. I once heard she stopped to see a boyfriend before she drove headlong into the water."

"She said I was a nice girl, but don't expect much from you. You like danger and put a lot on the line, but you're cautious. You aren't the settling-down type and you won't ever marry again. Without coming right out with it, she hinted I should find someone else." Twining her arms around his neck, she rubbed the back of his head. "No woman would ever match the love and respect you had for Addy, but she figured you were head-over-heels for me."

He turned her words over in his mind. Not marry again? Ever? Not quite. His perfect match was in his arms. And to let her get away? To find someone else? No sir, he didn't like that thought one bit. "She's wrong. A sweet woman I dated for a while, but she's terribly wrong about some of her conclusions. I trust her when it comes to animals, but not with my heart." He tipped her chin to gaze into her eyes. "Should I entrust my heart to you?"

Her lips parted a fraction of an inch. If he were home, he'd plunder her sweetness until they both screamed. At the hospital he needed to use decorum. People expected more out of cops, even when they were off-duty.

He brushed a thumb over her cheek, savouring her soft skin. All the things he'd seen in Addison blossomed in Jaden, but with Jaden, she didn't project an image—she was who she was. Addy had been on the edge of control. Jaden had lived through chaos and had risen above it.

Before he could explain more, a doctor came out into the waiting room. "Ms. Haydenweir?"

Jaden sat up and turned. "That's me!" She clamped a hand over her mouth once she realised she'd shouted. A couple of other people in the room turned and glared. She groaned. "Sorry."

Marlon rubbed her back. "It's okay. You didn't hurt anything. You just woke up a couple of other visitors. They'll deal."

The doctor, clad in buff-coloured scrubs, strode towards them. He yanked the cartoon character bandana off his head and ran his fingers through his hair. "You're Jaden Haydenweir? I'm Doctor Sam McDonald. I specialise in geriatric services." He cocked a brow. "You don't match the image in my head, which is odd because Judi can't stop telling me about you. I expected blue tights and an S on your chest or something."

She extended her hand. "I see. Nice to meet you, Doctor McDonald. This is my — this is Marlon Cross." Licking her lips, more in a nervous gesture than anything, Jaden stood. "I realise you can't share too many details because I'm not family, but when can we see her?"

Marlon shook hands with the doctor, stymied that Jaden had stumbled over her description of their relationship. After all his honesty and her declaration, was she not sure of her feelings? They'd sort a lot of issues out later, when things calmed down. Right now, he'd be her strength.

Jaden clutched Marlon's arm. Damn, she didn't do well under pressure. Thank God he offered her strength. She wanted to shout from the rooftops that she loved Marlon. Hell, she wanted to tattoo his damned name right above the lily tattoo at the base of her spine. Why had she fumbled? She had no idea, other than that his gaze had turned to ice when she'd refused to discuss her past. And now he looked like he could blow a gasket. Crap.

Dr McDonald tucked his bandana into his breast pocket. "Deputy Cross, I think I met you a couple of weeks ago when we had the four-car pile-up accident victims come through here. Next time, let's meet under happier circumstances." He stuck the chart under his arm and twined his fingers. "Long and short, Judi had a heart attack. She had two major blockages that I was able to open with stents. She'll recover, but I'm not sure she'll be able to go home. Her son can better make that decision. I tell you this because she insisted I should. Jaden, you take care of her, correct?"

She wrapped her fingers around Marlon's thick wrist. "I take care of her dog, but I live with her. We take care of each other, I guess."

The doctor grinned. "How sweet." His brow wrinkled. "You know, you look familiar. I'll bet you get that a lot. I just can't place it." He slid the chart from under his arm and shuffled the pages. "Her son is coming in, but I'll take you back. She's a little wrung out, so don't be surprised. She was asleep."

Jaden clung to Marlon and followed Dr McDonald down the hallway. She held back a step. "Marlon?"

His gaze, though hard, focussed on her. Whatever walls she'd breached with Marlon had filled in thicker than before.

"I'm sorry. This is really hard for me." She mentally pleaded for him to understand. But how? She wasn't even sure if she understood what was going on. One minute, she was cuddling with Marlon and Judi was fine, the next—

Hell.

He clenched his jaw. His face otherwise remained expressionless. "We'll talk about it later."

She wondered what was going through his mind. Her stomach churned. Was this how he looked during an interrogation? Marlon released her hand and shoved his fists into his pockets. Why did going into Judi's room scare her more than a gauntlet of paparazzi?

When she rounded the corner into Judi's room, she gasped. Her friend, once vibrant and full of life, lay limp and pale. Her heart clenched. If she could have traded places, she would've.

Judi smiled, faint, but there. "Sorry I caused such a ruckus. But you know how I like drama." She reached for Jaden's hand. "Doc says I probably won't make it home."

Jaden gasped. "Don't say those things." She choked back a cry. "You'll pull through."

Marlon smoothed his hand over her shoulder, giving her a bit of comfort. "You'll make it."

Though laboured, Judi smiled. "I'll pull through. Goodness. And I thought I liked a good dramatic scene! What I meant was that I won't be coming back to the house. They want me to go to a home where a nurse can keep an eye on me. They think I'm a flight risk or a something. I might try to walk a tight rope or two-step down at the Ricochet."

"But what about Sparks? Riley? They need you. I need you."

Judi patted Jaden's hand. "You have Marlon. I see a bright future for you two. Once you work out your issues, you'll be golden. And you have the dogs and the cats. I wasn't sure when I hired you that you'd take to Sparks. He smells, he's pushy, and he's noisy, but you did and you made me proud. Taking Riley in along with the cats warmed my heart."

Tears streamed down Jaden's cheeks. "But where will I live? It's not like I can keep the house or the animals."

Judi cocked her head. "Honey, you don't have to move until Steven sells the house, since he's assumed power of attorney. I'll fight him on it so you have a place to kip down. As for the critters, once he puts the house on the market, take them with you. If you can save them, then that's four animals that will have a better life."

Marlon touched Jaden's shoulder. The warmth in his grasp offered a little comfort. "If you'll give me a chance, I have an idea."

Jaden turned and wiped her cheeks. If she said anything, she'd bite his head off. He probably wanted her to send them to the shelter. Hell, no! She'd tell him to shove his ideas up his ass first. For the animals and Judi, she'd listen. Clamping her mouth shut, she glared at him.

He dropped his chin to his chest. "I have extra room and I like critters."

Jaden sniffled. Why the hell couldn't she keep it together? Even during that time of the month, she'd never been this hormonal. She took a deep breath. "I won't split them up. You can't make me."

Judi's voice, a bit stronger and harder, came from over her shoulder. "Jaden. Swallow your pride. You worked too hard to let this little setback knock you down."

She stared at the wrinkles on his T-shirt. "He doesn't trust me."

Marlon knelt next to her. "I'm offering you an out."

Judi clapped and tittered. "So does this mean I need to prepare for a wedding? I like the colour pink."

His eyes darkened, like when he was turned on. Jaden blinked back fresh tears.

Marlon laughed in his low voice. "I don't know that the boys will like the lack of a yard, but I insist you all live with me—at least for a little bit." He nodded to Judi. "You get better and I'll make sure you can wear whatever colour you like."

Jaden's heart fluttered within her chest. Had he just alluded to…? Did he mean…? She grasped the side rail on the bed to keep herself from dropping onto the floor.

A voice from the doorway interrupted their private moment. "Mom! Mom!"

Jaden refocussed her gaze on Steven. The stout man filled the doorway. His belly hung over his belt. A lock of thin, strawberry blond hair fluttered on the top of his head as he surged into the room. His brown eyes blazed. "You scared me. Was this because of the dog? I told you the doctors were wrong. Taking care of him overextends your strength and adds to your stress." He nodded to Jaden. "Why are you in my mother's room? Did the dog do this or was it the lunatic photographers that hang out outside the house because of you?"

Judi's giggles stopped. "Don't get your underwear bunched. Steven, you need to calm down before they give you the bed next door. There aren't any photographers outside my house. Jaden's taking Sparky home while I recuperate. Don't you dare give her static."

Steven grunted, making Jaden wonder yet again how Judi could have given birth to such a rude man. Maybe life had made him grumpy. She nibbled the inside of her cheek. Still, he ought to be thankful he had his mother around. Forcing a smile to her lips, she nodded to Marlon. "Why don't we leave them alone? It's late."

Steven nodded. "I'd appreciate that. She's not your mother."

Jaden winced. Nope, she wasn't. Judi couldn't even claim her as a granddaughter. She stood and gave Judi a hug. "I'll be back to see you tomorrow."

"You'd better. I'll miss my afternoon gossip shows and I want you to fill me in."

"Consider it done." Jaden forced a watery smile. "I'll even bring magazines." Maybe Judi wasn't her mother, but she was damned close. Heat, and not from Marlon, enveloped her. A rush of thoughts and emotions battled in her mind. She couldn't breathe. Gasping, she muttered a goodbye and escaped the room.

She burst through the stairwell door and stopped on the landing. The cold walls of the hospital reminded her of the last few moments with her mother. The pain settled low in her belly like a stone. She collapsed on the top step. Even though Marlon wanted her and the animals, he'd change his mind. Men always did. She had nothing other than the furry children—no money, no real home. And then there was Marlon…

God, her mind swam. He wanted her, but he didn't. She wanted him, but her fears of jumping into the great unknown prevented her from accepting his kindness. And if the circus of Hollywood made its way to Crawford…he'd leave her in a hot minute.

Stop being negative and move forwards.

She wasn't sure when he arrived, but Marlon's strong arms enfolded her once he sat down. His breath warmed her neck and his whiskers tickled her ear. She laced her fingers with his. A smattering of words teetered on her tongue, yet she remained quiet.

Marlon broke the silence. "Hey, Jaden Marie, you aren't in this alone."

Her chest heaved. "I don't want your pity."

Chapter Sixteen

Marlon nuzzled her cheek. So many things were so fucked up. So many questions unanswered. Why couldn't he either 'fess up to his feelings or walk away?

Jaden made his heart light, even when she asked too many questions and nibbled her bottom lip raw. He wanted to kiss every inch of her until she shrieked his name. Even Addy had never given him a rush like being with Jaden. And they'd had — what? A little more than a few weeks together? Each night of passion was ingrained into his permanent memory. Could he let her go? The idea scared him. Did he need her enough to make things permanent? Damn straight. She moved him like the air he breathed.

Her scent washed over him. She understood him and soothed him when he needed her arms to hold him. He wasn't himself without her to make him whole. "Who said anything about pity? Honey, I'm here for you. Life went berserk in the last twenty-four hours. Anyone would crumble. It's expected."

She sniffled, but didn't pull away. "You haven't fallen apart."

"I'm not perfect. I fuck stuff up all the time." He kissed her neck where it connected to her shoulder, drawing from her the feathery sigh he loved so much. He shifted his hips to relieve the ache in his heart. She brought out the best and the worst in him. "Summer doesn't lie. I'm not a relationship-slash-commitment kind of guy, but I am certainly cautious. I'd like to continue seeing you, but I can't when you won't tell me everything."

Turning, she cupped his cheek and rested her forehead against his. Her silky hair smoothed against his skin. "I come with a lot of baggage—and not just the furry kind."

"From the first moment I questioned you at the station, I wanted you. I'm game for whatever you can throw at me, Jaden Marie—as long as you're honest."

She sighed. "We need to get back to Judi's. The dogs will need to pee, I'm worn out, and tomorrow's Halloween. So much for passing out candy."

"Then let's go home." He nodded. *I don't have to work until seven tomorrow.* "I'll keep you and the critters company."

"Company? I'd love the company. Especially if we're—" Her eyes sparkled. "—naked."

He cocked a brow. *Oh, so she wanted to play dirty? He'd take that wager.* "Are you issuing me a challenge?" *One he could fulfil all night long? Hell, yes.*

Her shoulder barely moved in a shrug. "Maybe." She smacked her lips and grinned. "I mean, there is a trick to sex with an audience. Look how Sparks freaks when we kiss. Are you up for their challenge? I'm easy to sway since I liked you from the start."

Dipping in for a kiss, he cupped the back of her head. "If you're my prize, then I'm in for one hell of a time."

Jaden fell back against the sheets as Marlon prepared for bed. He tugged his jeans past his sculpted hips, baring snug boxers, sinewy muscle and the perfect sprinkling of hairs on his legs. The man's body was made for posing nude—not a flaw in sight.

Her mouth watered. For the time being, he belonged to her. She plucked at the edge of the towel she'd tossed on the foot of the bed. At her feet, Sparky and Riley shifted. Sparky grunted and began to snore, while Riley settled on his back. Playing house with Marlon seemed less like play and more like reality.

Although she'd never considered her bedroom in the Pennywood house large, Marlon's presence made it cosy. The pull and twist of his muscles as he eased the T-shirt over his head grabbed her attention. His hair stuck out at odd angles when he turned. If ever a man embodied sex, it was him. A shiver ran up her spine. And now he stood in her home, wanting to be with her.

A sheepish grin curled his lips. "What's running through that beautiful head of yours?"

She toyed with the hem of her shirt and sat up. He wanted to know, huh? Lifting the garment over her head, she shook her hair about her shoulders.

"Come here, gorgeous." His eyes lit up and he opened his arms. "Let me hold you."

She nibbled her bottom lip. His gaze on her body made heat rush through her veins. With Marlon, the act of foreplay held more weight, more emotion. She wanted to impress him, not to have him want her for her body, but for him to need the whole package. God knew, she'd fallen for him.

Edging over to him, she unhooked the front clasp on her bra. "Good?"

She drew in a ragged breath and dropped the lingerie onto the floor. Marlon groaned. "Oh, yes. Oh…yes." His hands roamed over her flesh, searing her on contact. Her heart pounded behind her ribcage. If they could stay in this moment forever, she'd be a happy woman.

"I'm thinking I've had a long night filled with the best highs, worst lows, and a few in-betweens." Hooking her fingers into his belt loops, she yanked him towards her. "Right now, I want to taste the man who makes me feel things I never imagined."

"Come here, little girl." He forked his fingers into her hair, massaging her scalp. Closing her eyes, Jaden brushed her nipples along his chest. He had her right on the edge, might as well share the tenuous hold on control.

Starting with his neck, she nibbled a path to his Adam's apple and down to his chest. When she laved her tongue over his flat nipples, he moaned and fisted his hands in her hair. The tiny buds tightened under her care.

"Oh, sweet baby."

Spurred on by his encouragement, she slid to her knees. His breath came in short puffs as he eased and tightened his grip. Jaden glanced at his closed eyes and the smile tugging the corners of his mouth. He liked it. His cock, long and thick, poked out from the gap in his boxers.

Jaden licked her lips and slid her hands under the waistband of his underwear. A primal growl ripped from his throat. "Oh, baby, yes."

His ass muscles tightened under her palms as she pushed his jeans and boxers to his feet. A bead of moisture glistened on the tip of his erection. Oral sex hadn't been her strong point, but for him, she'd make it her best effort. With one soft swipe of her tongue, she licked him clean and savoured his offering.

"Jaden." He drew her name out on a sigh and rocked his hips towards her. She obligingly took him into her mouth until his hairs tickled her nose.

"Fuck, baby girl." His hips moved in time with her ministrations. She took him as far as she could without gagging, loving the feel of his silky steel on her tongue. Oh sure, she'd given men oral satisfaction before, but none had treated her with such dignity and devotion. Each time he thrust into her mouth, she hummed her approval.

Grasping his ass, she took him to the back of her throat and hummed. He panted. "Jaden Marie, you'll make me come. God, I'm so close."

So he liked it? Hell yeah. She wrapped her hand around the base of his dick and cupped his sac, kneading his balls. His hips moved faster. He groaned. "Oh, fuck!"

When he jerked hard and held her in place, she lapped up every drop of his cum. Being with him felt like the right thing—the only right thing—in her life. Heat flowed through her veins, combined with new emotions. Love, yes, but she wanted a little bit more. She wanted him forever, not one night, not a month—the whole happily-ever-after package.

Leaning back, his erection slipped from her lips. She swiped her tongue over his taste, spice and salt. Marlon sank to his knees. His breath fanned over her skin when he leant forwards and rested his head on her shoulder. She crooked her brow. "I assume it was good?"

Gasping for breath, he responded. "Fucking...fantastic."

"Then next time, I get to play with your ass." Jaden wrapped her legs around him and stroked his hair. The feeling of the grown man in her lap, needing her comfort, made her smile and warmed her heart. The fact that she hadn't climaxed wasn't a priority. He needed her—not her money, not her fame—her.

"You can do whatever you want, little girl." His throaty voice vibrated down her spine.

Over his shoulder, she noticed the time on the clock. Five-oh-four AM. Her eyelids drooped with sleep. Still too early for the sunrise, but little time to rest before the animals needed to go out. She glanced at the dogs, both asleep on the floor by the door. The cats, cuddled together on the window seat, ignored her presence. Over their collective bundle of fur, she noticed a red light. She frowned. What the…?

I live on the second floor. It can't be a light next door. The nearest house is thirty feet away.

Straining around Marlon's sluggish frame, she tried to get a better look at the little red light that reminded her of…a paparazzi video camera! What the fuck?

"Marlon!"

He lifted his head, his eyes fuzzy. "What's wrong, Jaden Marie?"

Clipping her words in case someone was lingering outside her room, she spoke and yanked her shirt from the bed. "Outside. Someone's outside."

"What?"

"There's a light just like on a camcorder right outside my window. It's not coming from the Reardon's and the oak tree isn't close enough to put the camera in the fucking window. I need to call Bobby."

Slowly, he turned. But as he did, the red light died. Jaden gasped and fumbled for her phone.

"Shh." Using a hand signal, Marlon pointed to the light switch. Inching away from him, Jaden clicked the switch, bathing them in darkness. As her eyes adjusted to the low light, she noticed Marlon's form moving towards the window. Through the dim glow of the street lamp, she saw the outline of his face. He clenched his jaw.

She fought back the urge to shout, "Call for the police." Hell, he was the police. Still, she didn't want him to leave her alone in the house while he searched for the origin of the red light. That's why she'd hired Bobby—to keep the lunatics at bay.

Anger boiled in her veins alongside the fear. If her father had sent someone to spy on her, forgiveness wouldn't be an option. He might be more interested in money than in his own flesh and blood, and spying was totally within his range of actions—but spying on her? He wouldn't. And where the hell was Bobby?

Marlon's voice, a whisper, cut through the silence and her thoughts. "I don't see anything, but I'm going to call the CPD to check it out." Though she couldn't see him, she felt his arms around her after he crossed the room. "Has anyone tried to bother you? Think. Would the paparazzi seek you out, here in Crawford?"

She shook her head. "No, no one that I know of. But I've been wrong before."

"Does anyone want to hurt you? What's Bobby's role?"

"I've kept to myself since coming here." Glancing down at his naked torso, she couldn't help the nervous laughter. "Um, before you make that call, you do realise your pants are missing in action?"

After a long sigh, Marlon chuckled. "At least you aren't scared."

She rubbed her nose along his jaw. The prickles gave her a small measure of comfort—because they belonged to him. "I'm petrified, and you're the one person keeping me level."

"Why don't you lie down and stay out of sight? I'll call Bobby and then join you." He scratched his chin. "At this rate, we'll be asleep all day."

"Do you mind? You have to work tonight and I've been a bother." She chewed the corner of her mouth. She believed every word, but with the potential peeper watching her, things—and hearts—could change.

Standing naked as the day he was born, Marlon pressed buttons on his phone. "And wake up with a sexy woman in my arms?" He clicked his tongue. "I want to keep you safe so I can taste your sweetness all night—or in this case, all day long. Wild horses couldn't steal me away from you."

"Good."

Chapter Seventeen

When Marlon awoke, he rubbed his eyes. The scent of vanilla and flowers permeated the room. Something soft tickled his nose. Another deep breath, more for his own pleasure than recognition, revealed the scent of his Jaden. He sighed. His. She might not be his forever, but she was for the time being, and he couldn't be happier. He curled his toes. Something soft but soggy grazed his foot. Turning slightly, he saw the culprit—Sparky. Peeking over the edge of the bed, the Basset hound panted. Riley jumped up from the floor. His tags jingled as he jumped up onto the comforter.

Jaden groaned and threw an arm over her eyes. "Another ten minutes, guys, please?"

Marlon kissed her bare shoulder. "I'll put them out."

She jerked and flopped over. "Oh!"

"You forgot me. I'm hurt." He grinned. "See if I let you play with my ass now."

Clutching her head, she apologised. "Marlon, I'm so used to waking up alone that it's weird not to. I'm sorry."

He smoothed his hand along her arm, caressing her soft skin. "I see. You have fantastic sex with me, then forget I exist."

She smirked. "We didn't have sex. I went down on you. You fell asleep before returning the favour."

He tapped her nose. "All right for you, missy. I'll put these dogs out and have my wicked way with you. I'm dying for breakfast."

Before she could answer, he slipped from the bed and tugged on his boxer shorts. Leave her waiting to see what he had for a surprise. He whistled and both dogs followed him down the stairs. After the craziness of the night before, he expected a throng of reporters outside. When he saw none, he frowned. According to Sergeant O'Rourke's recon, no cameras or recording equipment were found outside her house. Not even a set of footprints. Still, she wasn't going to make something like that up…was she?

Marlon tapped the buttons on his phone to check his messages. No one matching the blond kid's description had been seen in the area of her house either. Well, fuck. When he went to the door to let the dogs back in, Bobby rounded the corner.

"Oh, hey man." Bobby's eyes widened for a split second as a thin smile curled his lips.

"Did you come with the CPD?" Marlon asked. "I just called them not a moment ago."

"Thought I'd stop by and see how Jaden was holding up. I heard the bulletin on the scanner. Don't over-think this."

Marlon narrowed his eyes. "See how she's holding up, or be her support?"

"You have to ask her. This is her thing."

"What did the CPD find?" Jaden wrapped her arms around him. "I know you told me last night, but I forgot. Didn't help that I had the world's worst nightmare. Bobby..." Her body tensed.

Bobby tipped his head. "I'm just leaving." He opened the gate and strolled down the back path.

What the hell was going on? A stalker, a suspected camera, and now Bobby I'm-sorry-I-fucked-your-girl Hutchins sniffing around? Marlon gritted his teeth. Jaden said she loved him. "I'm supposed to ask you why he's here," he snapped. "Care to tell me?"

"He's kinda like a cross between a parole officer and a bulldog. He's keeping me in line while keeping the crazies away."

She didn't trust him enough with her safety? Didn't think he'd take a bullet for her? What else had she hidden? "Then my job here is done." He stepped from her grasp and stomped into the house. "I can't be with a woman who doesn't trust me."

Jaden followed close behind without touching him. "There's a little bit more here than you know."

"Like...? I want honesty." He bit the words out. "All of it."

Jaden nibbled her top lip and picked at her fingers for a moment. "Everyone seems to know what's good for me—except me. Daddy's determined to get me back under his thumb. You don't think I trust you. Look, I had a fling with Bobby, yes, but that's all it was. When I decided to come back to Ohio, I called him to be a watchdog. I wanted to see you and the only way I could figure to have protection and your undivided attention was to use his brute strength. It had nothing to do with us and everything to do with gaining my freedom."

"Give me your phone."

"What?" Her voice came out in a squeak.

"O'Rourke said you were safe, although the camera probably wasn't your imagination. Eunice Lowry said she saw a prowler in the alley on the other side of her house. It's possible you saw the same person."

She picked at the hem of her sleep shirt. "So there is a stalker or someone who wants to intrude on my life. Why do you want my phone?"

"I want closure." Marlon tapped the buttons on the phone. "What's your father's number?"

"Don't call him. It's not worth your job. He will find your weakest point and exploit it."

"Bullshit." Marlon scrolled through the contacts. *Daddy four-four-seven-five-five-five-one-nine-five-six.* The nightmare had to end. He pressed send and waited for the call to connect. Jaden covered her mouth with both hands and turned away from Marlon.

"Talk to me."

Marlon snarled. "Is this Rexx Weir?"

"Who are you? Why do you have Jade's phone? I'm not paying a finder's fee to you."

Pounding his fist twice on the counter, Marlon unleashed his anger. "Listen, jackass. I don't know what sick thrill you get tailing your daughter, but she's scared out of her mind. Cut the fucking cord and let her live her damned life."

"You must be the cop she went back for."

"I am."

"Bobby, she's using you for sex."

Bobby? Fuck, fuck, fuck. "I'm not Bobby."

"Oh, you're Marlon. Even better." The line went silent for a moment. "You've dug your own grave, Officer. I know about your phobias and your skeletons. Don't fuck with me."

Marlon opened his mouth to answer, but was met with the click of a disconnected call. Son of a bitch. He slammed the phone down onto the counter a little harder than he intended.

"He plays to win."

Marlon turned. The scent of pan-fried toast floated around him. His stomach growled and some of his furore dimmed. "He knew about Bobby."

"He's probably got surveillance going right now." She flipped the toast over and, using the flour mill, she sprinkled powdered sugar on a plate full of French toast. "Hungry?"

"You never cease to amaze me." Marlon crossed the room and wrapped his arms around her. "You cook when you're upset?"

"How else do you think I gained all this weight?"

He swiped his finger through the fluffy sugar. "You can do whatever your heart desires." He tapped her on the nose with the sugary finger. "Like calming me down when I want to rip your father and Bobby limb from limb."

Jaden giggled and drew a heart in the spilled sugar. "Bobby isn't a threat, but Daddy is." She turned off the stovetop and placed the hot toast on another plate. When she turned around, she dotted his face with the confectioners' sugar.

"Eat and I'll talk." She shoved a platter into his hands. "I've got bigger things to worry about now, like where to live." She switched off the heat to the stove and moved the pan from the hot burner. "Granted, Steven hasn't kicked me out, but I know it's coming. It sucks. I haven't had time to move our things to your apartment—that is, if it's still on offer. Is it?"

Marlon placed the serving dish back on the counter and kissed her hard on the lips. To tempt him, she'd dressed in his T-shirt and, if his instincts were right, nothing else. He chuckled low in his throat. Moments earlier, he couldn't see past his frustration. With a bat of her lashes and a little powdered sugar, she'd reminded him of what he wanted. Could he get enough of her just being roommates? Never. He slid his hands under the shirt, smoothing them over her ass, bare as he'd expected, and lifted her into his arms.

She pressed her face against his neck, smearing the sugar. "What are you doing? You can't lift me again! I weigh one-forty. I'll break your back."

"Don't disturb me when I'm having my breakfast." He slid the napkin holder and the lacy placemats out of the way, placing her on the dark cherry dining room table. Her one-forty didn't bother him. He liked her with curves.

"You're a wicked man." Jaden licked the sugar from the tips of her fingers. "Filthy and wasting perfectly good sugar."

He wrinkled his nose and wiped the excess sweetener away from his top lip. "I'm your wicked, filthy man." Grabbing the arms of the chair, he nudged her thighs open and bellied up to the bar. Her junction glistened and a gasp rasped from her throat. So she liked a little mid-morning tryst? Nice.

With two fingers, he teased her outer lips. She shivered and writhed in his embrace. Very nice. He grabbed the hem of the shirt. "Lift that pretty little bottom of yours. I want to feast." Jaden did as he asked, propping her feet on the arms of the chair. Marlon shoved the shirt up over her breasts. An inch-long scar marred the underside of each breast. He traced the puffy pink line on her right breast.

"What happened, babe?"

Her voice came out in a gravelly tone that turned his insides out and sent his heart reeling. "I had my implants removed."

So she had gone down to her original cup size like the papers had reported. He liked the natural look. Threading his hands behind her back, he lifted her and urged her chest towards his mouth. He licked each nipple until both stood out like little arrows. Then he licked a path to her scars, kissing them as if his touch could mend the flesh. He wished it were possible. He'd get rid of all the scars in her life.

Tangling her fingers in his short hair, she cupped his head. "That feels wonderful. Don't stop."

"Never." He nipped the supple skin and left twin bite marks to cover the scars. Nothing mattered, not the ghosts in his past, not the speed bumps in her life — just the two of them and the love growing between them. While he gave attention to her breasts, he traced his index finger between her nether lips. Her slickness eased his journey until he pressed one finger into her hot channel. She bucked in his arms.

"Oh my...goodness. Take me."

Good idea. Leaving her breasts, he edged her down onto the table. She moaned with pleasure and opened to him. Her labia, pink and puffy, begged for his attention. He licked his dry lips. Yes, he needed to taste her. He rubbed his slippery index finger from her core to her clit, loving the way she keened for him. Her fingers tightened in his hair, pulling the short strands, but he didn't care. Her pleasure heightened his, cancelling out the pain.

Each tug on her clit, each dip into her channel brought another scream from her throat. "Marlon!"

Her hips wriggled against his ministrations, sending him into his own bliss-filled state. Time to up the ante. He used the cream from her pussy to lubricate his fingers and massaged her asshole.

Her chest bounced with her uneven breaths. "More."

Marlon caressed the puckered skin, easing his finger in a little further with each push. He pressed his face into her pussy and drank her sweetness. Honey dribbled down his chin as he reached up to pluck at her nipple. Dear God, she made love and life fun.

"Make love to me. I need to feel you in me." She panted and grabbed for him. "We need a condom."

"Can't wait." Planting kisses on her inner thighs, Marlon withdrew his finger from her ass and tugged her into a sitting position. He scooted her forwards onto his lap, punctuating the move with three slaps to her butt. "Want you without. You're mine." His cock jutted from the gap in his boxers, as if seeking her out.

"Are you sure?" A crease marred her brow. "I'm clean, but things can happen."

"Can't imagine being with anyone else." He threaded his fingers into her hair, massaging the back of her head. "I love you and I want to spend my life with you."

"I'm yours." She squirmed and the action pressed his length deeper into her junction. "All yours." Her liquid excitement eased their joining until she slid down to the base of his erection. She threw her head back and rode him — hard. Flesh slapped flesh, his hands smacked her ass and the combination of sounds bounced off the walls.

"Marlon." She spoke in a breathy voice he wanted to hear over and over. She wrapped her arms around him and bit down on his shoulder.

"I like that. Fuck, I love it." He groaned, grabbing her hips to pump into her. Her inner muscles grasped him as she climaxed, milking him of his seed and sending him to orgasm. When she looked up, the brilliant green of her eyes garnered his attention, not that he wanted to look away. Hell, he wanted her to mother his children. He wanted everything with her. Right now.

"Whoa." She slumped against him. "So…good."

Latching on to her neck, he suckled and sampled until his breathing slowed. When he pulled back, a purple mark marred the delicate skin. "Umm, baby girl, that was fucking wonderful."

She snuggled into the curve of his chest. "I kinda liked it, too."

He licked the hollow at the base of her throat, and the taste of salty sweat and Jaden danced on his tongue. "I love you, Jaden Marie. All of you. And I regret nothing. Absolutely nothing."

She sat up straight on his lap, offering her breasts. But instead of the declaration of love he anticipated, the joy on her face disappeared. Her eyes widened as she covered her chest. "Marlon!"

Struggling to find the source of her discomfort, he twisted in his seat. "What? What's wrong, babe?"

"Oh my God! Oh my God!" She panted and fumbled off of his lap. "Oh my freaking God!"

He grasped her shoulders. His heart pounded within his chest. "Talk to me. Tell me what the fuck happened."

Still covering her breasts, she pointed a shaky hand to the window. "A man…a man was outside the window with a camera. He saw us! He watched us! My dream came true. Oh my God."

Marlon yanked his shirt from the table and wrapped it around her. "Go upstairs. I'll call Mac, Bobby, and the CPD. This has got to end."

After she left the room, Marlon dialled his fellow officer. Three rings and the deputy picked up. "Hutchins."

"Where the fuck are you? You're at the top of my shit list, but I need a favour." Marlon stood at the back door. The dogs were still outside and if the peeper wanted to hurt her further, the animals were fair game.

"I'm on my way. Talk to me."

"Her peeper's back."

"I'll call Mac. See you in ten."

He tossed his phone onto the table and ran both hands through his hair. Jaden didn't deserve the intrusion into her life. She'd broken clean with Hollywood. What did they need her for when he needed her more? Her footfalls thumped on the carpeted steps.

"Did you catch him?"

Marlon snagged her in an embrace and kissed the top of her head. "Bobby's on his way and I'm staying here with you. We'll get the jerk."

Breaking the sweet moment, her phone rang. He placed his hand on hers as she reached for the cell phone. "Put it on speaker, babe. I have the feeling he's calling to gloat and I want to hear the asshole."

She nodded and flicked the phone open. "Hello?"

A male voice, gruff and low resounded in the room. "Are you ready to come home?"

Marlon met her confused expression. What the hell? He flicked his fingers to get her to continue the conversation.

Her bottom lip quivered. "Who is this?"

"My identity doesn't matter. Are you ready to come home?"

Doesn't matter? It sure did. Who was this clown?

Jaden grasped Marlon's hand, giving it a tight squeeze. "No. I'm not coming home when I am home."

The man cackled, sending a shiver up Marlon's spine. "The spoilt little rich girl is home with her hot cop? Not quite. You need to go back to where you came from. You owe people."

Jaden shivered and disengaged from Marlon. "What do you want?"

"I ask the questions, Officer." His voice grew lower. "I hope you enjoyed your afternoon delight and the late night snack. I did, and the viral community will, too."

Bile rose in Marlon's throat. The caller referred to him as 'Officer'. How did this jerk know about their lovemaking?

Oh God.

"You had the camera, you bastard." Jaden's words came out in a rush. "I want the memory card or the disc or whatever the fuck you used to spy on me! What I did isn't your business!"

"Too late, sweet cheeks. Anyone who pops your name into a search engine will see your brand spankin' new sex tape. That cop of yours won't have a job come the end of the day after everyone sees your drug fest. He's screwed—in every way possible."

Marlon froze. The veracity of the caller's words crashed down on him. Search engine... sex tape...cop...drug fest...no job... Oh fuck. "You can't do that." Shit. He hadn't wanted to tip his hand and let the cretin know he'd listened in.

"Hello there, Deputy. I'd say wear a shirt. You're awful pale." The caller chuckled. "You can't stop the clip. It's already posted. Now the world can see Jade Weir's biting fetish and snort session with a man of the law."

"Fuck you," Jaden screamed.

"Honey, don't shout. You'd better come to your senses, Jaden, and come home before the real damage is done. I'm tired of following your spoilt ass to make your ole man happy."

Before she could answer, the man clicked off the line.

She covered her mouth with her hand and sprinted from the room. Marlon followed, hot on her heels, as the caller's words etched themselves onto his brain. *Anyone will see your sex tape...* Acid burnt at the back of his throat. *Afternoon delight and late night snack...the world can see you snort up with a cop...* God dammit.

"Jaden?"

Curling over the toilet, she retched. Sobs racked her body as she sat on the floor slumped against the toilet seat and hid her face in her hands. The scrape of dog claws on the tile meant she and Marlon weren't alone. Sparky stuck his nose under her arms and licked her chin. She wrapped her arms around his head and continued to cry. Nothing seemed to go right—they'd made a breakthrough with the situation and their feelings for each other, but someone wanted them apart.

Marlon grabbed the washcloth from the shower. Kneeling next to her, he rubbed her back and wiped her face. There weren't many people who took the time to care for her. She wanted to lose herself in his arms and make the world go away, but when she met his gaze, her heart squeezed tight. Disillusion and disappointment radiated in his eyes. The damage had gone deeper than some ridiculous sex video.

"Things are so out of control." She scrubbed the back of her hand across her mouth and stood. Better to sever ties now than to have her heart broken when he walked out. "I think you'd better leave."

"You aren't the first person I've seen throw up. I'm not freaked by barf, blood, bones... Well, guts make me a little queasy, but I don't see any of those hanging out of you." When she didn't laugh at his bad attempt at a joke, his jaw clenched. He stood and tugged her close. "I won't deny I'm upset. Hell, my life is in the shitter. But I won't accept you giving up on us."

She sighed and wriggled away. God, it felt like the world had exploded around her. "Marlon, you need to get away from me and save your reputation. Get away before I ruin your career."

"What?" The screech of his cell phone split the air. Marlon grabbed his department-issued phone and punched the buttons. "This had better be fucking fantastic." She peeked around his arm at the screen. Images of her and Marlon in the throes of lovemaking, licking sugar off each other, and her splayed on the table flickered on the phone. A running internet link advertised where to buy the full sex and drugs video for nineteen ninety-five.

"Oh my God. Who would stoop this low?" He tossed the device across the small room. Still the screen played the images of them engaged in sexual activity as it slapped the wall a couple of feet away.

Riley strolled across the room and cocked his head at the screen. He gave it a sniff and lifted his leg, peeing on the device.

Grabbing the soggy phone, Marlon growled. "I'm going to lose my God damned job—all because it looks like I did drugs with you." He slammed his thumbs on the buttons. "Turn off, dammit." Glancing at the ceiling, he slammed the phone onto the Formica countertop, smashing the electronic equipment into pieces. "Piece of shit."

She winced. Marlon had every right to be angry. Hell, he had every right to be downright pissed off. She knew down at the molecular level who to blame, but calming Marlon down took top priority.

"I'm telling you to go." Jaden shoved Marlon from the bathroom and into the hallway. "You don't want to be seen with me. Without trying, I'm ruining your life. I can't do that to you, so get out while you can."

Marlon's eyes widened as he backed in front of the steps to the second story. He touched his ring finger and his voice came out soft. "You sound like Addy."

"I'm worse. I can't even stop this—at least not yet." For one of the few times since they'd become a couple, his strength didn't reassure her. The forces against them outweighed his power of authority.

The muscles in his jaw twitched as he sat down on the third step. "Not yet? How long have you known this was going to happen? Why didn't you tell me?" He threw his hands in the air. "I'm going through it again and I vowed I wouldn't. Dammit."

"Marlon, I'm sorry. But you have to know that I didn't orchestrate this." She sat next to him on the edge of the step and put her hand on his forearm. If anything, the angrier he got, the larger he seemed.

"I believe you, I do, but my ass is on the internet for anyone to see. I have to explain this to Mac. He'll shit a brick or ten. Unless he doesn't see it." He blew out a long breath and growled. "I can't get busted for drug use or possession again. I can't."

She scooted off the step and knelt between his thighs. She took both his massive hands in hers. "It's probably on his phone right now."

"God dammit." The words ricocheted through the silent house.

Jaden fell back on her bottom and skittered out of his way. "I didn't mean for this to happen."

He jerked off the steps and stood, offering his hand. "Come with me to the station and file the report. We'll deny it was us."

She leant heavily against the hallway wall and watched him storm into the dining room. Well hell, things made no sense. "It doesn't work that way—not with Daddy or his henchmen. I hoped the circus would forget me, but they didn't. Your best bet is to go out the door. Act like you hate me. Show the swarm of photographers on the lawn that we're through. They'll get tired of the absent drama and leave you alone. I won't lead them your way, either. You'll be safe and maybe one day we can try again."

"Jaden?" He shoved his wallet and keys in his pockets, only halted a moment by her words. "I don't buy it. We have something way too strong."

"What do you want from me? I haven't lied to you." She stood and brushed the loose strands of hair from her eyes. Why didn't this make sense to him? "I'd rather walk away than put you through hell. Splitting is best for the both of us in the long run."

"You're taking this way too easily." Marlon scrubbed his hand over his forehead. "Did you give up on us that fast or was it all a lie to begin with? I can't keep up."

She laced her fingers behind her head and braced her feet. "If I'm right about the person I think is behind this, our break-up will be the least of our problems. I won't let them screw with your career because I'm a has-been celebrity."

"So we're through? Just like that? End of discussion?"

"The world doesn't shine on your ass. Yes, it's the end of the discussion." She chewed the inside of her cheek to work through what she wanted to say. Going on pure adrenaline wasn't going to get through to him. "When dealing with my father, I have no other choice." She grabbed his hand. "The press and this clown want dirt. There's no chance for this to blow over if we're together, and I have a lot less to lose than you do."

Marlon dropped her hand and backed away from her. "Don't do this. Don't cut on me to make yourself feel better."

"Oh grow up." Her anger hit its peak. Her voice cracked and rose by an octave. "For all I know, the recording was just the beginning. He could have a tap on my phone and bugs here in the house just looking for ways to bring us down and ruin you."

The creases around his eyes deepened. He pinched the bridge of his nose. Why couldn't he just trust her? She knew how to manipulate the media. His brawn and badge were useless against her father's money and determination.

The veins in his neck bulged and crimson stained his cheeks. Raw anger and frustration hardened in his eyes. "Let me talk to your old man again. Since you ended us, I'm calling his ass out and putting an end to this shit."

"Marlon, look at what your initial intervention did. He's not listening to a word you say." She smoothed her hand over his cheek in an attempt to stave off some of his fury. "I'm so sorry, Marlon."

"You would be sorry. Your heart isn't flat on the floor." He wriggled from her grasp and threw his hands in the air. "And fucking hell, there's nothing I can say to change your mind. I don't believe this. I don't."

She'd tried tact and had given tenderness a go. Neither had got through to him. Attitude had barely dented his anger. Jaden fisted her hands on her hips and unleashed her emotions. "Unless you can pull an alternative universe out of your asshole, you're right. There's nothing you can do."

Marlon's mouth opened and closed. The red in his cheeks faded to a pallor. "I'm getting the hell out of here before I say something else I'll regret." He clenched his fists and pressed them against his temples. "I don't know whether to be more angry that I've been dumped, or that I now have to try to save my own career." His voice echoed through the cavernous room. "I need to see Mac and get this straightened out, dammit. I don't know if I can worm my way out of trouble."

"You probably can't."

Marlon turned on his heel and thundered through the house, collecting his clothes and wallet. He dressed in record time and grabbed his keys. "I won't stay where I'm not wanted. I'm outta here."

When he strode out onto the porch, the wave of lights flickered into the living room. Jaden choked back a sob and collapsed onto the floor. More than one person shouted his name, no doubt vying to get the first sound bite. She cringed when he spoke.

"No comment."

Whatever else he said blurred together as she succumbed to her emotions. She'd been through embarrassing photo shoots, slimy directors, men who didn't love anything about her other than her female genitalia. Marlon had cared about her until the shit hit the fan. Could she blame him for being upset?

No, but she could put an end to the madness.

Jaden sat up and wiped her damp cheeks. "What was the line of that old song, they can't take away my dignity?" She smoothed her tangled hair behind her ears and stood. "I earned my independence and dammit, no one's gonna take it from me." She crossed the room and snatched up her phone. "Time to deal with Daddy."

Chapter Eighteen

Jaden herded the dogs into her Mercedes. Four hours had passed since Marlon's departure. Since then, she'd managed to convince Cass to babysit the dogs and loan out her private jet in return for eight days of babysitting over the course of the next year. Keys in hand, Jaden tapped her fingers on the roof of the car. "Where the hell are you, Bobby?" She sucked in another breath and puffed it out. Her hair fluffed over her forehead. Dust swirled around her in the humid air. As soon as Bobby arrived, they could head to the airport. Until then, the dank garage kept the media at bay.

A knock came from the main door to the house and Bobby peeked through the lacy curtains. Jaden slid into the driver's seat and engaged the garage door opener. As she turned the engine over, Bobby slid into the passenger seat.

"Sorry, I had to clear the time with Mac. Marlon's madder than a wet hen."

"He'll get over it." Despite her curt remark, her thoughts travelled to Marlon. Somehow she wasn't so sure they'd weather the break. Losing him would be a wound no amount of time could heal.

The sex clip had spread around the country faster than cheap gossip. She'd silenced her phone after the fifteenth call. The voicemails, even after a whopping four hours, were all the same—who would be the man in the next video? When she'd turned on the television for noise, one of the tabloid shows subsidised by Delish claimed she'd staged the whole incident to catapult her career back into the limelight. Photographers stood guard outside the house to catch a shot of her to run in the next day's magazine.

Jaden eased out of the garage and honked her horn to part the sea of photographers. "I'll never have Marlon or my own life if I don't face them. Living in a cave won't stop the craziness."

The dozens of flashbulbs popped amidst the chorus of her name. She blinked and continued down the drive.

"Is your AC busted?" Bobby twiddled with the knobs and his hand brushed her knee. "It's hotter than hell in here."

"Roll down a window," she grumbled. Bobby got the window down, but the crush of paparazzi practically climbed into the car. Someone wore thick cologne and the biting scent of body odour churned her stomach. She prayed she'd make it down the concrete pad without running someone over. She could just see the headline: Jade Weir slaughters paparazzo while driving drunk. Within the hour, shots of her would grace countless e-zines, gossip sites, and minor news stations.

Stomping on the brake, she shook her head. I was a celebrity for years, I can wear the persona for a little longer.

When someone, she wasn't sure who the arm belonged to, shoved a digital recorder in her face, she plastered a smile on her face and waved. "Thank you for your support in this very difficult time. I love you all." The lie tasted sour on her tongue. But it would pacify the gossip mongers.

Biting back tears, she backed the car onto the road and shifted into drive. She cast one last look at the Pennywood house. So many happy memories flooded her mind. She'd walked into Judi's home a virtual child, full of hope and a wide-eyed expectation of the future, only to emerge a woman—hurt and disillusioned by life.

"Say goodbye to our house, kids. We'll visit Judi and then we're going to go on an adventure." Sparky barked and Riley growled. The cats cowered in their carrier.

A shadow darkened her driver's side window. When she turned, a scream ripped from her throat. The blond man peered through the dirty glass. A smile curled his thin lips, his sky blue eyes vacant. Pressing the button on the locks, she stomped on the gas pedal.

"I've got my gun," Bobby said in a calm voice. "Go. He won't hurt you. I'm here."

Not relieved by his demeanour, she shivered and peeled out. Before she got too far down the street, she glanced in her mirror, seeing nothing. A cop probably sat at the end of the street ready to nab her for reckless driving or speeding. She'd adopted the ditzy glamour girl image and hesitantly embraced her newfound bad luck. She peeked again. Still nothing but dull, grey pavement.

"Honey, you're gonna run into this kind of crap until you decide what you want." Bobby patted her thigh. "We'll get you through this crisis."

With shaky hands, she drove to Cass's house. Oh sure, Cass listened and tried to understand, but Judi was more of a mother figure. Cass was just an older, doting sister-type.

She zipped around town, taking side streets and backtracking to leave the swarm of paparazzi in her dust. After an hour, her tactics had worked enough for her to stop at Cass' to drop off the animals. With help from Bobby and Cass, Jaden got the dogs into the run with Cass' dogs, and the cats into the house. She scratched Sparky's ears. "I'll be back in a couple days. Promise. I won't leave you for long—ever."

Jaden said her goodbyes to her friends and made her way to the hospital. There, she found a spot near the door. She gave a cursory visual sweep of the lot in case the creep was back or the wide range lenses were poised to capture her. With Bobby by her side, she rolled her shoulders and willed her pounding heart to slow. *I can do this.*

One of the nurses, a brunette named Joy, grinned. "You're early. Wonderful. Judi hasn't stopped bragging about you." She shook Bobby's hand, but spoke to Jaden. "Now are you her daughter or granddaughter?"

Shoring her courage, Jaden shook her head. "I'm just the girl who took care of her pets. She's got a son named Steven and a daughter-in-law named Peggy."

"They must've been by to visit," Bobby added.

Joy clicked her tongue. "Huh. I've never seen them, and I've got the shift that gets the most visitors. You and Cass Malone are about it. Judi loved playing with Julian last night. He brightens the whole place. And his giggles are contagious. I love it." She started down the first hallway. "Do you mind me asking—"

Jaden bit her tongue and waited for the sex tape question. Or better yet, who was her new dish. Her stomach churned.

"—I hear you got two cats. Where from? I know there are a few patients in the geriatric wing downstairs who are allergic, but I think a couple of cats and a dog or two might brighten their days. I know it would be a boost for the staff."

Jaden sighed and thanked God she'd dodged the bullet. "I got them at the Sunny Retreat Animal Shelter. Summer Tyler told me there are too many animals coming in each month that belonged to older folks who can't take care of their pets. You'll find some great critters there."

Joy stopped short. "Summer? You mean Marlon Cross's girlfriend? Well, no, she's his ex, I think. I didn't know she ran the SRAS. I guess you learn new things each day."

Jaden winced. Just the mention of Marlon's name stung. Hearing his name in conjunction with another woman hurt like hell. Bobby grinned and rubbed circles along her back. Maybe having him come along wasn't a good idea.

"I heard you and Marlon have a thing. Well, no, Judi told me so. She's practically got wedding dates picked out. You know she wants to wear pale pink during the ceremony?" Joy stopped in front of a waiting room. "Why don't you and your friend spread out here? I'll get Judi. Be right back."

Jaden waited for the nurse to leave the room before she let her true emotions loose. She blinked back tears and sat on a nearby couch. Bobby grabbed her hand and rubbed circles over the top of her palm. The gesture made her feel a little better, but not warm and gooey like Marlon's touch.

"Shit," Bobby muttered.

Jaden turned when Bobby stopped moving. She expected to see Judi. Her smile faded.

Marlon.

He frowned and shoved his hands into his pockets.

She forced a small wave.

Closing his eyes, he shook his head.

"I'll stay over here." Bobby grabbed a magazine with a football player on the cover. Jaden stood and hurried to the door. "Marlon?"

He paused a couple of feet from her, but didn't say anything.

Forcing her pride aside, she spoke. Maybe a couple of kind words would help them on the road to mending the friendship. "I didn't expect to see you here. How'd things go with Mac?" She snapped her mouth shut. If he wanted to speak, then he could continue the conversation. If not, she'd leave him alone. Watching the play of muscle under his snug polo shirt, she longed to smooth her hands over the tension in his shoulders. How could she tell him about the baby? She gulped air. "I guess you don't want to talk. I'm sorry to bother you. Have a good one."

As she turned to open the door, he stepped into her personal space. "Why?" His green eyes blazed. Creases marred his forehead. "I just spent the last several hours pissing in a cup and explaining why I didn't deserved to be fired. Until the test comes back, no one believes me it was just sugar and innocence. No one."

She gazed up at him. "I'm sorry, but there is so much you don't understand." What else could she say? The sex tape debacle wasn't her doing—not that he believed her.

The interview accompanying the video had been faked—nothing but clips strung together and played over still shots taken by the paparazzi.

With a sigh, Marlon tucked a lock of her hair behind her ear. "I'm sorry, too. I'm sorry I didn't fit into your lifestyle. I can't be so casual with my mine. I want a woman to want to be with me because she loves me, not because she can further her career." He dipped his head. His words came out in a murmur. "Why would you—I mean, how could you make that clip for the news? I believed in you."

"Then let me explain. There's a lot you don't know, but I've not given up loving you."

"I want to believe you, to believe that you didn't pull this stunt, but no matter how much I may or may not love you, something in my heart won't let me give us a try." His words came out broken. He cleared his throat. "I'm a cop and a damn good one. I can't do my job with my privates all over the internet. What happens if the information on my computer or phone is stolen because the paparazzi want dirt on you? That puts so many people in jeopardy."

"I had no idea." Sure, Jade Weir personified the camera-hogging celebutante. Anything to get her name and picture into the paper in the past...but Jaden? The only time she'd cut loose was with him. Nothing had ever been simple in her life, but to put others in danger... She nodded, unsure of what else to do. He wouldn't listen to her explanations when he had his mind made up.

"I'm not trying to be a dick, but I can't live looking over my shoulder to keep an eye on anyone who wants to catch me in the middle of some faked illicit act. As of right now, I've been stripped of my badge." His voice wavered and he glanced away a moment.

"I hope you find that one man who makes you tick."

The words teetered on the tip of her tongue. She itched to tell him the truth.

I already did.

As she watched his sculpted body disappear around a corner, she heard the nurse approach. With Bobby right behind her, Jaden followed Joy down the hall and entered Judi's room.

"Jaden, honey! I thought you forgot about me."

Swallowing a cry, she wiped her damp cheeks and plastered a smile on her lips. "Hi Judi."

Once the door had snicked shut and the nurses had left, Judi frowned and pointed to Bobby. "Then the rumour is true. You made a bad movie, broke up with Marlon, and got a new man. I don't believe it, but I know it happens. What I don't understand is why? You're so good together."

Bobby aimed his thumb at the door. "I'll go try to talk to Marlon. Be back in a moment." He exited the room, leaving Jaden alone with Judi.

Jaden sat down in one of the chairs. "Where should I start? Marlon and I argued, made love, and some lunatic turned it into a viral video. He's convinced I lied to him. I can't change what happened, so he's through with me and I can't blame him. If I saw the spectacle, I wouldn't want to talk to me either."

"Do you love him?"

"Bobby? He's still just acting as a bodyguard."

"I meant Marlon."

"I love him with all my heart."

"And you aren't going to fight for him?"

"Yes I am, which is why I'm here. I'm heading to California." Jaden slapped her thighs and stood. "It's

Daddy's doing. I know it. He dismissed me like a spoilt child and it drives him crazy to not have me under his thumb. I won't do it." Despite her best attempts to keep her true feelings under wraps, the truth bubbled to the surface. "I want Marlon and I want this nightmare over with. I'm tired of being synonymous with failure."

"I'm disappointed in you." Judi narrowed her eyes. "The girl I know doesn't give up like this."

"I haven't given up. I just don't have a real firm plan on what I'm going to do."

"Do you have access to your wealth?"

Jaden tipped her head. "Money isn't the answer to my Marlon problem. He hates me and my father's money."

She shook her head. "Not for him. I want you to promise me you'll do something good with it." Judi shifted in her seat. "Do you remember my bridge buddy Estelle Lowry? Her sister Eunice lived a couple of houses down from us."

Jaden nodded. "Eunice is a sweet lady. Estelle had a bulldog, didn't she?"

"Bruiser and she had a cat named Charlie." Judi removed her glasses and wiped her eyes. "She loved the both of them very much. When the doctors' tests came back with cancer and they made her live in the rest home, her daughters sent the cat to the shelter. Bruiser went with the oldest girl. She called me the other day. It seems he won't eat. I think he misses Estelle."

"So what can I do? I'm not a vet."

"I know, so hear me out. What did you tell me when you left the shelter after you got Tantrum and Unruly? You told me all the animals had the same look in their eyes—please remember me. Maybe you can use that money to help them."

"How?"

"You have to figure that out on your own. I can't tell you."

She reeled. How Judi expected her to care not only for her four animals, but a whole passel of other ones when she'd just got her own life more or less on the tracks? Grief. "Why are you saying these things?"

"Because I don't have much time left. I dreamt of my Collin last night. He told me I needed to come home soon. I miss him. I miss his arms around me when I sleep. I miss his kisses." Judi blotted her eyes. "The doctors say I'll live a while longer, but I'm not convinced. Please, do this something for me. Help the animals in remembrance of me. I know you'll figure out what to do."

Emotions from way down deep welled to the surface. "I'm nothing but a spoilt rich kid who failed at everything she tried. I pushed everything good in my life away!"

"You're wallowing in your drama. Snap out of it. The cats, the boys here, all think you're doing a fantastic job of caring for them. You need to face the drama head-on and obliterate it."

Jaden rubbed her face with both hands. Judi had a point. Running away from California hadn't solved her problems. It had made them worse. But she'd also learnt how to grow up. She'd figured out how to take care of herself. She'd found the strength to love.

"So did you decide what you're going to do?"

Jaden stood and folded her hands in front of her mouth. "First thing I'm going to do is read my father the riot act. I didn't when I lived in California and I should've. As for the money, well, that's about half-formed. I can't take the critters with me for a short trip, but they're being taken care of."

"Who?"

"Cass and Logan have agreed to have them at the farm for a little while. What I have to do won't take long." She hugged Judi. "I'll miss you, but if it's time to be with Collin, then you should. I'll make you and the furry kids proud. I promise."

Judi clapped her hands. The smile returned to her face, followed by a bout of the giggles Jaden loved so much. "See? I told you things would work out. Go put that plan that isn't formed into action. You'll be unstoppable."

"You bet! Love you, Judi."

"I love you, too, honey."

As she walked out of the door, a cloud of peace settled around Jaden. The niggling feeling she wouldn't see Judi again ate at her mind, but she shoved it aside and nodded to Bobby as she passed him in the waiting room. She'd make Judi proud and she'd find her purpose in life.

"Don't give up on me, Marlon. I haven't given up on you," she murmured and strode out of the hospital. "This roadblock isn't enough to extinguish my dream. Before I'm done I'll make you all proud of me!"

Chapter Nineteen

Twenty-four hours after visiting Judi at the retirement centre and seeing Jaden with Bobby, Marlon sat splayed on his couch. The thought of her laying with Bobby unnerved him. He tossed his third beer can into the recycling bin at the far end of the room. Drinking wasn't dulling the pain of Jaden's betrayal. It made it worse. He glanced at the laptop perched on his stomach. According to leading search engines, his name had surged into the top one hundred searches overnight. The video was the talk of every major online tabloid newscast. It hurt to see the object of his affection plastered all over the television and internet.

Out of curiosity, he searched her. Over a thousand sites, many fan-generated, popped up — all with nude or nearly nude images of his love. Some mentioned him by name. Others called him her 'stud with a badge'. He groaned and watched the interview once more. Her hairstyle changed during the course of the clip. Even the fullness in her cheeks streamlined. The whole thing seemed faked, but he wasn't sure how.

She'd said she loved him and, God, he wanted to believe her. But every thought of the ninety-second clip chipped away at the tender feelings he had for her.

I trust her. Secrets and acting aside, I trust her.

I just can't be with her.

Marlon closed the internet window and stared at the sheriff's badge image on his desktop. Indefinite unpaid leave. What a crock of shit. Mac's words burned into Marlon's brain when he delivered the good news. "You're worth the trouble because I can count on you in the clutch, but I can't condone what happened. It's too close to what happened before."

Seeing Jaden ripped the scars on his heart wide open. Each time he thought about the love he'd believed they shared, he winced. Common sense dictated she wouldn't stoop so low as to have their lovemaking posted on the net, but the rawness in his heart begged to differ. She'd readily admitted she'd lied when she'd come to town to break up Logan and Cass's burgeoning relationship two years previously. At the same time, she'd lied about being involved with Dex Rose. Who knew if she was lying now? As much as he wanted to be with her, his gut dictated he stay far away.

He glanced at the silent television. Maybe today he'd find regular programming to dull his heartache. Maybe today he'd get through the sunlit hours without having a horde of cameras thrust in his face. Or Jaden would stop by to tell him the charade was over.

Fat chance.

When he sat up and closed the laptop, the bell rang at his door. As much as he didn't think he'd see Jaden yet, a tiny part of him hoped she stood on the other side. Her appearance a couple of months ago had changed his life in so many ways, good and bad, but he wouldn't trade the memories.

Peeking through the peephole, he sighed. Not Jaden.

He engaged the chain and opened the door. "Hi, Sabrina. What's up?"

Sabrina stood on his stoop. Although she still looked attractive, the sparkle was gone from her eyes. "Can I come in a moment?"

"I'm not in the mood for company." He braced his arm on the doorframe and shifted his weight. "What's the matter? You aren't going to make a pass? I won't know what to do with myself."

"I'm not going to bite." She nodded. "Open the door."

Against his better judgement, Marlon flicked the chain loose. The sigh escaping his lips came out in a combination of defeat and disillusion. He felt like a man without a country—without a soul.

Sabrina wrapped her arms around her waist and took a step across the threshold. "Are they really gone? I didn't see any cameras or news vans outside."

Marlon dipped his head once. "She's back in Cali."

"She moved on? With Bobby?" Sabrina took a deep breath and a wide grin curled the corners of her mouth. "Then she won't mind me doing this!"

Before he realised what was happening, Sabrina launched herself into his arms. She pressed wet kisses all over his face while her hands smoothed over his chest. His cock hardened behind his zipper. For a moment, Marlon considered letting her have her way with him. A warm, willing female stood in his living room showering him with physical affection.

What was a horny and slightly drunk man to do?

If said man was lucky, he'd stop before things got out of hand and realise that Sabrina only offered physical love.

She wasn't about emotional connections any more than he was about one-night stands. He clenched his mouth shut when she fused her lips to his. Pressing the issue, she bit him, making him open to her. Her taste, one of too many breath mints, made his stomach churn. He missed Jaden. Longed for her. Loved her.

Fuck, being with Sabrina was wrong on too many levels. He gripped her shoulders and wriggled from her tight embrace. "Sabrina, you don't want to start something we'll regret."

"No?" She grabbed the remote control and clicked the television on. "See your sweet Jaden? She's out on the town with Bobby. He fucked Addy, and he fucked me. She's just another notch in his belt."

Marlon gasped. Pictures flashed on the screen. Jaden arm in arm with Bobby. Bobby holding her. Bobby kissing the side of her head. The bastard making love to her.

"She's moved on, so you can, too," she shrieked. "My life wasn't complete without you. You're my soulmate."

"No." Before he could argue with her further, his cell phone rang. "I need to get that."

"Is it Jaden?"

He snarled. "No, it's Logan."

"Malone? The movie star? Here in Crawford?" Sabrina's eyes lit up. "You know Logan Malone?" Her voice dripped with sugar sweetness and venom.

Marlon rolled his eyes. Typical. When the grass—no matter how married—seemed to be greener, Sabrina stood first in line to jump ship. He pressed the buttons to answer the call. "Hey man."

"You're an ass." Logan's words, clipped and curt, resonated down into his soul. He was an ass for letting her get away, for not following through on his promise to keep her safe from the peekers and the invasion of the cameras.

Walking away from Sabrina, Marlon stuck his finger in his ear. "I beg your pardon?"

"You're a grade-A, number one ass."

"We're not exactly bosom buddies, so what the hell?" Ire up, Marlon let his anger loose. "Fuck you, too." Logan wasn't the cause of his foul mood, but his call placed him in Marlon's emotional gun-sights.

"Don't get lippy with me. Jaden didn't orchestrate that movie. She's conniving on occasion, yes, but she loved you. Still does, as far as I know. The interview, if you bothered to really look, was staged, faked, and spliced together."

He grunted. "I'm sorry. And you know this how? She ruined your life before she waltzed into mine."

Logan growled. "What do you expect? She's twenty-three. She made a few mistakes, but if it weren't for some of those poor choices, I wouldn't be with Cass. So don't get holier-than-thou on me. She goofed up, but she didn't wreck your life on purpose. The voice-overs don't even match up. It was a shitty cover-up to piss you off and it worked."

"Get to your point."

"Give her another chance. She's not with the rent-a-cop. Read her body language."

"Fuck you!" With the last word in, Marlon punched the buttons to disconnect the call. Who the hell was pretty-boy Logan Malone to tell him how to run his life? His career wasn't in the toilet because of a sex tape.

Sabrina appeared behind him and began rubbing his shoulders. "You're tense, honey bear. Let me work it out for you. I know what you need."

He let out a long breath. Sabrina didn't have a clue. "Why do you want me? I'm no good at love. You swore you'd never talk to me when you left because I broke your heart and danced on your dreams in golf shoes. I made you go fishing, tried to teach you how to use a lawnmower, and insisted you go with me to the dirt races. You don't like any of those things, yet you keep coming back and changing your mind. Why?"

She stepped around him to gaze into his eyes. "Because when you love someone, you make sacrifices. I hate pretty much everything you love, but I'm willing to fake it to keep you happy. Now smile for the cameras."

Fake it to make him happy? Hated what he loved? Including Jaden? He wrapped an arm around her shoulders. Desperate times called for evasive action, including pandering to her ego. "Sabrina, this is a side of you I never thought I'd see." He strolled to the door. "And I'm glad I saw it. I understand you so much better."

A barrage of flashbulbs popped. The cameramen and reporters surged forwards to gain access to the former Mr Jade Weir. Smiling slyly, Sabrina hooked her fingers in his front pockets and rubbed against him like a cat in heat. "When are you coming over to play good cop, naughty girl? We have an audience, just like you like."

He shook his head. "Never again. I have some heavy thinking to do and I need to concentrate."

"So you say." She nibbled the corner of her mouth. "Then find me when you're done. I'll be waiting." She blew him a kiss and stepped off his stoop, into the throng of cameras.

Closing the door, Marlon leaned against the cool barrier. Well, hell.

Chapter Twenty

Shoring up her courage and smoothing her dress suit, Jaden stepped from the limousine in front of the garish golden Delish building. She'd been away from the dogs, the cats, from Ohio—from Marlon—for thirty-six hours, but it felt more like an eternity. So far, she had nothing to show for her plans.

Her second day in California and all attempts to speak to her father ended up ignored. Would he ignore her if she made a public statement in front of his magazine empire? Probably. She clicked her tongue. Long ago, the white marble columns had reminded her of a palace. Now, she wanted to throw up. All the excess Rex Haydenweir had spent trying to become Rexx Weir and rise from his humble beginnings. Would her mother approve? Probably not. Darby Hayden-Weir had hated false praise and facades.

Be who God meant you to be, not who money made you.

Jaden nodded. Although she should've listened to her mother's advice long ago, she finally took it to heart. "I'll be myself, Momma."

She considered placing a call to Marlon just to tell him she cared. Palming the phone in her purse, she kept on her course. Each time she dialled the phone, clicks popped on the other end of the line. No way would the cretins bugging the phone catch her telling the truth before she was ready to let it out.

A woman passing on the street turned to stare at Jaden. "Oh my God! Jade's back!" her voice rose above the noise on the busy road. "Jade! Sign my shirt, please?"

Paparazzi swarmed her position as Bobby wrapped an arm around her. Jaden gave the woman the autograph she desired. When the woman withdrew from the throng, Jaden turned and smiled. "I'll be back, boys. Bobby will make sure you get great shots of me leaving. Deal?" Like hell. Screw the camera-aiming vultures. She planned on using the underground exit and getting away with her dignity.

Before anyone could shout more, Jaden raced on spindly heels into the building with Bobby glued to her side. Once inside, she took a deep breath. No wonder she'd given up the ultra-glam. Being on her glamorous game took too much work, especially when a man like Marlon liked her natural. She clenched her teeth. At least she had fond memories.

"Wait a second." Bobby wrapped a thick hand around her arm. "Can we talk?"

Jaden nodded to an alcove next to a gathering of potted palms. "What?"

"What do I mean to you?" He stepped closer and drew an imaginary line along her cheek and toyed with her lapel. "We have something between us. It never really died."

"Something? We had a one-night stand that ended in you leaving before I woke up. That's not anything to build a relationship on."

"You're really in love with him."

"You make it sound like an accusation."

Bobby dipped his head, capturing her in a kiss. Instead of curling in to him, she stood rigid. No tingles shot down her spine. No warm fuzzies cocooned her heart. When he broke for air, his heavy-lidded gaze did nothing for her libido.

"You taste like candy," he murmured.

When she didn't respond, his gaze hardened. "There really isn't anything." He looked away and shoved his fingers into his hair. "I thought maybe my service and devotion would be enough to prove to you I still think about you — more than the others."

She stared at Bobby. More than the others? Which others? "You slept with Addy and Sabrina, didn't you?"

"I've sowed my share of wild oats, just like you."

Clips of her life flashed in her mind. The times she'd used men for one night, the times she'd been used in return. The moment Marlon had walked away for good.

Bobby made a good bodyguard, but not at all what she wanted in a long term lover. Wasting time with him wouldn't fix the problems in her life.

"Marlon gave up his chance. I'm here with you." Bobby hooked his fingers under her chin. "I've got your back."

"Wait for me outside." She marched away from her spot in the alcove. "I've got my life to settle."

The woman behind the main desk smiled when Jaden made her way forwards. Though she'd never bothered to acknowledge the woman in the past, she remembered her name. Jaden walked with sure steps to the desk. "Hi Patsy. Is my father in? I don't have an appointment, but I do need to speak with him."

Patsy's blue eyes widened. "You—you remembered my name..."

Jaden stuck out her hand. "I'm sorry for being so rude in the past. You work hard and deserve kindness. Please call me by my given name, Jaden."

Without tearing her gaze from Jaden, Patsy pressed buttons on the intercom. Rexx's secretary, Glynnis, answered. "This is the office of Rexx Weir. What can I do for you, Patsy?"

Patsy fumbled for a moment. "I have Jaden here and she'd like to speak to her father."

"Who?"

Jaden chuckled and nodded to the phone. Patsy angled the device so Jaden could speak in the range of the mic. "It's me, Glynnis. I want to talk to Daddy."

Appeased, Glynnis laughed. "Ah, Jade. So you are home. Come right up. Your father has a surprise."

Patsy pressed the buttons to end the call. "It was nice to meet you."

"Likewise." Jaden grinned. "Make sure Daddy gives you a raise. I'm sure he's not paying you enough. And when he complains, tell him I said to use the crowbar to pry open his wallet."

As she strolled to the elevators, her spirits lifted, then wavered. Being personable with the Delish folks wasn't nearly as hard as she remembered. Maybe her mother wasn't so off when she insisted manners weren't so bad. But a surprise? What did he know? Better yet, what did he have to do with the internet fiasco?

The man in the elevator waved his hand, ushering her into the car. As they ascended the floors, he cracked his knuckles. "I know this isn't my place, but why did you make that movie?"

"You're pushy." She pressed her lips together. Nice, I'm supposed to be nice.

"Just curious."

Reaching around him, she pressed the emergency stop button. "You asked, I'll answer. Do you mean the internet clip?" What did this man have to say that she hadn't already heard?

He nodded and folded his arms. "Yeah. I'm no gentleman and I like my dirty movies when the mood strikes, but that wasn't a run-of-the-mill skin flick. You looked like you really cared about him. Why put that on the 'net?"

Folding her arms, she mocked his stance, but not his intentions. "Plain and simple, I did—do—care about that guy a lot, and I didn't post that clip. Someone peeped through my windows and taped it. I didn't find out until it was over, but I don't see why you care."

"You can't shit a shitter, Jaden." He cocked his head. "You don't remember, but we went to high school together."

Studying his features, she remembered the kid with shaggy black hair and vibrant blue eyes who'd always carried around a notebook for doodling and had asked her to go with him to one of the dances. She gasped. "Ron? Ron Harlan?"

He nodded. "One and the same."

Details flew into her mind. He'd given her drawings in study hall and made it a point to tell her she looked pretty. When she'd left and begun the tutoring, he'd stopped by her father's office to say hi and keep her up-to-date with gossip. Even as a teen, he'd always had the inside scoop. "You wanted to be a reporter. Why are you working the elevator here instead of writing comics or thought-provoking stories for the ten o'clock news?"

"Comics... I miss those." He clicked his tongue. "I write in the evenings. I'm in charge of a horror blog called With Teeth and Claws. I reviewed your flick Vampires Unleashed. It wasn't that good."

She cringed. "I hated it, too." Tapping her lip, an idea came to mind. The perfect merging of his talents and her schemes. "Can you write that blog from anywhere?"

"Yeah, why?"

"I'll need a press officer—someone who can write a great release for a pet shelter. I can't pay much yet, but I can guarantee a place to stay. Sound like something you'd like to do?"

His blue eyes widened. "Here in Cali?"

"Nope. In Ohio. Want in? The old office building has five floors, three of which will be the shelter. My private suite will be the top floor if all goes as planned." She grabbed a piece of paper from her purse and jotted down some numbers. "Here's my cell."

A grin blossomed on his lips. "You tell me when and where and I'll be there."

"You mean it?"

"Sure. Blogging by night, working as a press agent by day. Might even get some time in to go back to creating those comics."

"Good. I'll call you next week if the plans pan out." She stuck out her hand. "Isn't it great to have friends in all sorts of places?"

"You bet."

After Ron started the elevator car back up and took her to her father's office on the top floor, she rolled her shoulders again. Why did talking to him seem so impossible? Because the man could eat nails for breakfast and shit roses in full bloom. She checked her makeup and hair in the foyer mirror, fluffing the golden strands. *I can be me and do something worthwhile.*

She pushed open the glass door and mustered her courage. Glynnis, the svelte secretary with piercing brown eyes and hair the unnatural colour of a fire engine, smiled. "So it is you. You're a bit fuller than before? I assume you're eating well out in the sticks."

Jaden narrowed her eyes. "I'd like to speak to my father, please." Some people deserved human kindness, but after the cutting remark, Jaden wanted nothing to do with Glynnis Martine.

The petite secretary rose from her chair. "I'll let Rexx know you're here. He's not happy about the interruption. He's very busy making popular culture come to life. But I'm sure he'll be glad to talk to you."

"A father should want to talk to his child, but I can take care of myself." Instead of giving Glynnis and her father the upper hand, Jaden pushed past the secretary. "He's probably got his flavour-of-the-month girlfriend with him."

"Excuse me, but his flavour is Pia Reardon."

"Oh, he's still with her?" Jaden yanked the door open and spoke over her shoulder. "Great."

Glynnis gasped when Jaden shut the door in her face. When she turned, her father sat on his couch with a platinum blond crouched over his lap. His-button up shirt barely covered his chest where the woman plastered ruby red lip prints over his almond skin.

"Daddy, really!"

Rexx sat up, his hands moving from Pia's butt to her waist. His blue eyes blazed and his mouth opened and closed. "Jade! I told Glyn to let me know when you were here!"

"Jaden! We've missed you." Pia rubbed her slightly protruding stomach. "Does she know our news?"

"I haven't had time," Rexx growled. "Give me a moment with her and then we'll see."

Primping, the woman stood. "I hope you'll accept me in the family." She stuck her hand out, and Jaden just nodded. Pia shrugged. "I'll be back later, Rexie. Miss me when I'm gone."

Jaden forced the bile from her throat. So her father had the right to want human contact. Yes, he was a grown man who had primal urges…but with the blonde bimbo? Sheesh. Darby Haydenweir would pass out if she wasn't rolling over in her grave.

When Pia left the office, Jaden sucked in a long breath and spoke. "So… this is what you do with yourself when you're—" She hooked her fingers in the air. "—working. I'll bet you get a lot done. Are you going to make her an honest woman?"

Buttoning his shirt, Rexx stood at his full six feet. "You aren't an angel, my dear. I see that little video of you has over seven hundred thousand hits. Nice job. I knew I could count on you to take one for the team." He slid his arms through the suit jacket sleeves without looking her in the eye. "I hadn't planned on the clip showing quite as much. For that, I'm sorry."

"You masterminded it?" Her blood ran cold. "I don't believe it."

"I wanted a little necking, some petting. Not nudity and absolutely no drug use. Still, he was a bit below you. He's a cop, for God's sake. He's nothing more than a public servant. If you wanted a man of the law, I'd call your friend Bobby or maybe Jeremy. He's playing a cop on Daytona Homicide. He's a much better suitor."

Clenching her fists, Jaden stepped in front of her father. "Marlon's a damned good cop and he lost his job on account of me."

"Good. He's a shit. He protected my little girl from the prying eyes of the public too well. The world's a better place."

Realisation washed over her like a splash of ice-cold water. "I didn't want to believe my instincts, but it was you all along. You sent that jerk to ruin my chance of having a life of my own!"

"I did no such thing—this time." He adjusted his collar and rolled his shoulders. "Besides, it's nothing you haven't done in the past. Call Joe a bad decision I regret. Bastard cost me an extra fifty K."

"That's it. You sent the blond fan to hunt me down and when he found me, you sent another guy, maybe the same one—I don't know—to follow me. You allowed them to record me and for what? The magazine? Who the fuck do you think you are?"

"Your father."

"You of all people should've protected me from creeps like that—not encouraged them. That was a special, private moment and you stole it from me."

"Hank did his job and should leave you alone. If Joe's bothering you, then I'll have Hank take care of him."

"What? Are you now a mob boss, too? Tell your goons to leave me alone. I'm not a celebrity any longer. I'm Jaden Haydenweir, regular citizen."

"You're right." Rexx picked up his phone and spoke in low tones. After a long moment, he dropped the handset onto his desk. "Your little follower is all gone and you can call off Hutchins. His services aren't needed. Now, what did you come here for? I know it wasn't for a touching family reunion. My relationship with Pia hasn't gone public yet."

Relationship not public? Every magazine and pop culture outlet had images of Rexx and Pia Reardon. "Even if I wanted to say I missed you, I can't. I came here for my trust money."

"I assumed as much. You have to use it for charity. Enlighten me with your scheme, if you have one. How will that benefit the magazine? What are we going to see Miss Jaden Haydenweir, public citizen, do to get the press to pay attention?"

"Walk out of here with my head held high and go back to peace in Ohio. You can have your piece of ass and I can have my freedom." She snorted. "I'll leave you alone so you can make the tabloids churn."

A flicker of emotion lit his eyes for a split second. "Is that all you think I want you for?" His voice cracked.

"No, I know it is." She grinned. She'd got under his skin. Good. She rolled her tongue around her mouth. The furry kids needed her, and if she worked fast enough, Judi would get to see her wishes come to fruition and Marlon would be in her arms. "Why don't we discuss the terms of my trust fund money?"

Rexx snorted. "Your mother wrote it into her will that once you turned twenty-one, you received two million dollars, but you have to use it for a philanthropic purpose. Fat lot of good that did. She also stipulated that I can't touch it. I was her husband! I should've been in charge."

"If you're not, then who is?"

"Your Uncle Gene."

"Fine." Uncle Gene liked her as she was. Heck, he practiced law in jeans when he wasn't in court. He'd help her in an instant. "I'll give him a call and let you have your life."

"Rexx?"

Jaden glanced over her shoulder as Pia re-entered the office, clutching her belly. "You need to feel this! The baby kicked. Our baby moved."

Baby? Our? The handful of crackers Jaden had eaten in the car made their way up her throat. She wasn't sure whether to be happy that her father had someone or sick because she knew what future lay in store for the baby.

"I'll let you have your privacy, Daddy." Jaden flicked a lock of hair from her eyes and forced a smile. "It was nice to see you."

As she left the front office, Glynnis followed her to the elevator. "You can't walk out on your father like that."

Again Jaden spun on her heel. "I didn't, but why do you care? He wants his only daughter—his only child until now—to bare her body for the sake of his magazine? I'm supposed to be a cokehead, riding around drunk in the back of a limo so he can sell glossies? Come on. I'm sorry I took this long to figure him out, but I'm not sorry I'm leaving. I deserve better!"

"She's right."

Jaden's eyes widened. Her father, with his hands folded and his head down stepped into the foyer. "Glynnis, please run down to Mr Gaughan's office. I want to see the prelims on next week's spotlight."

Glynnis snorted and pressed the elevator button. When Ron opened the car, she walked in, but not without a final snarky comment. "He should've given you up when he had the chance. Worthless brat. You're just like Ira."

Ron rolled his eyes and closed the door, shutting out any further comments. Jaden shuffled her feet and stared at the black carpet. She hardly knew Glynnis, so why did the woman hate her so?

"She's right and she's not."

Jaden crossed her arms. "How? She's a raving lunatic."

Rexx sat on the desk. His shoulders sagged. A long sigh escaped his lips. "Honey, it's complicated." He crossed his arms. "I can't live the lie."

Gripping her handbag, Jaden edged to the chair in front of Glynnis' desk. Her heart pounded behind her ribcage. "What lie? And why is she talking about someone named Ira?"

Rexx dropped into the seat next to her. "There's so much you need to know and so many things I did wrong. It's high time you found out the truth." He rubbed his forehead, the creases deepening. Crinkles formed around his eyes. "An hour ago, your former boyfriend called and read me the riot act. He was completely right and I deserved his anger. And just a few moments ago, I stood there caressing Pia's stomach, feeling the glimmer of life I helped create, and it hit me right over the head. I can't screw up another life. I won't."

Folding her hands, Jaden studied her father. The cool demeanour melted. For the first time, she noticed the streaks of grey lacing the jet-black strands of hair and the thinning areas at his temples. The sparkle that once lit his eyes had diminished.

"Marlon's got a mouth on him, but he cares about you." He span the ring on his middle finger—his one reminder of Jaden's mother. "I'm not even sure how to tell you. It's a cluster-fuck my Delish people would love to get their hands on."

"Tell me, Daddy." Even if she didn't want to hear it, she needed the truth.

"Here goes." He sat up, squaring his broad shoulders and nodding. "I'm not your father."

She slumped in her seat. "Yes, you are. You're my dad as much as you are to Pia's baby." Not her... Things didn't make sense. Tears pricked her eyes. "What are you saying?" She clenched her fists. Her words came out in a scream. "Who, then? Who do I belong to?"

He sighed again and his voice cracked. "Your mother never wanted you to find out. She wanted me to keep the secret because Ira Lambert was such a jackass. He beat the living hell out of your mom because he could. He slept around on her and refused to believe you were his. When I met your mom, she'd just finished making the movie Mirabella and had broken things off with Ira. She wasn't looking for a relationship, but the moment I saw her, I dropped to my knees and professed my undying love. She was so beautiful and full of life." He paused and scrubbed his palm over his mouth. "She was pregnant with you when we married. I didn't care. I wanted a little girl to spoil."

Thoughts raced through her mind. Ira Lambert? The photographer from back in the Hamptons? No wonder she'd screwed up her life—it was in her genes. Maybe that was how she'd allowed things to go to hell with Marlon...

And now she was in the same predicament—pregnant and alone.

"When you were five and your momma got sick, I got so angry. The damage from Ira's beatings took their toll on her body. I knew it wasn't your fault, but my anger won out against my common sense." Rexx pinched the bridge of his nose. "I'm sorry. No one knew about the discrepancy until Glynnis found the adoption papers. Ira never wanted you and your mother insisted I adopt you. I did in a heartbeat, but every time I looked at you after she passed, I saw him. I'd lost her despite my best attempts to save her. In my anger, I took it out on you."

Jaden covered her face with her hands. So many crushing moments came to mind. Ira Lambert had worked for Rexx and never bothered to tell her the truth. He didn't want her any more than Rexx had. Even though her heart broke, she needed more answers. "So why let me run wild? Why did you let me act like a fool in front of the entire world?"

"Because I thought I didn't care. Each time you screwed up, I blamed it on Ira. I couldn't bring myself to believe I allowed you to run loose."

She swallowed past the lump in her throat. "But you're my father."

"And I'm sorry I ruined your childhood. My actions screwed up everything." He shook his head, leant forwards and braced his elbows on his knees. "The reality of Marlon's phone call and Pia's pregnancy made me see things in perspective. This little person will grow up and make choices. I can't allow the same stupid decisions I made with you ruin another life. Things between you and me will never be perfect, but I'd like both my children to know I love them."

Stunned by his confessions and his apologies, Jaden's voice broke into a whisper. "So why did you have that man create that internet clip? You not only destroyed my faith in you, you obliterated Marlon's life."

"I told him to catch you two in the act of making out—not sex. Too many things happened with Pia, finding out she's was pregnant, doctor's appointments... I let the goons have too much leash and they bit me in the ass for it. Blinded by my own stupidity, I tried to believe that he somehow got your okay for the video, even though I knew otherwise in my heart." He crossed the room and wrapped her in an embrace. "Please let me make this up to you. I can't bring your mother back and I can't fix my mistakes, but I can help you with your dreams."

The change in his demeanour shocked her. She couldn't process the gravity of his statements, but if he wanted to be a part of her life in a positive way, she'd make him work for it. "You want to help with my wishes or buy my love?"

Rexx's Adam's apple bobbed as he cleared his throat. "Little girl, I can't buy what I don't deserve."

"You're right." She stood and smoothed her skirt. "You don't deserve my forgiveness."

"Jaden, please?"

He'd said the magic words. She turned slowly and looked him straight in the eye. "Let one of your many vice presidents—one you truly trust—take over the magazine for a while and come with me to Ohio. Bring Pia. The fresh air clears the mind and heals the body. Call it a honeymoon of sorts."

Rexx bobbed his head. "Might be a good place to raise the baby."

"Good place to be a grandpa, too."

He froze and his eyes widened. "What? Did you say…?"

"That's the funny thing about the video. I can't erase it, but it hardly seems important in the grand scheme of things, and no, I'm not pregnant." She brushed the tears from her cheeks. "Even if I don't get Marlon, it was worth it."

"Did you know he called me?"

"I was there. I heard it all."

Rexx rubbed the dusting of hairs on his chin. "I don't think so. He called about two hours ago. Made a pretty convincing case."

"For what? Your head on a platter?"

"For your hand in marriage. He said the children needed a stable home. How—how did I not know about four children?"

"I have two cats and two dogs. Four furry kids." She spun her mother's ring around her middle finger. Marriage. Marlon still wanted her? Even after everything? "I hope you told him it was my decision."

"I did."

"Good. I'm not ready to be married anyway."

"You put the man through hell and won't marry him? You've got your mother's sense of humour." Rex stood and tugged her out of her chair, wrapping his arms around her. "You look more and more like Darby every day. I'm glad I didn't lose you completely, too." He stroked her hair. "You said you had a plan for your money. What do you want to do, honey?"

"Create an animal oasis for older folks who don't want to give up their pets and a shelter for pets whose owners can't take care of them anymore. It'll be a place for those animals who have done nothing wrong but have nowhere to go—kinda like me."

"I'm so sorry I made you feel so alone." Her father tucked loose strands of hair behind her ear. "I'm in. What do I need to do?"

"Come with me to Ohio. There's someone I want you to meet, but first, can I use your phone? I need to make a call."

Chapter Twenty-One

"Sunday nights suck."

Marlon checked the blank screen on his cell phone as he walked out of the department towards his Jeep. After the three months since the fiasco at the hospital and the phone call to Rexx, he still felt like shit. He'd got his job reinstated, so he should've been on cloud nine. He replayed Mac's words over and over. "Your drug test came back negative and the clip looks spliced. Your record in the last ten years speaks for itself. I'm glad to say, welcome back."

Orange sunlight glistened off the windows of the department, but the chill of the November evening stirred around him. Without Jaden, things weren't so sunny or warm. Who could he blame? The media? Not entirely. They intruded on his life, but they hadn't shot the video. Her father? Damn straight. If he'd sent the goon, he could rot in hell. Still didn't take the sting away.

The urge to call her and apologise for walking out nibbled under his skin, yet he didn't press the buttons. She'd escaped enough stints in rehab and lied her way out of hospitals the last time she'd been in California. Would she ever really kick her habits?

As he neared his vehicle, the aroma of flowers danced on the bitter breeze and a figure moved in his peripheral vision. He knew the scent. "Jaden?"

His former lover, in the flesh and clutching an enormous navy purse in front of her stomach. She still glowed, but the light wasn't as bright in her eyes. "Hi."

"Hello." His heart ached at the need in her voice and the way her chin quivered. Loneliness barely scratched the surface of his feelings.

"I thought we could clear the air a little."

"You know my number."

"What I need to say has to be said in person. Want to go to the diner? It's warmer."

"I'll be all right here in the open."

"I'm not sure where to start, but I just need you to listen." Her knuckles whitened as she tightened her grip on the bag. "I love you, but I can't accept your asking to marry me

"Because you're seeing Bobby?"

"Bobby has nothing to do with the fact that you don't trust me." She dropped her voice to barely above a whisper. "You need time. I need time. Plain and simple. But I thought we deserved closure."

A beep split the tension and made Jaden jump. "Oh my God. Dammit."

"What?"

"It's Bobby. One of the goons is unaccounted for."

"Does he have a location on this person?" He braced his feet and shoved his hands into his jeans pockets. Marlon rubbed his temple and glanced at the line of cars parked on the opposite side of the street. "What did the missing goon look like?"

"Mid-twenties. Craggy eyes with thick brows. His name is Joe Sutton." Her gaze snapped to his. "You have a bead on him, don't you?"

He dropped his voice to a whisper. "Look to your right. Is that him?"

She turned her head a fraction of an inch and the colour drained from her face. The man fitting Jaden's loose description sat in the driver's seat of a green dented late eighties model Ford, a smile curling from ear to ear as he waved a silver device in his hand. His other hand rested inside his jacket. Did he have a gun, too? Marlon wasn't sure and he refused to find out without some sort of backup.

"Take my phone and call Mac. Speed 2." He placed his cell in her hand. "Get behind me and then crouch behind the car so he can't hurt you."

Based on the size and shape of the object, either Joe had a bomb detonator or a recording device. Both could do maximum destruction.

"What do I say?"

"I need back-up. The man suspected of videotaping Ms Weir is sitting outside the station. Could be armed."

"I love you."

Her words went straight to the empty spot in his soul. She still cared. Never stopped. If it killed him, he'd keep her safe. Then he'd smother her with kisses to make up for their time apart.

Moving as little as possible, Marlon removed his Glock from his shoulder holster and kept it hidden in his jacket. If this was indeed the cretin who'd taped them, he'd go down for invasion of privacy.

"Joe? Joe Sutton?" Marlon nodded to the man and palmed his gun. "Step out of the car."

Using the hand holding the recording device, Joe pushed the door open. "Go play cops with the big boys. Forget I'm here."

"I want to talk to you in connection with Jade Weir." Inching across the quiet street, Marlon palmed his weapon. "I want to see both hands."

"She's here and I have a job to do." No flinch, no backing down. The guy had guts.

"Rexx didn't ask for a skin flick, now drop your weapon." Marlon ground his teeth together. Where was Mac?

"Ain't no law saying I can't have a piece." Hand still in his jacket, Joe clicked a button on the recorder. "I got a hundred K for that video. Easiest money of my life. Made a fool of both Weirs. Now it's your turn."

A pang of guilt surged through Marlon. She had told the truth. The private moment was meant to be just that—private. "You invaded her privacy."

"She's a public figure with a public 'figure' and I'm cashing in."

"I don't see a press pass. Are you admitting you illegally taped Ms Weir engaged in sexual activity? Why do you need a gun?"

"I said it was easy money. Her dad paid me more to shut it down, but I kinda like this lifestyle." Joe shrugged. "I gotta stay safe."

Marlon clicked the safety on his gun. "Hands up so we can talk."

"You can't touch me, asshole." He tipped his head. "Now move to the left."

"You don't give the orders." Marlon's heart hammered against his ribs. "Drop it." Controlling his urge to attack the man, Marlon stared at Joe as Mac moved up behind the goon.

Joe's eyes flashed in the orange light of the setting sun. "You fucked her and now it's my turn to fuck you." Yanking his jacket open, he tossed the recorder and aimed the gun. "You made a good blip, but her life was so much more exciting when you weren't around." The click of the safety disengaging split the air. "Goodbye."

Marlon ducked as Mac charged Joe. The wild shot whizzed past his ear.

"No one kills my officers under my watch," Mackenzie growled. The handcuffs glinted as he clicked them around Joe's wrists. "Marlon, is Jaden okay? Check on your girl. I've got the son of a bitch."

"Fuck." Marlon jerked around, searching for Jaden. If she was hurt, he wouldn't be held accountable for his actions. "Babe?"

"Down here." Tears streamed down her cheeks as she gave him two thumbs up from her crouch next to the car. "You did it. You got rid of my peeper."

Marlon dropped to his knees and wrapped her in his arms. Fuck the rest of the world for a few moments. She was safe. He breathed in the flowery scent of her hair and basked in the softness of her body. God, he'd missed her.

"You'll squeeze me to death." Her muffled voice vibrated against his shoulder.

He inched back, releasing her from his tight grip. Tell her you love her, the voice in the back of his mind urged. "We need to go fill out paperwork."

"Of course." Grabbing his hand, she stood and brushed loose strands of hair behind her ears. "This makes you a hero."

Her hero?

She wobbled and grasped his sleeve. "I need to sit."

"You okay?" A quick glance from her head to her toes revealed no blood. He swallowed past the lump in his throat. "I can call the EMT."

"I'll be fine. Just a little dizzy."

"Then let's get you inside."

"No, I came here to do something and I'm going to do it." She took a long breath and let it out slowly. "When I came to Crawford, I felt complete. I felt like I was the woman I'm supposed to be. I can't get rid of the circus, but I liked being lowbrow. I liked being with you."

She sighed, the sound drawn out as she bowed her head. Resignation?

"Marlon, the internet leak wasn't of my making. If I had my way, I'd erase it from public viewing. One of Daddy's goons shot the footage. The order was to stop at sex, but he didn't. I lost a part of me when that went viral, but I never meant to hurt you."

She'd offered her heart and bared her soul. The words I love you lingered on his tongue.

"But we're not meant to be. You think Bobby's in the picture and I can't be sure Sabrina's not."

"What are you saying?"

She placed her hand over his heart. "Please remember me when you find the woman of your heart. I want you to look back at our time together fondly." Tears glistened on her cheeks. "Goodbye, Marlon."

He moved his mouth, but no sound came out. She offered him a wobbly smile and wandered into the department to give her statement. Running after her sounded like a damned good idea, but his feet refused to move.

The woman of his heart had slipped right through his fingers.

* * * *

Eight hours later, Marlon sat at his desk digesting the turn of events. He clicked the button on his pen. In her own way, Jaden had saved his life. Dropping the writing instrument, he closed his eyes. God knew he needed the vacation. He had an ass-load of paperwork to catch up on first. Dammit. For one of the rare times in his life, he hated his job.

The squeak of footsteps on linoleum broke his train of thought.

"Jaden left something at the house and Mom asked me to deliver it." When he opened his eyes, Steven stood before Marlon's desk, hands behind his back. "You want it?"

"I don't know when I'll see her again." His thoughts turned to Jaden. The moment she'd told him she loved him in the living room. The times she'd called him names on the front porch. Making his heart soar while sprawled on the dining room table. Damn. He missed the sounds she made while laying next to him. Remembering each whimper, sigh, and hum jerked at his heart.

The more he thought about it, the more he realised she'd always been a part of him. With Jaden around, things were fun. She turned to him when she needed someone. Not the celebrity playboys, not the millionaires she ran with before. She chose him.

Her smile, something so simple, brightened his life. She might not be in the same room, but she was part of him just the same. She filled the holes in his soul. Through every oddball incident, every smile and tear, he loved her all the more.

"Mom's adamant this is yours to give Jaden, so take it." He pushed the box across the desktop with one finger. "I hope you're part of the bomb squad. I was forbidden from opening it."

Drawing Marlon's attention from his musings, Steven plopped down in the plastic chair.

"Right." Marlon shook his head. "I'm not the bomb squad, but I'll check it out."

"Mom's delirious." Folding his thick arms, Steven leant back a bit in his seat. "Said you had to have it in order for Jaden to get it. Why she waited three months is beyond me."

Rubbing his hands on his jeans legs, Marlon stared at the object. Wine-coloured lace festooned the outside while a pearlescent ribbon kept the lid closed. Steven leant forwards in his seat. "Open it already. I didn't think they had this kinda crap at the home and I want to know what it is."

Narrowing his eyes as he glanced at Steven, Marlon tugged the slippery ribbon. The sides of the lid popped open, revealing a letter and a smaller box. He withdrew the envelope. The side was torn as if someone tampered with it. He unfolded the crinkled paper, grinning as Judi's distinctive scrawl lined the page. He smiled and set the box aside to read.

This gift is intended for Marlon Cross. If you're Steven, put this back or I'll cross you off the list in my will. I'm not dead yet and I will have Marlon arrest you for tampering. (If you're Marlon, you can do that, right?)

Marlon — when I first met you, I knew you'd be over a lot. She's part of you and you can't forget her no matter how hard you try. I want you to do something for me. In the little box, you'll find something given to me a long time ago. It's mine to bestow. You'll know when you need to use it.

Don't wait too long. You both deserve to be happy.
Love,
Judi

Marlon slumped in his seat, the weight of the page heavy in his hands. Love. The bad things didn't really matter any longer. It was time to get down to loving her the way she deserved.

He reached for the smaller box. The dark brown felt contrasted with the pale complexion of his palm. Once again, he glanced around the room. Open the box or wait. Might as well know. He flicked open the lid and the wind rushed from his lungs. The emerald set in the simple gold band matched the green in Jaden's eyes. Judi had given him the ring out of love. Could he in turn, give it to Jaden? She'd turned him down once before.

"You gonna sit here and gaze at that piece of costume jewellery or you leaving to do what my mom wants? Dinner's on the table at home and I wanna go."

Marlon glared at Steven. If he wasn't mistaken, the gem wasn't manmade. "Costume jewellery?"

"Dad used to give her frilly crap like that after a fight. He'd say, 'Your mother means more to me than any coloured rock, but if it makes her smile, it's worth every cent'. It's junk, the jewellery, the line, all of it."

"Thank you for bringing it by. I'll make sure she gets it."

Steven grunted and stood. With a nod, he limped out of the station.

Marlon toyed with the ring and sat back in his chair. So Judi found value in 'junk'. Hadn't Jaden said she was little more than 'junk'? According to Judi's note, he'd know when to give Jaden the ring.

She'd said she needed time.

The scent of her perfume, the taste of her kisses, the feel of her body against his came to mind. She permeated his life and damn, it sucked without her.

Across the room, Carol Ann sat at her desk pounding away on the computer keyboard. She held up a piece of paper "Deputy Cross. Message."

He jumped out of his seat and snatched the note from her hand. "You're being awfully formal."

"You are a deputy and I am to address you as such." She cracked her gum. "I'm delivering a message and trying to finish this report. Mac wants it by the end of the day and that's only a couple of minutes away. Besides, it's Saturday and I've got a date with Craig tonight." Her mouse clicks echoed in the room. "Oh, and you have a visitor in the interrogation room. He showed up while you were talking to Mr Pennywood. The guy says he won't leave until you—and only you—speak to him, so you have to stick around."

"Does this him have a name?"

"Rexx Weir."

He froze. Rexx…Weir? Dear God. Jaden's father. Marlon clenched and unclenched his fists. He faced murderers, robbers, angry drunks, and the occasional coyote. He knew how to use a gun and had passed his proficiencies with the highest marks. Even Addy's alcohol-fuelled tirades hadn't scared him. He'd argued with the asshole three times over the phone. Why not air things in person?

"If you need me, I'll be in I-one with him."

Carol Ann waved and returned to her report. For a man who generally had no fear, Marlon was currently an equal combination of hard-ass and scared shitless. He knocked on the door and strode into the cramped room. "Mr Weir, I'm Deputy Cross. I hope you're enjoying your time in Jarvis County. Here in Crawford, we strive to show you the cream of the crop of Ohio. Now, the secretary says we need to chat. What's on your mind? You aren't filming this for future use? I'm not ready for my close-up."

Rexx scooted back in his chair. "Call me Mr Haydenweir." His salt-and-pepper hair glittered in the harsh fluorescent lighting. He wrinkled his nose, making his moustache twitch. Folding his long hands, he crossed his legs. "I owe you an apology, although after your comments I wonder if it's deserved. I came here with the intention of making peace, not adding to the problem." He sighed. "And meeting you in person, I see why you're the problem."

Marlon crossed his arms. "I'm the problem? I beg to differ. I didn't post nude photos of her online or ruin an innocent man's career." He gritted his teeth. He wanted her back, not to push her further away. Arguing with her father wasn't going to win him points.

"Uh-huh." Rexx stroked his chin. "You're a jerk, you're callous, and despite your bravado, you're determined to prove you aren't hurting as well."

Marlon crooked his brow. "You got all that out of my short statement? Maybe we need you as an interrogator."

"I'm in the business of people-watching. I have an uncanny ability to tell when people are uncomfortable. You, my friend, are so out of your comfort zone, it's not funny." He chuckled. "I have to give my girl credit. She got under your skin. She's good at that, just like her mother."

Ego deflated, Marlon sighed. "She did, but with the Hollywood circus surrounding her, I don't know where I fit in. If I'm to believe her, she's not mine to worry about."

"What if I told you I've been in your shoes and know you're making a mistake by letting her go?"

"I'd laugh."

Rexx stood. "Want to try this again? I can see it in your eyes—you're not ready to let her get away." He withdrew a piece of paper from his breast pocket. "This is an invitation to the grand opening of Please Remember Me, tomorrow night. You are cordially invited, and I highly suggest you attend. It's black tie, so you might want to rent a tux if you don't have one."

Marlon folded the cardstock invitation and stuffed it, along with his hands, into his pockets. "I'll see what I can do. I'm on call tomorrow night."

"You've got an evening to think things over." Rex stabbed a finger at Marlon. The creases around his eyes deepened and a frown marred his lips. His voice held a hard edge. "Don't be an ass because you think it makes you look right. Take it from me. You'll have a lot happier life if you give in to her and let her smother you with love.

Looking right when you're completely wrong feels like shit."

Marlon palmed the invitation as Mr Haydenweir walked out of the station. What the hell was Please Remember Me? And why did Rexx swear he needed to attend a gala? He didn't have a tuxedo and wasn't keen on dancing or mingling with the upper crust of Crawford society. He raked his fingers through his hair and sighed. He had to stop the nervous gesture or he'd be bald soon. The silence in the office suffocated him.

Time to go home.

He shuffled out into the parking lot, but stopped. Bobby Hutchins sat on the hood of the Jeep. Marlon rubbed his forehead. "Aren't you supposed to be somewhere else?"

"You gonna go?"

"Go to hell, Hutchins. You've done enough damage, I never want to see your ugly ass again."

Bobby slid off the hood and finger-combed his hair. His gaze didn't quite meet Marlon's. "I didn't sleep with her."

"Give it a rest."

Groaning, Bobby looked up. "Yeah, I'll admit it. I fucked Addy. I snuck around with Sabrina and I had one God damned one-nighter with Jade, but I never, ever slept with Jaden once she came back. She told you the truth and I'm sorry I was a shit."

"Bob—"

"I put the moves on her and she turned me down."

Marlon's mouth went dry. She'd turned Bobby down? His world tilted on its axis. He drew a hard breath into his lungs and let it flow over his lips. "I have to go and think."

"Don't take too long."

Chapter Twenty-Two

"What do you think, Sparks? Is it beautiful?" Jaden rubbed her brow and dropped the paintbrush back into the empty can. Three months of hard work translated into a nearly complete remodelling of the building and the completion of her dream. The dog barked, his nails scraping on the hardwood behind her.

"I like it, too." She nodded and drew a satisfying breath. "What do you think, Judi?"

Hands clapped to her right. "Oh, I love it. Who knew hunter green could be so pretty! It makes the whole room seem warm, like a giant hug." Judi snickered and wheeled up next to Jaden. "I never thought I'd see the day. Your half-formed plan is fantastic."

Jaden turned and grasped Judi's hand. "Well, you gave me the idea. I'm glad I ran away and moved to Ohio. PRM is the best thing I ever did."

"You're sure you're okay?"

"Never better." She gave Judi's hand a squeeze. "Marlon dances to his own beat and my pushing won't help. I'm giving him space."

"You've become a wise girl since you moved here. How is Pia? Did she have a boy or girl?"

"Neither. The doctor said it was false labour pains and she's still got another month to go. She's upstairs lying down. The flight was too much for her, even with Daddy's personal physician on board."

"Have you talked to Marlon?"

"I nearly got him killed. I'm sure he wanted to talk, but I ended the relationship before he broke my heart."

"I love your flair for the dramatic, but I really think you need to talk to him again. It's the only way."

"I want to call him, but I'm scared I caused too much trouble and wasted too much time. For all I know, he still thinks Bobby's a threat for my attention."

A voice called from the great room. "Jaden!"

"Oh dear. You'd better help the help before they go rogue!" Judi giggled again. "We need all the hands we can get."

Jaden rushed into the adjacent room. Logan, Corbin, and Ray Russell stood in the middle of the space holding an enormous oak desk. "What's going on, guys? It looks great."

Corbin groaned. "We wanted you to give the okay on this. Is this finally where you want the welcome desk? 'Cause it's getting heavy and these two are pansies."

She pointed to the floor. "Right there is perfect."

After the men edged the oak desk into place, Logan jabbed Corbin in the arm. "Pansy, my ass. This thing is heavy. Would've helped if you'd put your back into it."

Ray scrubbed a hand over his bald head. "I think you both got soft." He turned to Jaden. "How many animals are slated to be here?"

"Besides my four, five will be here to start. The nursing home wants to work with us to bring in at least three more. I'm also planning on adopting a couple more cats from the APL to give Unruly and Tantrum someone to play with besides terrorising the dogs."

Corbin stepped back from the cabinet and blew a puff of air over the end of the drill. "It's screwed down, nice and tight. So you like?"

She applauded. "I love it. Judi! You have to see this!"

Footsteps echoed on the hardwood floor. A man's voice rang through the room. "We have the photograph!" Cade and Melanie Nicholson strolled into the foyer. Cade placed the large frame on the now-stable desk. "This is one of Mel's best pieces."

Jaden took a deep breath as Cass wheeled Judi and Julian into the room. Time for the good news. "Well, since you're all here — well, save for Les — I have some things to say and no, Pia didn't go into labour. If she had, Daddy wouldn't be here." She clasped her hands together to keep them from trembling. Marlon should've been there. He should've helped her. She forced those thoughts aside. No need to dwell on what couldn't be. "You all know or have some good ideas about where my head was about three years ago. Since then, I found my heart and the woman I was always meant to be."

Starring at her hands, then at her friends, she continued. "First I want to thank Logan for dumping me like hot lead. I don't like knowing I slept with an asshole, but I learnt from the experience. Cass, thank you for being that big sister I needed a long time ago. If it weren't for you, I'd be homeless and friendless right now. I'd thank Bobby, but he's on patrol. Ray, Corbin, thanks for being my muscle. We've had a rocky relationship at times, but I still think you're the best. Cade, Mel, this photograph and many more of yours will decorate the walls of this shelter, bringing joy to all those who visit. Thanks. I owe you all big time for spending your free time helping me learn to paint and lay hardwood flooring without making a huge mess."

Nodding to Cade, she helped him stand the paper-covered photo on the floor. "Now this is a bit large for me to hold, but it'll be great over the desk. Judi, this is thanks to you and Sparks for not giving up on me when no one thought I could do anything."

Starting from the corner, she ripped the paper aside. The image of Judi and Sparky filled the frame. Judi covered her mouth with both hands. Tears streamed down her cheeks. As if he knew the tears were for him, Sparky threw his head back and howled.

Rubbing the slight swell of her stomach, Jaden crouched next to her friend. "I know you can't live here, but between Daddy, Cass, and I, we got the permits, equipment, and funding that anyone, regardless of their situation can come in and be with their pets. It's my way of saying thank you to you and a remembrance for all those who had to say goodbye to their furry friends. My goal is that no more cats, dogs, birds, or other small animals will be abandoned."

Having said her thank yous, Jaden collapsed into tears. Her father wrapped an arm around her. "I'm proud of you. Even though you took my best elevator operator, I'm proud."

"Thanks, Daddy." She brushed her hair from her eyes. "Your scheming helped make this possible, too."

The room erupted in applause. She blotted her tears with the back of her hand. "You think this was a sob-fest, wait until tonight. Daddy's throwing a black tie gala in honour of the grand opening. You all have to come as my guests of honour. I've even reserved tuxes for Sparks and Riley."

Logan cleared his throat. "What about Marlon?"

She sighed. The topic of Marlon had to come up sometime. She'd severed ties with him and yet he cropped up in her mind almost every other second. Jaden glanced at her father, who shook his head. Smacking her lips, she nodded. "Crawford PD has agreed to cordon off the street during the event. I even have some of Daddy's security staff from Delish coming in to provide their services. After the shooting, Marlon and I decided we needed some time to think and decide what we want. I want him here, but if he attends, he attends. If not, then not." She waved her hands as if to dismiss her crestfallen emotions. "But that's not important. In less than forty-eight hours, we're going to open and celebrate and tonight we'll have a great time."

Once again, the room erupted in applause. Still, she fought back tears and clutched her belly. Maybe Marlon really didn't need her any longer. He hadn't called to convince her she'd made a mistake. For all she knew, he was on-call or still tying up loose ends on the Sutton case. Jaden needed Marlon—not to live, but to make life better.

Judi squeezed Jaden's hand. "Have some faith. Things don't always happen the way you want when you want, but good things do come to those who believe."

Dropping her forehead to the top of Judi's head, Jaden laughed. The warmth of Judi's advice wrapped around her like a verbal hug. "Then I'll believe."

Chapter Twenty-Three

Twenty-four hours after his meeting with Rexx Weir, Marlon drove down Main Street. If asked, he'd say he was drawn by the searchlights dancing across the darkened sky. In truth, his curiosity had got the better of him—he wanted to see Jaden. He scrubbed a hand over his chin. Jaden could make anything a huge party. He skidded through the light coating of snow on the road. He wondered if she thought about him. According to her father, she missed him. Thinking about the recent past made him cringe.

Marlon parked in the farthest spot in the jam-packed public lot. Across the way, the former Buchanan Building now bore a stylish sign reading, Please Remember Me. Marlon scratched his head and replaced his hat. What a stupid name for a nightclub. The more he stared at the neon blue lettering, the more he realised it was the name on the invitation. What did Rexx Weir aka Rex Haydenweir have to do with anything in Crawford, Ohio?

Unless his daughter was behind the remodel. Could Jaden really be there?

Locking the cruiser, he zipped his parka and trudged across the snowy street towards the party. At the door, he nodded to the bouncer and flashed his badge. "Hi. I'm Deputy Cross. What's going on? Is this the party for Please Remember Me?"

The bouncer, a bald behemoth with a heavy silver hoop in his left earlobe crooked a thick black brow. "Are you on the guest list?"

"I should be. Rexx Weir hand-delivered my invitation."

"Cross?" He flipped pages on the black clipboard, the sound rustling against the string music filtering out of the building. "You're name isn't on my list, but since you're the law, I'll let you in." Stuffing the clipboard under his massive arm, the bouncer unhooked the red velvet rope. "But, if you give anyone trouble because you're drinking and getting rowdy, I don't care who you are, you'll be out on your ass."

Marlon nodded. The man couldn't touch him, but still — better to avoid a confrontation. He stepped past the ropes and into the great room of the building. How the hell had Rexx and Jaden planned the shindig without him even getting a murmur?

Streamers of black, red, and silver draped from the ceiling. An eight-piece string orchestra sat in the corner providing mood music, something from the late nineties if he wasn't mistaken. Glittering lights sparkled on the guests and the hunter green walls. The men wore tuxedoes, while the women had donned evening gowns. He groaned. "I don't belong," he muttered. "I've gotta change."

"So you did show!"

He whirled around. "Well, hello, Summer. How are you?" Okay, he'd been spotted. Leaving without embarrassing himself wasn't going to happen.

Summer, decked out in a strapless crimson dress, grinned. "I didn't think you'd make it. You've been kind of grumpy as of late."

"It happens." He scoured the crowd. Who else would spot him? About ten feet away, his fellow deputy Bobby Hutchins danced with a redhead whose name he couldn't recall. Rexx Weir stood on the small platform laughing with a woman Marlon didn't recognise. Whoever she was, the way Rexx caressed her stomach and smiled, she had to be someone important. Marlon snorted. Rexx didn't strike him as a decent father figure. Still, the loving gesture made him miss Jaden all the more.

Time to stop missing and start making amends.

Summer rested her hand on his shoulder, pulling him close. "You might as well get comfy. You're stuck. Sabrina's here and Jaden's on the platform with her father and his fiancée, actress Pia Reardon. She looks adorable pregnant. Speaking of adorable, Jaden looks awesome in silver. I should be jealous, but I'm not. She's quite a lady."

He focussed on the platform. Sure enough, Jaden strode across the dais arm in arm with a raven-haired man. Her grin spread from ear to ear as she spoke to the new man. Marlon's heart thumped against his ribcage. Was she involved with him? They appeared rather cosy. Jealousy slid through his veins. He wanted to make her smile. He clenched his fists. The silver gown draped over her creamy shoulder and flowed over her form, clinging to her more ample curves.

He'd waited too long.

"Oh, and I'll warn you, Sabrina's ready for a fight. She showed up with that B-list actor, Fallon Stone, but he—like every other man in the county—is interested in Jaden. It's a big mess." Summer chewed the corner of her mouth. "You aren't still involved with Sabrina, are you?"

He shook his head. "She was a mistake. As for Jaden, I see she's doing well without me."

Summer snorted. "I think you should ask her to dance, for old time's sake."

"You're kidding?" His mouth gaped open. "I'm in uniform. I stick out in this crowd, not that I belong here to begin with."

"Then she can't say she can't see you coming." With that, Summer gave him a nudge forwards.

Making his way through the throng of people, Marlon headed for the dais. Summer's vague words played over and over again in his head. Yes and no. Could Jaden want him forever? He'd never know if he didn't come right out and ask.

As he neared the fringe of partygoers, Jaden's voice rose above the others. "What would I do without you? This is as much your doing as mine." He glanced at her position. Closing her eyes, she leant in to the raven-haired man's arm and rested her head on his shoulder. Marlon's heart shrivelled within his chest. She'd moved on.

Another voice caught his attention. "Marlon! Honey!"

He turned. Sabrina, decked out in a black-and-white striped wrap dress strode to him. Cringing, he forced a smile to his lips.

Pressing her breasts against his chest, she wrapped her arms around his neck. "You are so hot in your uniform. It makes me want to yank you out back for a quickie."

Her alcohol-tinged breath warmed his face. He gagged. When in hell had he found her attractive? When he didn't have an alternative and his life had been at rock bottom. He might be low, but he wasn't falling for her crap any longer.

Marlon sneaked a glance at the dais. Rexx and the blonde woman danced and laughed, but Jaden wasn't in sight.

"You won't find our former fuck friend up there." Sabrina wobbled on her stiletto sandals. "She's right behind you."

Trying to disengage from Sabrina, Marlon turned. Jaden stood before him. Her smile appeared forced. "I'm glad you could make it, Marlon. I hope you enjoy the rest of the gala. Sabrina, I wish you the best. Thanks for supporting us."

Before he could stop her, Jaden walked away. The sight of her ass in silver silk made his mouth water. Her practiced, poised response jarred him. Something wasn't right.

Sabrina cackled. "I do believe you are now back on the market, and I'm ready to take you home."

With a snort, Marlon wriggled from her grasp. The sight of sadness buried in Jaden's green eyes felt like a kick to the gut. He caused her sorrow—him and the mess he'd made of the life he had with her. Enough was enough. "Sabrina, I'm not a piece of meat and I'm not on the market. If you want a man in a uniform, why don't you chase down one of the bouncers? They can handle your strong-arm manoeuvres better than I can. I'm sorry I can't stay and listen to your lies and stories. I'm going after the woman of my dreams."

Jaden swallowed past the lump in her throat. In his uniform, he took her breath away. She'd severed the relationship and taken the high road, but it didn't diminish the urge to forget her pride and admit to the public she loved him. Maybe she'd been wrong to walk away. He made her feel safe, protected her in the clutch, and claimed to love her in return. As she left the great room and headed for the solace of the cuddle room, footsteps echoed on the hardwood floor.

Without looking, she spoke. "Ron, I'm fine. The morning sickness passed. I just wanted some air."

"Morning sickness?"

She froze. Marlon's voice slipped over her senses, sending a shimmer through her veins. Although she didn't turn around, his warmth enveloped her. He deserved the truth. "Yes, morning sickness. I'm fifteen weeks along."

Behind her, Marlon gasped. Using his large hands, he turned her to face him. His touch warmed her chilled skin. "Does the father know?"

Worry etched his face, crinkling around his eyes. His jaw clenched. Even angry, hurt, and sad, he turned her on. What should she say? You can do the math? Nah. Remember our tryst on the dining room table? Not quite. I still love you and want to raise our child here in Ohio? Nibbling her bottom lip, she found the words. Forget the world around them. Marlon was the only person who mattered.

"You do now."

His eyes widened and he inched away from her, wobbling a bit. "Me?"

Twining her fingers together to hide the shaking, she nodded. "I wanted to call you so many times, but I wasn't sure what to say. Whatever I'd have told you would've been on the evening gossip shows. I refused to let you find out any way but from me. I'm sorry I waited so long."

His mouth opened and closed like a fish. "I wish you'd have told me right when you found out." His shoulders sagged. "I'm gonna be a dad and I had no idea."

Tears pricked her eyes. The weight of her mistakes pressed down on her heart and tore at her soul. "I tried to be strong and stick to my decisions, but so many other things happened—Daddy and Pia and the baby. I didn't know what to do and I refused to lose my independence." The words came out in a blubbering rush. "Things aren't the same as they were three months ago, and I'm sorry I wasn't strong enough to deal with it."

"Start at the beginning." Smoothing his hands over hers, Marlon helped her to the nearby couch. "I think we have a lot to talk about."

She mumbled the first thought in her head. "Are you with Sabrina?"

The smile on his lips lit up his eyes. "I haven't been with anyone else since the day you showed up on my doorstep."

She reeled. No one else? "But Sabrina insisted—"

He placed a callused finger over her lips. The salt of his touch lingered on her tongue. He leaned in close. "She's trying to make trouble like a certain former socialite did for someone else we know. If you slept with Sabrina, fine. If not, that's fine, too. We all have bits and pieces of our lives we're not proud of, but we learn from them."

She whimpered. As much as he was right, he was so wrong. "You sound like a psychobabble greeting card." She smoothed away her tears with the pad of her thumb. "I know I'm not the woman who makes your heart beat.

I'll never live up to the memory of Addison and I can't erase my past. I don't want to be another reminder of mistakes in your life, so I'll drop a note in the mail when the baby comes."

Cupping her jaw, his thumb caressed her cheek. "You'll do no such thing."

"What?" He couldn't want to take the child. She'd fight him tooth and nail. The baby hadn't arrived, but she loved him or her just the same.

"I love you, Jaden Marie."

He what? She shook her head. No way he meant what he said. "You can't. I saw you with Summer and Sabrina. You want your freedom and safety and solace. I'll tie you down. And what if the media shows? I'll screw things up."

"Sweetheart, I've had a lot of time to think and be an asshole. Here's my truth. Tie me down and keep me forever. Addison is a part of my past I'll never forget, even if it wasn't my brightest moment. Saying you're like her was a mistake. Summer is a good friend. Sabrina means nothing to me." Drawing her close, he rubbed his nose on hers. "But you—you are my future. I want the picket fence, two dogs and two cats, toddler strolling around the house, happily-ever-after life with you. You make my heart beat and my cock throb. I'm glad the farce is through. I missed you too much."

He nibbled on her lips, tempting her for more. She opened for him and her sigh filled the room. The man addicted her like no drug or drink could. His strong arms tugged her into his lap. She shivered and twined her fingers through his hair. His erection pressed against her bottom, not that she complained. Things were far from perfect, but at least she'd found her home, safe and secure.

When they parted for air, Marlon kept her close. "What's in your heart, Jaden Marie? Who is in your soul?"

Between gasps, she told him her truth. "You."

Before he could respond, the door to the cuddle room slammed shut. Jaden jerked in her seat. Sabrina plastered herself against the wooden barrier, a pair of beautician's shears in her hand. Her eyes blazed. "You can't have him. He's mine and I'll rip your bloody little heart out if you try to challenge me!"

Jaden clutched her stomach. Sabrina could beat the living hell out of her as long as she didn't harm the baby. "You're better than this, Sabrina."

Marlon edged out from under her and stood. He put himself between the couch and Sabrina. "What are you doing?" With his hands in the air, he inched towards her. "You're going to ruin all the things you worked for, like your spot at Callum and Callum. Jaden's right. You're a good actress and accountant. Don't throw your new career away over me. I'm not worthy of you."

Although she knew he was pumping Sabrina's ego to calm her down, Jaden winced. Her gaze darted around the room. Why the heck hadn't she put a phone near the couch? Pushing herself off the sofa on unsteady legs, she edged towards Marlon. If she slipped his cell phone from his belt, she could call for help. She held Sabrina's gaze as she moved forwards.

"No you don't." Sabrina surged towards Marlon and slapped Jaden's hand from his waist. "I'll stab him through the heart if you try something so stupid." Her eyes narrowed to angry slits. "My life was perfect until you showed up. Marlon and I had a rocky time, but we were on the verge of working it out. Then you came along and shot my world to hell just like on the set of Kicks. I won't have my heart ripped apart again."

From the corner of her eye, Jaden noticed Logan and Corbin strolling down the hallway. Gain their attention. Her gaze vacillated between Sabrina and the door. Now or never.

"Help me!"

"Bitch. I loved you." Sabrina lunged at Marlon, swinging the shears. At the same time, Logan shoved the door open. As the barrier gave way, Marlon strong-armed Sabrina into a headlock. The shears slipped from her fingers, plinking across the floor. "Don't do this to me, Marlon! I love you. We belong together."

Logan sprinted into the space, his footsteps muffled on the carpet. "What the hell? Are you hurt, Jaden?"

Collapsing into Logan's arms, Jaden forced her gaze to Marlon. He had Sabrina on the ground with her hands behind her back. "That's what you get for trying to hurt my fiancée," Marlon snapped. "Never again."

Corbin knelt next to Marlon. "I called nine-one-one. Back-up should be here in a second." He tapped the floor near Sabrina's face. "That'll teach you not to fuck with the law. Marlon knows mixed martial arts."

"Your fiancée? Jaden? Should I know something here?" Logan did a double-take. "I don't know martial arts, but I have your back."

"I don't know what's going on." Jaden stared at Marlon. "I need to sit down."

Before she could say more, two uniformed officers and the bouncer from the door stormed into the room. Dropping her head to Logan's shoulder, Jaden let the tears flow. Blame it on the hormones and the never-ending disasters in her wake. Logan caressed her shoulder with the pads of his fingers. "Marlon's got this under control. He's a good man—a little slow to come around, but a good guy."

Wriggling from his arms, she collapsed onto the couch and buried her face in her hands. After what seemed like an eternity, but was probably only a few minutes, a pair of putty-coloured knees edged between her sandal-clad feet. When she looked up, Marlon smiled his crooked grin. He smoothed his fingers over her jaw. "It's all over, Jaden Marie. You're safe."

Her resolve shattered as the gravity of the events collapsed down around her in a landslide. "Safe? What's safe? You mean no paparazzi chasing me to get pictures of me doing stupid things, no strange women threatening me with scissors because they thought we'd had a romantic relationship, no more forcing those who care about me to leave me because I'm a hot mess?" Fresh tears slid down her cheeks. "I just wanted to create a place for animals to go when no one wanted them. I wanted them to be happy. I wanted to be happy and free from Daddy's constraints."

Wiping her tears away with kisses, Marlon rested his forehead against hers. "And you created it."

"Create? I wreck everything I touch." She picked at the buttons on his shirt. Her voice caught. "Why do you love me?"

"I can't explain why, I just know I do." He cocked his head. "There's more going on in that beautiful head of yours. Let me in, baby girl."

Time to unburden herself. "Rex isn't my father. My life is one big lie."

"How?"

"When I went to California, I asked for my money—my trust from my mother. Long story short, when Pia's baby kicked, he realised all the mistakes he'd made with me and how much he still loved Momma. He said until that moment, he'd forgotten how much I meant to him, because he only ever saw my real father when he looked at me. He'd wasted sixteen years of my life allowing that hatred to sour our relationship. I don't want that with you or the baby."

Pulling her down astride his lap, he wrapped his arms around her. "No way in hell. I finally got you back in my arms. I'm not letting you go. Ever."

A cross between a laugh and a cry escaped her throat. She pressed her face in to his neck. Her world righted on its axis. Marlon loved her. He wanted her—forever.

His hands smoothed over her hair. "I love you, Jaden Marie. In front of the press, in the eyes of God, our friends, yeah, I love you."

Looking him straight in the eye, she dragged air into her lungs. "Do you want the baby? Tell me you want us."

He rubbed the knuckle of his middle finger over her belly. "A mini Cross? You bet—and his or her mother. We're a pretty damned good team."

Tears of joy fell from her eyes. "I love you, Marlon."

"Then marry me."

"Before the baby comes?"

"Whenever you want, baby girl, as long as you're willing to be Jaden Cross."

Covering her mouth with her hands, she cried yet again—this time happy tears.

"I know this is probably a hormone overload, but is that a yes? 'Cause if you want to wait until I walk out to the cruiser, I have a ring—a very special one."

She threw her arms around his neck. "I can't wait to see it."

"I have a question or two. We arrested Joe and impounded his Ford. Who is this new, mysterious, black-haired guy, anyway?"

"That's Ronny Harlan, my publicist for the shelter. I went to school with him, but he's not a threat. He's got a thing for Goth chicks."

"And Bobby?"

"Was a mistake I wish I could take back."

"What's going on in here?"

Jaden and Marlon turned in tandem. Judi sat in the doorway, with Sparky and Riley on either side of her wheelchair. Both dogs barked. "What's going on? The party isn't fun without you..." A bright grin spread across her face. "Marlon! So nice to see you. And I assume you have that piece of jewellery you found."

Jaden's gaze vacillated between Marlon and Judi. "You two conspired."

"Apparently, she wanted to make sure when I actually proposed, it would be something special." Marlon nodded. "I'm sorry I waited too long to show you I really love you."

"You both needed the time apart. It was for your own good, Jaden, honey." Judi folded her hands on her lap. "When I saw that you weren't happy because he strolled out of your life, and that he wasn't acting right because he needed you, I instigated a little Judi-intervention. Have you asked her? Because I wanted to see you ask her."

Chuckling, Marlon nodded again.

Judi cocked a brow. "And what is your answer, missy?"

Jaden glanced at Judi, then the dogs and finally at Marlon. The things she wanted the most in life were right at her feet. All she needed to do was grasp them with both hands and live. Easier done than said. "Sparky has been lonely without you. He won't shut up, barking at all hours of the night and day, and in this building, it echoes." She nibbled her bottom lip. "Would you be willing to live with us upstairs? I have the top floor of the building all to myself. And if you are, there's a garage and everything so we don't have to park in the street."

He silenced her with a kiss. The joining turned primal in an instant. She whimpered and melted into his embrace. She belonged with him. Her stomach did flip-flops...or was it the baby? Hell, she wasn't sure. When they parted for air, Jaden gasped. "I'll marry you. I love you, Marlon."

"Hot damn! I'm going to get to wear pink after all!" Judi clapped her hands and grinned.

"Do you think Sparks will walk me down the aisle? He helped bring us together."

"I'm sure of it."

Chapter Twenty-Four

Kicking her feet up, Jaden leant back in her blessedly overstuffed office chair. If anyone had bothered to tell her about six months earlier that having a child was so labour-intensive, she might have shied away from the task. Between the bouts of morning sickness that took place at any time of the day but morning, the backaches, and the horse pill-sized vitamins, she wasn't sure she liked the idea of being pregnant. Then again, she didn't need the implants to increase her cup size, much to Marlon's delight.

Glancing at the wedding photo on her desk, she sighed. The past month seemed like a dream. After marrying Marlon at the now-infamous little stone church, she had settled in at the shelter as the director. With twenty pets in the building and four on loan to the nursing home, the idea was a success.

She flipped pages on her clipboard. More volunteers sent in applications each day. Due to Marlon's insistence, she had rigourous background checks done, in case anyone who might hurt the animals or the other volunteers slipped through the cracks. In the alcove under her desk, Sparky snored. Lump, Marlon's cat, sprawled across her desk with Tantrum and Unruly in a furry grey and black conglomeration of cat.

A knock at her office door startled her. Sparky barked and Tantrum darted under the couch. Lump opened one green eye before curling up again and resting against Unruly's back. Jaden took a deep breath. "Yes?"

Ron poked his head around the frosted glass door. "Calm down, Sparks. It's just me." He strolled into the room and knelt to scratch the dog's floppy ears. "See? I'm not a masher. Hey, I have the new release for Delish, and the local news channel called. They'd like to interview you for their Person of the Month column. Are you up for that?"

Sparky trotted around the desk and jumped up onto the couch. He circled the cushion once and plopped down in his sleeping spot.

Jaden scratched her belly. The baby kicked, pressing against her ribs. "Junior's busy today. I think he's going to be a gymnast or do mixed martial arts. He's certainly got the legs for something athletic."

"He's a fighter like his mother." Grinning, Ron stood and folded his arms. "So are you sure he's a boy?"

"I have no idea. Marlon doesn't want to know and I'll be happy when he or she's in my arms, not kicking my bladder."

Ron chuckled. "And once he or she is, you'll want another. Speaking of children, Marlon's on his way back. I do believe he's got a present. Oh, and the bus from the retirement centre should be here in about ten minutes if you want to see Judi today."

She nodded. "Thanks. I'll be out there in a bit."

He dipped his head and disappeared through the doorway.

With Ron gone, Sparky vacated the couch and strolled to her chair. He dropped his chin on Jaden's lap. Without looking down, she closed her eyes and scratched his head. "What do you suppose the surprise is?"

When she opened her eyes, Marlon was seated on the edge of her desk. She screamed. "You'll give me heart failure."

He shrugged. "I know mouth-to-mouth. I can resuscitate you. No sweat." He held one finger up. "Second thought, there'd be a little sweat, but we'd both end up sated."

She stared at him. In his uniform, the man could stop traffic—figuratively and literally. But in a simple long-sleeved T-shirt and jeans, he made her body flush. He made love to her each night and held her when they had finished. Her heart swelled each time she saw him.

He folded his muscle-corded arms. A hank of copper hair slipped across his brow. "Don't you want to know what the surprise is?"

"I always want to know what your surprises are."

"Well, it's really a two person surprise." He turned to the door. "Bring her in, Ron."

In the doorway, Ron appeared. He whistled. A caramel-coloured Basset hound with black freckles on its legs ambled into the room. "Meet Mrs Nesbit."

The new dog barked in a throaty voice. Sparky sat up and struggled to stand. Mrs Nesbit sat and panted, her long pink tongue dripping doggie slobber onto the floor.

Jaden squealed and clapped. "You got Sparks a girlfriend!" She struggled to her feet and rounded the desk. Marlon's hand warmed her lower back. Wrapping her arms around him, she kissed his neck. "What a fabulous surprise. I love her and I think Sparks does, too."

Feathering a kiss over her temple, Marlon chuckled. "Good thing. She belonged to an elderly gentleman over in Jarvis. When he passed, the family opted to put her down. But they read the ad for PRM and decided to drop her off here instead. Looks like she'll fit in just fine. What do you think?"

Jaden sighed. What did she think? Life was perfect. "I have the dogs, the cats, a baby on the way, and a building that's paid for. I'm good."

"What about me?" Marlon wrapped both arms around her and rested his forehead against hers. "Am I good?"

"You're the icing on my cake."

"I love you, Jaden Marie."

"I love you, too."

About the Author

I always dreamed of writing the stories in my head. Tall, dark, and handsome heroes are my favourites, as long as he has an independent woman keeping him in line.

I earned a BA in education at Kent State University and currently hold a Masters in Education with Nova Southeastern University.

I love NASCAR, romance, books in general, Ohio farmland, dirt racing, and my menagerie of animals. You can also find me at my blog.

Wendi Zwaduk loves to hear from readers. You can find her contact information, website details and author profile page at http://www.total-e-bound.com

Total-E-Bound Publishing

www.total-e-bound.com

Take a look at our exciting range of literagasmic™ erotic romance titles and discover pure quality at Total-E-Bound.

CPSIA information can be obtained at www.ICGtesting.com
Printed in the USA
BVOW022322021012
301890BV00001B/7/P